# CODE BLOOD

## KURT KAMM

Published by MCM Publishing, a division of Monkey C Media
www.mcmpublishing.com
Book Design by Monkey C Media
www.monkeycmedia.com

Edited by Denise Middlebrooks

Printed in the United States of America

Publisher's Cataloging in Publication Data

Kamm, Kurt L.
      Code blood / Kurt Kamm. -- San Diego, CA : MCM Publishing,
      c2012.
      p. ; cm.
      ISBN: 978-0-9798551-3-9 ; 978-0-9798551-4-6 (ebook)
   Summary: A Los Angeles County fire paramedic responds toa fatal accident in
which an unidenified woman's foot is severed and stolen. During a weeklong search
to find the victim's identity and her missing foot, he encounters an underworld
of Goth fetishists, body parts dealers, a woman with a full upper body tattoo,
a killer, and a strange Chinese woman involved in stem-cell research.

      1. Emergency medical technicians--California--Los Angeles County-
-Fiction. 2. Accident victims--California--Los Angeles County--Fiction. 3.
Los Angeles County (Calif.)--Fiction. 4.Mystery fiction. I. Title.
      PS3611.A4686 C63 2012               2011935091
      813/.6--dc23                    1201

A LL OF US HAVE WITNESSED the spectacle of blood, and we know that the experience is something which, to varying degrees, imparts to us feelings of dread, fascination, discomfiture, mystery and even terror or horror. However much we try to overlook or normalize the experience, the sight of blood always invites a moment of disequilibrium. Perhaps this is because we know that life's equilibrium depends on blood, and so, to see blood is to find oneself reminded of the tenuousness of existence.

*—Jonathan Wender, keynote address to the Western Society of Criminology, 2006*

# CODE BLOOD

# ONE

A N ORANGE GLOW APPEARED on the horizon. As the incandescent light spread, the ocean turned blue and separated itself from the sky.

She welcomed the sun—she had been awake all night and was about to explode with the energy flooding her body. The bare wood of the Colony Beach Club deck chair hurt her back. Still, she felt safer than the night before, when she lay on the beach, fearful that the men who lived beneath the sand would reach up and cut her with their long knives.

She looked at her pink plastic watch, which matched her pink backpack. It was 6:30 a.m. In another hour, the September sun would begin to bake all of Southern California. In two hours, the beach club members would begin to arrive, but she would be long gone.

The ladies' room on the deck was unlocked—a godsend. She picked up her backpack and went inside. She slipped out of her leather sandals, stripped off her clothes and gazed at her thin reflection in the mirror above the sink. Her blue eyes were crystal clear, reflecting the strength and power she felt, but her short blond hair needed washing. She twisted her torso from side to side and stretched her hands above her head. She couldn't see it yet, but it was there, in her belly. She had known for six weeks. There was no doubt.

She washed herself as best she could in the sink, using the scented soap from the dispenser and wiped away the water with paper towels. She stuffed her dirty sweatshirt into her pack, pulled on her grimy white shorts and the brilliant blue CALIFORNIA T-shirt she had found on the clubhouse deck. She let the water run over her toothbrush and scrubbed her teeth.

When she left the washroom, the sun was in full ascent. She slung her her one shoulder, carried her sandals in her hand and walked off the deck and far enough out into the water to make it around the fence. She stopped for a moment to empty the bottles of Seroquel and lithium into the ocean and then scrambled up over the rocks onto the shoulder of Pacific Coast Highway.

In the early morning, the road was deserted. She felt she could walk from Santa Monica to San Francisco without stopping. After a mile, she made a detour through a parking lot and dropped the pink backpack behind a row of steel trash dumpsters.

# TWO

S TATION 88, *squad and engine respond to vehicle accident on Pacific Coast Highway at the Surfrider Restaurant.*

When the tone sounded, Colt Lewis was replacing the IV bags in the drug box. A surge of adrenaline pulsed through him. He ran to the engine bay, stowed the box in the side-panel of the squad—the paramedic truck—and pulled on his gear. Brian, his partner and preceptor during his eight-week internship in the field, slid behind the wheel and grabbed his headset. Colt punched the red button on the wall and jumped into the passenger seat as the heavy metal garage door rumbled up.

"You good?" Brian asked. He hit the lights and siren.

Colt nodded and heard the deafening wail before he put his headset on. They rolled down the driveway onto Pacific Coast Highway and turned right. It was an early Sunday afternoon in mid September and PCH was crowded with people coming to the beaches. Colt was living his dream. He had just become a Los Angeles County Fire paramedic stationed in Malibu. He was part of the firefighter brotherhood. The men on his shift replaced the family he no longer had.

Vehicles moved aside to let the squad pass. Brian wove through the sea of traffic to the center divider lane and picked up speed. "Squad 88 responding," he called in. "What have we got?"

"Single vehicle accident," dispatch radioed back.

Colt's adrenaline spike subsided. He shook his head. You never knew what you might find when you were toned out. People drove at high speeds on PCH and collisions were common. The worst were the devastating MVAs—multiple vehicle accidents. During his two years as a firefighter before becoming a paramedic, Colt saw several MVAs with torn flesh and metal spread across the pavement. A one-car accident at the Surfrider sounded harmless. An old woman with blue hair probably bumped her head when her husband touched the brakes in the parking lot.

In his side view mirror, Colt watched the LifeLine ambulance fall in behind them. Farther back, he glimpsed the red lights on top of 88's engine, caught in the traffic. The squad screamed past Ferraris and Porsches, SUVs, motor homes with satellite dishes, Jeeps with surfboards, Harleys and sport bikes—all trying to squeeze over into the right hand lane. A black and white from the Sheriff's Department made a sudden U-turn and preceded them for the short trip down the coast. After five years in California, Colt was still amazed at the congestion. In Wyoming, where he grew up, the land was empty. The entire population could be on the highway and no one would notice.

A mile from the Surfrider, traffic was backed up to a standstill. Sheriff's deputies had placed their cars diagonally across the highway in front of the restaurant, stopping traffic in both directions. Brian swung out into the center lane again. As the squad approached the Surfrider, Colt saw a metal light pole lying on the ground, one jagged end in the parking lot and the other, with a smashed streetlight still attached, sticking out into the right-hand lane of PCH. A silver pickup rested on the cement pad where the pole had been anchored. The impact had driven the front bumper, grill, and hood halfway to the windshield. Colt looked for the telltale circle of smashed glass and blood and hair on the inside of the windshield, but saw nothing.

Brian pulled into the parking lot and stopped. Several feet away, a crowd from the beach wearing bathing suits, restaurant customers wearing shorts and tank tops, and the Surfrider staff dressed in black pants, white shirts, red suspenders and bow ties, had collected. A surge of excitement pulsed through the throng. People shaded their eyes to get a better look, pointed and spoke to their companions. Several took photos with their cell phones.

Brian was out of the squad before Colt had his hand on the door handle. "Let's go," Brian said. "Glove up."

Colt grabbed the orange drug box and followed Brian.

The ambulance arrived seconds later and the LifeLine EMTs trailed after them across the parking lot. The crowd parted as they approached. Colt saw a deputy kneeling next to a girl wearing a blue T-shirt, lying on her back.

The next thing he saw was what remained of her right leg—a stump with shreds of muscle and tendons in place of her foot and ankle. Blood from a severed artery formed a puddle on the ground next to the deputy. Colt felt a new rush of adrenaline.

The deputy turned toward them. "Glad you guys are here," he said. He had pulled everything off his belt and was using it as a tourniquet. His flashlight, radio, mace, gun and holster, two sets of cuffs and bullet clips lay in a pile at his side. He held the thick brown belt tight around the girl's right calf, but blood continued to leak from her severed limb. Nervous sweat ran off his face, dripped onto the blacktop and mixed with the blood. His tan shirt had dark rings of perspiration under the arms.

Colt couldn't take his eyes off the stump of the girl's leg. His job was to help those who needed it. Although he would never admit it, sometimes when he knew the victim had done something stupid, Colt was a little less concerned. The person lying in front of him wasn't one of those reckless jerks injured in a motorcycle crash, or some lunatic who raced down Pacific Coast Highway weaving through traffic. This victim was a girl, badly injured and bleeding out from a severed foot. Although surrounded by sheriff's deputies and curious strangers, she seemed alone. Colt didn't see anyone trying to comfort her.

Brian pulled a tourniquet from the drug box and tightened it around the girl's leg above the deputy's belt. "How long have you been here?" he asked the deputy.

The deputy loosened his belt and slipped it off the girl's leg. He wiped his face on the shoulder of his shirt and looked at his watch. "It happened about fifteen minutes ago, say around 1420. The dispatch was a Code 3. They should've said it was a Code Blood."

Brian wrote the time on the tourniquet with a black marking pen. The medics in the ER would want to know how much time had elapsed since the accident.

Colt realized the girl was wearing a blue CALIFORNIA T-shirt. He paused and stared at the vivid blue color with the white letters.

"Colt, damn it," Brian said. "Get her vitals."

Colt knelt down. "Miss, can you give me your name?"

Her eyes were open and she turned her head slightly toward him. Her lips barely moved. Her voice was inaudible. Colt had seen the glazed look of shock before. It was not a good sign.

"Do you know your name?" he repeated, and leaned toward her. He thought he smelled scented soap on her skin.

"Bibi," she whispered.

"Bibi," Colt said to Brian. "She says her name's Bibi." He turned back to the girl. "Do you know where you are?" She looked at Colt but said nothing. He read the response in her eyes: help me.

He touched her palm. She had a delicate hand and white skin, but her nails were dirty and ragged. "Can you squeeze my finger?"

She could not.

"A-O times one," Colt said, giving the paramedic shorthand assessment of her alert and oriented condition.

Help me.

"You writing this down, Colt?" Brian didn't ask, he ordered.

"Uh … yeah," Colt said, looking away from the girl's face. He pulled out his pad and began to make notes. The LifeLine EMTs stood by, listening and making their own notes on the girl's condition.

The deputy stood up, dangling his belt like a dead snake between his gloved thumb and forefinger. He looked at the spots where blood had stained the leather and shook his head. While his partner picked up his gun and equipment and took everything to their patrol car, the deputy coiled up the bloody belt, held it in one hand and pulled the latex glove inside out over it. He pulled the second glove off over the first, creating a casing of latex around the belt.

"Get a C-collar on her," Brian told Colt. When Brian was in action, there was no idle chatter. He spewed out staccato commands and expected immediate execution.

Colt took out the collar, gently wrapped it around the girl's neck and immobilized her head. Trying to stay ahead of Brian, he yanked two saline bags and IV kits out of the drug box, bent over the girl, found a vein and inserted the first needle into her arm. As he hooked up the saline, Colt glanced at her face again. Ocean blue eyes looked back at him. Colt had never seen such a beautiful color. She appeared to be in her early twenties, had short blond hair and a California tan. She could have been a cheerleader from nearby Pepperdine University. Her white shorts, probably spotless when she put them on that morning, were spattered with blood and soiled from the dirt on the parking lot. The blue CALIFORNIA T-shirt matched her eyes and reminded Colt of a picture of his mother wearing a similar blue T-shirt.

Colt leaned toward her and held her hand. "Don't worry," he said, "we're here to help you." He squeezed her hand gently, then moved to her other side, held her arm and searched for another vein. He worried they might be collapsing from lack of blood pressure. He watched the blue T-shirt rise and fall as the girl took quick, shallow breaths. Colt pressed his fingers against the radial artery above her wrist and felt her pounding pulse. It only took a few seconds to count the beats. "One-thirty-two, she's going tachy," he said to Brian. Colt pressed his wrist against her forehead. In the warm afternoon sunlight, her skin felt cool and damp. Her body was shutting down and shunting what blood remained to her main organs. She was going into hemorrhagic shock from loss of blood. It was a standard case study from his training.

He found a vein and started the second IV.

"Cold," she whispered. "Cold."

For a split second, he thought she had uttered his name, Colt, and that she knew him. He took her hand again and held it in his own for a few seconds, trying to give her a sense of reassurance. "We'll take care of you, Bibi." He looked at her. "Don't worry. It'll be OK, I promise." He wasn't so sure it would be OK, but that's what he was trained to say. "Get us some blankets," he called to one of the LifeLine EMTs. "She needs blankets."

As he bent over the girl, Colt's peripheral vision registered the bare feet, sandals, tennis and running shoes and the shined sheriff's boots surrounding the girl. Where was her foot?

An EMT returned with a gray blanket. Brian took it and spread it over the middle of the girl's body. He stood up, stretched his back, and turned to one of the deputies. "What happened?"

The deputy lowered his voice and looked at the silver pickup. "That asshole was texting when he veered off onto the shoulder. He had to be doing close to 50 because that's what it takes to bring down a metal pole." The deputy shook his head in disgust. "He's lucky he had his seat belt on or he'd have gone through the windshield and ended up on the other side of the restaurant. He passed a breathalyzer test, but he's definitely on something. This poor gal was standing out here and the pole sheared off her foot when it came down. It happened so fast she couldn't get out of the way. We were parked in the lot and saw the whole thing.

"You saved her life," Brian said.

So far, Colt thought.

Brian radioed a size-up to Captain Ames, still caught in traffic a minute away. "We've got a trauma case, severed foot and we need the AirSquad."

Colt looked at Bibi's face again. He looked out at the white sand and the water beyond. It was a beautiful afternoon. The sun was warm and the sky was blue, sprinkled with the thin cirrus clouds that hover over the Southern California coast during the late summer. The surf crashed onto the beach throwing up a fine mist. The smell of saltwater hung in the air. Gulls circled and fought for scraps of food from the restaurant's trash bins. Two lifeguards with deep tans and wearing red shorts had run up from the beach to check out the situation, one of them carrying another drug box. How terrible is this, Colt thought. This beautiful girl is lying here on the blacktop bleeding out when she should be down on the sand enjoying the last hours of the weekend. Instead, some moron had taken her down.

Colt wiped the sweat off his face and motioned to the other EMT. "Hang on to these," and handed him the saline bags with the drip lines inserted in the girl's arms. Colt began a quick assessment. He didn't have to pull her jaw open to make sure her throat was clear, she had already uttered a couple of words, but he ran his hands along her body to check for broken bones and further injuries. He remembered the half-joking words of one of his instructors: "Trauma calls look dramatic, but just splint the twisted stuff, plug the holes, start an IV, immobilize the back and get the patient to the trauma center." Right now, it didn't seem so simple. How do you plug this hole, Colt wanted to know.

Brian finished briefing Captain Ames, put his radio away and called out to the crowd, "Is anyone here with her? Does anyone know this person?" No one responded. Brian lifted her arm, placing his fingers above her wrist. He tried to find a heartbeat, then dropped the arm and stuck his fingers on her carotid artery. "Her pulse is dropping," he said to Colt. "It's down to 60." Brian frowned.

Engine 88 finally rolled into the parking lot and Colt waved them over. Moose jumped out, took one look at the situation and ran to the squad to get the backboard. Captain Ames joined them clutching his radio. Colt heard him talking to the AirSquad stationed in the hills above Malibu.

"We've got a trauma run," Captain Ames said. "A female patient, foot amputation. She's going into shock. We're at the Surfrider Restaurant. The SD's clearing a landing zone on PCH. This is ALS, repeat, advanced life support."

Colt heard a small chopper. It sounded like a lawnmower. He knew it couldn't be the AirSquad and looked up. A news helicopter circled overhead. He saw another coming up the coast from Los Angeles. In minutes, news crews in vans would arrive, extend their satellite transmission poles, broadcast pictures of the accident and fan out to find people to interview. In the process, several spectators would have a moment of fame on Los Angeles network television. The accident would be a good lead-in on the 11:00 p.m. Sunday night news, but the anchors would be disappointed that a Malibu celebrity wasn't involved.

Moose joined them with the backboard and laid it down next to the girl's body.

Brian checked the C-spine. "Ready guys? On my count."

The men prepared to roll the girl on her side.

"Be careful," Colt said.

Brian gave Colt a quick look and said, "One, two, three."

In unison, they rolled her onto her side, Moose pushed the board in toward her and the men laid her back onto it.

Colt thought he heard her utter a faint moan. While Brian secured the head brace and straps across her body and prepared her for transport across the beach, he looked at her bloodied leg again. "Where's the foot?" he shouted. "Does someone have her foot?" She still wore one delicate leather sandal.

"We can't find the sucker," one of the deputies told Colt.

"Can't find it? How's that possible?" Colt said. The girl needed her foot. They had to ice it down before the tissue started to die. It might be reattached. "It has to be here somewhere." He went over to the damaged pickup.

The driver of the truck sat with his head down, behind the metal screen in the back seat of a black and white. A sheriff's deputy stood outside, questioning him through the window and writing on his notepad. Colt interrupted. "Where's the foot?" He was met with a shrug and a blank stare from the deputy. Colt looked at the driver of the pickup, a man about his own age, and hated him.

Colt walked around the pickup. Glass shards from a headlight and pieces of plastic lay on the ground. He knelt in a pool of green coolant dripping from the smashed radiator and looked under the front of the truck. The foot wasn't there. He stood up and looked around. Thirty or forty people stood in the parking lot watching the activity.

Colt grabbed the arm of the deputy who was questioning the driver. "Help me out. We have to find her foot." The crowd backed away as Colt and the deputy walked a circle around the truck and the cement base of the pole, scanning the ground. Colt shouted to the crowd, "We have to locate this girl's foot. Has anyone seen it?" A few heads shook as a buzz went through the crowd: a foot was missing. A severed human foot was somewhere in the parking lot.

Colt scanned the crowd of spectators, hoping for a response. He noticed a short man holding a take-home food bag, wearing a black hat, dark sunglasses, tight black pants and a long sleeve black shirt, buttoned at the neck and wrists. Standing among the people wearing shorts, swimsuits and T-shirts on a beautiful hot day at the beach, the guy looked like someone from a Goth horror movie. Next to him was a girl wearing a skimpy tank top with tattoos covering her neck, shoulders and bare arms. Colt did a double take and ran his eyes over her body before he resumed looking for the foot. While the deputy continued to circle the area, his eyes glued to the blacktop, Colt searched the area around the end of the light pole and saw the blood on the sharp, ragged metal.

Colt looked over at the deputy, who shrugged his shoulders and said, "Nothing."

The deep whack, whack, whack of one of the AirSquad Blackhawks echoed as it flew in over the hills. It stopped overhead, hovered and began to descend slowly onto PCH, tail and nose bobbing up and down, threading its way between power lines and telephone wires. Bystanders near the road turned their backs on the sandstorm and debris kicked up by the rotors. The backwash sandblasted a few cars and sent blue and green plastic trash containers flying.

In a well-rehearsed rescue ballet, the rotors had barely come to a stop before the AirSquad crew in dark blue flight uniforms and white flight helmets opened the side door and jumped to the ground. The EMTs and the men from 88s, trailed by Brian holding the IV bags, carried the girl on the backboard across the parking lot, up along the shoulder of the highway and across the pavement to the waiting helicopter. As the aircrew took charge and loaded her inside, the engines gave off a high-pitched whistle and the rotors began to turn again.

One of the AirSquad medics shouted from the door, "Where's the foot?" Brian shook his head.

Everyone backed away as the departing Blackhawk churned up another sandstorm. When it lifted off, Colt was still searching the parking lot. He looked up at the belly of the yellow and black bird as it headed for the California University Hospital. "I hope you make it Bibi."

When Brian returned from the beach, Colt told him, "We looked everywhere. Her foot isn't here."

"It has to be," Brian said. "Let's check again. It didn't just walk away." He gave Colt a small smile.

Colt was still unaccustomed to the paramedic "crispy critter" jokes. He understood humor was a way of coping with the terrible things they saw, but to him the jokes made everything seem worse. They walked the area again and came up empty. Reluctantly, they returned to the squad.

It was time to write reports. While the girl in the AirSquad was fighting for her life, everyone on the ground had a form to fill out. The sheriff's deputies had to record the details of the accident and the people involved. They were already measuring the distances between the base of the light pole, the spot where it fell and the place where the girl was injured. One deputy had to submit a request for a new belt. The driver of the pickup was already on his way to the Lost Hills Sheriff's Station for booking and a drug test. The LifeLine EMTs sat in their ambulance and prepared their own run sheet, even though they had not transported a patient. In the squad, Colt grabbed the metal clipboard with the patient assessment sheets. He looked at the list of questions. He knew so little about the girl and had so little to report:

Name – Bibi?

Address – unknown.

Age – 23? Colt made a guess, and then crossed it out.

M/F – F. At least he knew that.

Assessment – Severed right foot. Not found.

Colt went on to fill in some of the vital signs they had recorded earlier and to write a brief description of the accident. He wanted to add: life of a beautiful girl ruined by speeding idiot on drugs.

The entire incident had taken less than an hour, but the expenditure of nervous energy was enormous. Now that the girl was someone else's responsibility, Colt could relax and begin to decompress. He felt exhausted. Activity in the parking lot returned to normal. The news crews finished their interviews. The spectators dispersed—some departing, others returning to their meals at the Surfrider. A tow truck prepared to haul the pickup away. The crew from 88s helped direct traffic while they waited for Caltrans to arrive and drag the pole off the highway.

Colt finished the assessment sheet and decided to circle the area around the cement base of the pole one last time.

The deputy who interviewed the truck driver joined him. "Did you find her foot?" he asked.

"No."

"Someone probably picked it up."

"Picked it up? Colt was incredulous. "Who would do that? Not possible."

The deputy shrugged. "You never know. This is Los Angeles. Plenty of nut cases running around."

On the way back to the station, Colt said to Brian, "'Bibi.' I wonder what kind of name that is." He couldn't stop thinking about the foot and wondered if it could have even been reattached. They were trained to retrieve any severed body part—fingers, toes, hands, feet, even a penis—put it on ice and get it to the trauma center in a cooler as fast as possible. From that point, it was up to the surgeons to do their best. Colt refused to accept the fact that the foot was gone. A body part didn't just disappear from the scene of an accident. He was disappointed. It was his first real life-and-death situation as a paramedic and he felt he had failed. He promised Bibi with the ocean blue eyes that he would take care of her. She had been his responsibility while she lay injured on the blacktop. Now someone would have to tell her that her left foot had disappeared from the parking lot at the Surfrider Restaurant.

# THREE

THE DOPAMINE WAS FLOWING and Markus felt electrified. He was SOARING. He jumped into the passenger seat and pulled the door shut. Behind his oversize dark glasses, he squinted from the glare of the sunlight and creases spread from the corners of his eyes. He held up the plastic take-out bag in one hand and looked underneath to see if it was leaking. The bottom was clean and he placed it on the floor mat between his feet. He opened the glove box of his PT Cruiser, took out a bottle and squeezed disinfectant gel on his hands.

"Unfuckingbelievable," he exclaimed, and rubbed the gel over his fingers.

"Oh my God, you're freaking me out," Audra said, as she drove out of the Surfrider parking lot. "I can't believe you did that."

"It was nothing."

Did you get blood on your hands? "Aren't you afraid of—?"

"Pathogens? No." Sure, Markus was afraid of blood-borne pathogens, but he wasn't about to admit it to Audra. Besides, when the gods offered up a severed foot to him, he was bound to accept it.

"Glad I made you come?" Audra asked.

Markus didn't answer. He looked at her over the top of his sunglasses, revealing his red irises. "It's so bright at the beach, it hurts my eyes. Vampires burn up in sunlight like this."

Audra returned his gaze. "Except you're an albino, not a vampire."

"Albinos burn up in this light too." Markus took off his sunglasses and rubbed his eyes. He looked inside the plastic bag at the girl's delicate foot. The fibula and tibia, severed just above the ankle, shone white through torn flesh. "I don't think we're gonna want the rest of the halibut," he said. Most of the blood had run out onto the parking lot blacktop, but a small amount still dripped from the torn flesh onto the white Styrofoam container with the remainder of their lunch. Markus rolled down the side window and squinted again. He reached into the plastic bag, eased the bloody sandal off the foot with his thumb and forefinger and tossed it out onto the dirt on the side of Pacific Coast Highway. He closed the window again and leaned back. "This is epic!" he exclaimed.

Someday he would have a hearse, but for the time being, the funky old PT Cruiser would do. When Audra was with him, she insisted on driving. She claimed his weak eyes and heavy foot on the gas pedal made her nervous. He humored her.

During the 20-minute drive from the beach to his apartment near the California University campus, Markus leaned against the passenger side door and admired Audra's body. He wondered what she looked like six years ago, without her tats. She must have been hot even then. Some days he hated the bitch, but today she looked particularly delicious. She was wearing her cut-off jeans, short enough to show the beginning of the curve of her awesome ass, and a tank top that revealed the colors and mosaic of her upper body tattoos. Her long black hair cascaded down over her bare shoulders. While everyone in the parking lot was staring at the accident or looking at Audra, it was easy to pick up the foot.

He touched his prize through the thin plastic bag. He felt the toes, the arch, and cupped the palm of his hand against the ankle. The look of Audra's body, the image of the blood spilling out onto the blacktop and the foot in the take-out bag sent a wave of sexual excitement through Markus' body. He forgot about the discomfort of the bright sunlight and felt the familiar tension build in his groin. By the time Audra turned onto Albion, a short street filled with APARTMENT FOR RENT signs that ran between the Los Angeles National Cemetery and the edge of the California University campus, Markus had an insane erection.

"I'll be up in a second," he said when Audra drove into the carport. Markus jumped out with the plastic bag and walked into the alley. He lifted the lid of one of the metal dumpsters, pulled out the Styrofoam container with the halibut and tossed it away. Markus shivered with excitement. He was certain he would remember this as one of the great days of his life—the afternoon he walked out of the Surfrider Restaurant in Malibu and picked up a severed human foot. He ran up the stairs to Unit 2.

Inside, Markus went into the kitchen, took off his dark glasses and hat, rolled up his long sleeves and scrubbed his hands in the sink. He took latex gloves out of a drawer, pulled them on and spread some old newspaper on the counter top. He drew his treasure out of the bag. It was a right foot. Rigor mortis hadn't set in yet and he could still bend each toe. He marveled at how delicate and perfect they were. The nails were dark pink and the second toe was longer than the first, something Markus found kickass. He thought it would be wicked to see what it looked like with Audra's runic toe ring. He held the foot at eye level and saw a nicely shaped ankle below the broken stumps of bone. The girl lying on the blacktop had looked delicious. It would have added so much to his enjoyment of the foot if he knew what she looked like naked.

"I'll be there in a minute," he called to Audra in the bedroom. He turned on the kitchen faucet, held the foot underneath the spray and rubbed off the sand and congealed blood. He dried the foot, put it in a plastic bag and placed it in the freezer next to the bag containing the hand, nestled among the frozen peas. It was a left hand, and he had not yet paid for it, which was a problem. Now that he had a beautiful foot, the hand meant nothing. The squirrel head in the third bag meant less than nothing.

Markus went into the gloomy living-dining room where he did his Internet hacking. Software disks in plastic containers littered the floor. On the table, covered with black velvet and a dozen dark red candles of different sizes, he kept his computer, monitor, extra hard-drives, two printers, an unused router still in its box and an assortment of motherboards and other components. A tangle of wires and cables plugged into surge protectors hung off the edge of the table. This equipment allowed him to pry into people's private information. Markus considered himself a great hacker, but he desperately needed some new malware. Firewalls were becoming more sophisticated, well beyond his own ability to surmount them. The Russians and Indians sold the best stuff, but it cost money, thousands of dollars, and Markus was low on funds.

When he worked his way through firewalls to ransack personal files and information, he sat on his throne, a wooden chair adorned with carved gargoyles. He rested his feet on a black Los Angeles County Coroner body bag purchased on Craigslist for $34. The website had advertised the body bag as "used." A trio of unmatched black wrought iron chairs surrounded the table. Heavy black drapes covered two windows that looked out onto Albion Street. The walls and ceiling were pale blue because the property owner wouldn't let him change the color, but in the semidarkness, it wasn't a problem. There was one floor lamp in the room and the shade was covered by one of Audra's black shawls. He rarely turned it on; the light from the computer screens was enough.

Markus did a quick check of his e-mails. He had accounts under different names with several carriers and ran his own SMTP server. His most confidential e-mail address, reserved only for close and important friends, was fangs@ markusblood.com. He hit SEND/RECEIVE, but on a Sunday afternoon, nothing but spam showed in his inbox and he deleted everything. The important communications came at night when his vampire friends were stirring.

He turned on the MP3 player anchored in a speaker base and the death-rock sound of Fear Cult filled the apartment. Markus loved his Goth dungeon. It would satisfy any vampire. During the six weeks since Audra moved in, she had improved the décor and the dark mood. She added the black and dark red velvet, the black lace, the candles and the roses. Audra loved roses. Bouquets the color of blood, dried and preserved with hairspray, hung on the walls. Best of all were the roses on her body.

Audra had lit the candles and he could smell the aromatherapy scent drifting out of the bedroom. He didn't like it nearly as much now that he realized she had the same scent on her hands from the massage oil when she came home from work. He paused at the door of the bedroom and saw her lying face-up on top of the bed wearing only a bra and panties. He watched her stretch, keeping one leg flat and bringing the other up at a right angle. She held on to the piece of old wrought iron cemetery fence they used as a headboard. A small patio table on one side of the bed functioned as a nightstand. A weathered church pew and a massive Victorian dresser with spiral-turned legs were the only other pieces of furniture. Before Audra dragged him to the Salvation Army to buy furniture, Markus slept on a mattress on the floor.

Markus was eager to get it on with her—his body needed some nasty sex. He stripped off his pants and sat down on the bed. Sexual electricity swept through him and he forgot the things about Audra that annoyed him. He ran his finger up her thigh and across the tattoos on her stomach. Tattoos were almost as wicked as blood, and Audra had the tattoos. Audra looked way sexy lying there. Markus thought about the girl lying in the parking lot, blood spurting from her leg. A girl with blood on her skin was sweet. The sight of blood aroused him. The taste of blood excited him. Blood play—cuts, punctures and bites—drove him wild. Sharing blood with someone you were really into was a fantabulous experience.

He bent over and kissed the ring in her bellybutton. "I wanna suck a few drops of your blood and do you," he whispered.

She pulled away from him. "Not now, I need some rest. Besides, I can't keep going to work with bleeding fingers." She looked at the clock on the nightstand. "It's almost six; I have to be at work in two hours."

"I'm all rammy. I want you. You have to—"

"Just chill. Wait until I get home."

Markus clenched his teeth and lay down next to her. He tried to think of something that would extinguish his craving. He thought about Audra's exotic dancing at the club—that was a real buzz-kill. He wanted her to quit, but there was no way she would give it up. The first time he saw her at the Alley Kat, with black and red tattoos, he couldn't get over her intense body. He dreamed about her. He thought about her. He kept coming back to look at her like all the other men and even some women. Everyone liked to inhale Audra's body and fantasize about what they wanted to do with her. He decided he had to have her. He wanted her to belong to him. Now she had moved in with him, but he still had to share her with everyone else at the club. Markus couldn't bear to go back and watch her dance while everyone ogled her tats and reached out to touch her.

Markus moved toward her on the bed. "It's time," he said.

"I said wait until I come home from work."

"No, I mean it's time to stop dancing."

Audra sat up, gave him a look and laughed. "Right. Like, you're gonna take care of me? I need to earn a living."

"They said the tattoos would cost twenty thousand," Audra had told him the first time she stood naked in front of him. "Where could I get that kind of paper? I was 16 and had $10 when I got off the bus in L.A. Dancing's the only way to make good money, especially with the extra stuff."

He wondered what else Audra was doing at the club. He had a good idea what the "extra stuff" was, but she wouldn't tell him. She didn't have to; he knew her job was to bring strangers' fantasies to life. He had picked up girls like her in the clubs for years. Audra was a good lay. Actually, she was a great lay, but what if she brought home an STD? Even though he knew she took care of herself and had regular checkups, Markus was becoming increasingly concerned. The thought of catching an STD frightened him. He had already seen enough doctors in his life. His excitement was gone. The electricity in his groin petered out. Markus rolled over and closed his eyes.

When he awoke, it was 8:00 p.m. and Audra was gone. He got up and walked naked into the kitchen. He opened the freezer and pulled out the plastic bag containing the foot. It was a blue-gray color now and hard as a rock. Markus admired it for a moment, whispered, "Dee-licious," and put it back in the freezer. He opened the refrigerator and took a container of vanilla yogurt mixed with raspberry jam. It was his favorite— when he swirled the jam around it looked like coagulated blood on a girl's immaculate white skin. On the way back into the bedroom, he opened the container and licked the jam with his tongue.

Markus rummaged through his closet and pulled out the olive duffel bag hidden under a pile of dirty clothes. He unzipped it and took out the rubber arm, syringes, needles and plastic tubing, all wrapped in a towel. The arm was excellent. It wasn't real, but it worked and made it possible for him to learn how to insert a needle into a lifelike vein. After he became proficient inserting the needle into the plastic arm and drawing out the colored fluid, he began drawing blood from his own arm. The first time, he missed his vein and stabbed his flesh. The pain was terrible, but he clenched his teeth and poked around with the needle until blood began to flow into the syringe. On the second try, he hit his vein immediately. As the days passed, he kept practicing on the back of his hand and on his arm until he was certain he could do it. He had become a vampire paramedic. Audra would be very impressed, but this was not anything she needed to know about.

He took a sterile syringe out of its package. There were two left, both of which he would take with him tomorrow night. Markus tied the rubber tube around his biceps, trapped the blood, patted his vein to make it stand up and stuck the needle in near his elbow joint. He pulled the plunger up just far enough to see blood start to fill the syringe and then yanked the needle out. The entire process took about 15 seconds and Markus was satisfied he could do it in his sleep. He didn't expect any problems. His prey, the China Doll, was young and would have healthy veins that were easy to penetrate. Sometimes veins rolled sideways under the skin. If that happened, he would just have to keep trying—that's what the medical technicians did. The China Doll wouldn't know the difference anyway.

He finished his yogurt, wrapped everything in the towel, stuffed it into the duffel bag and buried it again under the debris on his closet floor. It was 8:45 p.m. and the night stretched out before him. Markus felt restless and edgy, fueled by his unsatisfied sexual arousal. He got dressed and went out.

On nights when Audra was dancing and he wasn't working at CU, Markus often walked the short block down Albion Street to the Los Angeles National Cemetery. The entrance was secured after dark by enormous iron gates almost a mile away, but he knew a spot where two of the 8-foot high metal bars on the fence were missing. He had his own private entrance.

During the day, the cemetery belonged to the mourners and visitors who strolled among the thousands of tombstones that ran off in straight and diagonal lines. At night, the cemetery was dark and grim—it belonged to the dead, the undead and to Markus. His weak eyes were no handicap in the gloom and he wandered the narrow streets—across Constitution Avenue, up Chateau Thiery, across San Juan Hill—stopping with a small flashlight to examine the names and ranks on the gravestones.

*Arthur Rodriguez, SSgt. U.S. Air Force, 1957*
*Robert Bensinger, Cpl. U.S. Army, 1917*
*Alex Nicholas, Capt. U.S. Navy, 1912*

Markus tried to imagine the unique death of each person and the way the blood might have drained out onto a battleground or dissipated into a cold sea. Six months ago, he discovered a tombstone for Audra Barnes, Lt. U.S. Navy, 1988. When he met Audra, he thought it was an omen.

He drifted between the rows of tombstones and listened to the wind blowing through the branches of the tall eucalyptus trees. In the distance, the whine of the cars on the 405 Freeway became the wail of lost souls. Markus became Vlad Drackula the Impaler, living on his estate in 15th century Transylvania. He stepped up onto a gravestone and addressed his followers: "Come, follow me fellow vampires, through this lonely gothic forest. I will find victims for you and we will gorge on their blood. When we have sucked them dry, we will dismember them and place their heads on the spikes of the fence surrounding my property." Markus surveyed their glowing eyes and sharp teeth. They were impatient to begin the hunt. "As protector of this pack, you will bring me the most beautiful woman. I will ravish her, then rip open her white neck and feast on her crimson elixir." The vampires standing around him stamped their feet and nodded in agreement. He was their undisputed leader. It was time to begin the blood hunt. Markus looked up into the clear California night and heard the sound of the wings of thousands of bats that would accompany them on the hunt.

On his way home, Markus climbed over the fence on the far side of the cemetery and walked around the perimeter toward Albion Street. At the corner of Sepulveda and Wilshire, he passed the homeless man who lived under two grocery carts with filthy blankets wrapped around the sides and covered with strips of building insulation. Markus knew how easy it would be to surprise the vagrant, rip the blankets away, jump on him and kill him before the old man could even cry out. The guy was filthy, smelled and might be HIV positive. Markus reconsidered. Not even the hungriest vampire would touch the vagrant's blood.

He walked along the sidewalk and thought about Audra's body. He thought about the foot in the freezer and about the rare Bombay Blood running through the body of the China Doll. Audra wouldn't be home for several hours and Markus was totally jacked. Instead of heading home, he continued down Sepulveda to the titty-bar that advertised: FULLY XPOSED WOMEN – BUSIEST CLUB IN LA – FREE ADMISSION SUNDAY NIGHTS.

# FOUR

O<small>N MONDAY MORNING</small>, the day after the incident at the Surfrider and the second day of a three-day shift, Colt turned himself inside out with the rest of the 88s during the physical training hour. He and Moose were in the midst of their weekly sit-up contest. Colt was just over 6 feet tall, thin and wiry and had great endurance. The problem was that Moose was bigger and stronger and built like a pro football wide receiver. Colt hadn't won the challenge in the five weeks since he'd joined the B-shift. Each week, he tried with new determination. Each week, Moose was still crunching away after Colt was exhausted.

"You lose again, pussy," Moose said. He stood up and wiped the sweat from his face. Looming over Colt, his 6 foot 3 inch body looked like a telephone pole on steroids.

"Damn," Colt groaned, "I'm done." He rolled over, forehead on the cement, waiting for his stomach muscles to stop cramping.

Brian poured half a bottle of water on Colt's back. "I just don't know what's wrong with young people these days," he said. "You're such weaklings."

"OK guys, turnout gear and SCBAs." Captain Ames came out the back of the equipment room. "We're gonna work on air management." He rolled a tractor-sized tire partway down the street behind the station.

Colt groaned again. "Can I test mine here on the cement?" Full gear and the SCBA—self contained breathing apparatus—weighed 65 pounds. For this drill, they had to run down the street in full gear, carrying sledgehammers, stop, pound on the tractor tire several times, run back and repeat the process until their air was gone. Colt stood up and went into the station to get his turnouts.

While they suited up, Captain Ames joined Colt and said, "You can't practice this enough. You've got to know breathing control and how much air you have."

"I know, I know," Colt said, waving him away.

Captain Ames persisted. "You'd be surprised how many experienced firefighters make mistakes. There's air in the tank for maybe 13 minutes going into a structure and 13 minutes coming out. If you get stuck in a fully involved fire with 6 minutes of air, you're in deep shit and you may not even know it. You have to monitor your air gauge."

Colt knew the various tricks like skip-breathing to save oxygen, but as he ran back and forth on the street, swinging the hammer, his respiration increased. He was having trouble breathing and was gulping air. His lungs were on fire. As he slowed down, Captain Ames, Brian and Moose ran past him at full speed. If he were climbing a smoky stairwell in a burning building, lugging tools and extra air bottles, he would be in trouble. Colt checked the time. Only eight minutes had passed; something was wrong. He felt lightheaded, staggered to a stop, loosened the straps on his mask, yanked it off and sat down on the curb, sucking deep breaths of fresh air.

While Moose and Brian continued their workout, Captain Ames came over to Colt. "What's the problem?" he asked.

"I can't breathe. I felt like I was going to pass out."

"Oh yeah?" Captain Ames stared at Colt, with a smirk on his face. "What a surprise. Did you check your air valve?"

"I—"

"No, you didn't. Righty tighty, lefty loosey. Your valve is halfway shut."

"It is?"

"Yeah. It is. I know, because I tightened it and you didn't check it. That's a rookie's mistake."

Colt took the tank off his back, laid it on the ground and checked the valve. Captain Ames was right. He turned it three revolutions to the left to open a full flow. He looked up and shook his head.

"Finish your workout, Einstein," Captain Ames said.

After inserting fresh air tanks in the SCBAs and leaving their gear in the engine bay, the crew gathered in the kitchen to cool down, rehydrate and eat breakfast.

The station, number 88 of 187 fire stations in Los Angeles County, was one of the smallest. It was tucked in behind a shopping center off Pacific Coast Highway in the heart of Malibu. The kitchen was a walk-in closet. When the men sat at the table, they could lean their chairs back against the stove and dishwasher on one side and the refrigerator and cupboards on the other.

Colt shoveled oatmeal into his mouth. He paused for a moment and said, "Someone took it home."

"Took what home?" Captain Ames said, washing down a handful of vitamins with black coffee.

"You still thinking about the foot?" Brian said.

"Forget it," Moose said. He took alternate bites of sections of an orange and a peanut butter and jelly sandwich.

Colt finished his oatmeal and reached for a donut. "One of the sheriff's deputies told me people sometimes steal severed limbs. It's a crime, aggravated mayhem, but people do it."

Captain Ames leafed through the morning's incoming e-mail from Command and Control while he drank his coffee. "Are they investigating?" he asked.

"The Sheriff's Department?" Colt said, and shook his head. "No. Low priority. The deputy said it would be a wild goose chase. Of course, if I found out who took it, I could always make a citizen's arrest."

"A citizen's arrest?" Moose said. "Gimme a break. What TV shows have you been watching?" He dripped purple globs of jelly on the table.

Colt looked at him. "That's disgusting. Why don't you eat something healthy, like a donut?"

Moose held up a piece of the orange. "You know," he said, "I think you're suffering from Sexual Dependence Transference. The medical term is SDT."

"What?" Colt said.

"You and your girlfriend break up and two weeks later you're obsessing about some girl involved in an accident. Someone you don't even know. If that's not SDT, I don't know what is."

"I've heard of an STD, but never SDT," Brian said.

"That's because I just made it up," Moose said. He walked around the table, locked one arm around Colt's head and ground his knuckles hard against Colt's scalp.

"Hey!" Colt squirmed.

"Forget about yesterday and find yourself a new girlfriend. You need to get laid," Moose said.

"Speaking of getting laid," Captain Ames said, "did you get a look at that chick with the tattoos at the Surfrider? In the tank top and shorts? I'm on the radio calling AirSquad about a life-and-death situation and I'm thinking about what she looks like with her clothes off."

"I thought when you're over 30 you lose interest in sex," Moose said.

"How about the guy standing next to her?" Colt said, rubbing his head. "At the beach, in the summer, it's 80 degrees and he's dressed from head to toe in black. How come there's so many weirdos in Malibu? No one ever dressed like that in Wyoming."

"The foot'll turn up," Brian said. "In the next couple of days, someone'll drive over it in the parking lot and have a heart attack. We'll be called back."

Moose made another sandwich and washed it down with Gatorade. He wiped the jelly off the table, looked at the clock, stood up and said, "I'm gonna go check the engine."

Colt, Brian and Captain Ames remained at the table.

"I just filled out your four-week review," Brian said to Colt.

"I'm going down on Thursday to meet with Nurse Sandy," Colt said.

Nurse Sandy was Colt's field coordinator at the Paramedic Training Institute. She supervised the new paramedics and conducted two face-to-face reviews during their 20-shift internships in the field. She was a no-nonsense woman who had been around forever. She had the power to extend an internship, or even terminate it. She was fair, but tough, and had chewed a second asshole in more than one newbie. Colt was nervous about the upcoming meeting.

"Don't worry," Brian said, "I gave you pretty good marks."

"Pretty good?"

"You're doing great on the skills, but you're still a little stressed."

"I'm still getting used to being responsible for whether a person lives or dies," Colt said. "What if I screw up and make a mistake? What if I forget to do something? There's so much to remember." Colt got up, filled his coffee mug and looked out at PCH through one of the small windows in the kitchen. "Like yesterday. That girl, Bibi, was lying on the pavement and her foot's cut off. There's no one with her and she's looking at me with those deep blue eyes.

So I tell her everything's gonna be OK. Then we can't find her foot."

"That's what I mean. You're a little stressed," Brian said.

"You do everything you can," Captain Ames said, "but if you can't pull it off, it's not your fault. You can't perform miracles. You're gonna lose some people."

"Yeah, but—"

"Don't second-guess yourself," Brian said. "Don't get emotionally involved with your patients. If you start asking 'what if,' it never stops. You have to wall it off. You understand what I'm saying?"

Colt nodded. "I guess so. I just don't want to let anyone down."

"You're gonna see stuff on a day-to-day basis that most people don't see in their lifetimes," Captain Ames said. "It'll start coming back at you in your dreams if you let it. It'll tear you apart. When I had paramedic training, we spent a week at County Hospital. All the homeless people came to the ER for treatment. They had everything you can imagine. The pediatric cases were the worst. I remember one little girl, she couldn't have been more than 9 or 10. She comes in with her crack-head mother. They're both filthy and they stink. The kid had live maggots in an open sore on her leg. They were eating her flesh. I couldn't think about anything else for a week. That's when I realized if I let it get to me, I would never make it."

"Thanks for sharing that over breakfast," Colt said.

"Let's get to work," Captain Ames said.

Monday was a slow day for the 88s—there was only one serious incident, late in the morning. Brian and Colt responded to an accident in which a motorcycle tried to pass an SUV and clipped the side view mirror. The old Harley flipped over and the rider went down hard. The bike, low-rider bars twisted, lay in pieces on the highway. The gas tank, painted with a yellow and red flame design, had ripped away from the frame and left a trail of fuel as it tumbled over toward the center divider.

Colt and Brian arrived and went to work. The rider lay in the middle of the right-hand traffic lane, moaning in pain. He had severe road rash and raw flesh showed through the shredded leather on the right side of his body. He also had an exposed fracture on his right leg and half a dozen sheriffs' deputies were already on the scene, stopping northbound traffic, standing over the injured rider, interviewing the shaken driver of the SUV and clearing the biggest pieces of metal debris off the pavement.

Brian immobilized the biker's neck with a C-collar while Colt checked his vitals and started an IV. When they were certain he was stabilized, Brian put a splint on the injured leg. Colt began to cut off the bloody clothes. They didn't even try to remove the carbon-fiber reinforced motorcycle boots.

"Don't ruin my leathers," the biker said between grunts of pain.

"Sorry man, they're already ruined," Colt said, and continued to cut. "Just take it easy, we're gonna fix you up and get you to the hospital." Colt looked at the biker. He saw pain in the dark brown eyes, and maybe a little fear, but not death. Colt knew he would survive the crash.

"What about my bike?"

"The Sheriff's Department will take care of it," Brian said.

When Colt removed the biker's shirt, he saw the flesh scraped away from shoulder to hip. The man had a large belly and a mat of black hair grew over an eagle tattoo on his chest. Colt thought again of the stunning girl with the tattoos standing in the Surfrider parking lot.

Within 20 minutes, they had the injured biker in the LifeLine ambulance and on his way to the ER. Brian filled out the run report while Colt replaced their gear in the squad. They stood around for a few minutes, made small talk with the sheriff's deputies and then headed back to 88s. In the squad, Brian radioed the station, then said, "The guy's lucky he didn't end up under the rear wheel of that SUV."

Colt wasn't listening. "I Googled the name Bibi," he said. "It's a French name; it means 'a lady.'"

"Well, the lady was in the wrong place at the wrong time. It happens."

"I'm gonna go see her."

"What?"

"I'm going over to the hospital to see her."

"No, you're not. No way." Brian glared at Colt. "Drop it. You don't even know her. Did you hear anything we said this morning? You can't get involved in this stuff."

Colt stared out the windshield, avoiding Brian's gaze.

"Don't be so damn stubborn Colt, it'll only lead to trouble. As your preceptor, I'm telling you not to go. Our job is to rescue and stabilize injured people and send them on to the hospital. It stops there. That's it. You don't owe anyone more than that. If they make it, fine. If not, that's the way it is." Brian honked at a car making a left hand turn in front of the squad and swore under his breath. "You're not supposed to look into the eyes of an accident victim and start to care. Got it? End of discussion. I can still change your four-week evaluation report."

Colt kept thinking about Bibi and was quiet during the remainder of the shift. When it was over, he left the station without saying anything and drove to the California University Hospital on the west side of Los Angeles. He parked his pickup near the emergency entrance, placed his fire/paramedic sign on the dashboard and went through the double doors to the ER. Two Los Angeles City Fire paramedics preceded him, rolling a woman in on a gurney. Colt glanced at her face. Her eyes were closed. The eyes always bothered him. Colt preferred that the injured be unconscious. Even if they couldn't speak, when their eyes were open, they pleaded for help, like his father had done.

The hospital was a modern facility. The ER was spotless. Compared with the two trauma centers where Colt had done his clinical training, both of which were crowded and chaotic and where patients spent a lot of wall time in the halls waiting for an examination room, this was spacious, almost luxurious. Colt walked in past the sign with instructions printed in 12 languages.

Paramedics and EMTs from various fire departments and ambulance services stood talking, drinking coffee and filling out endless forms.

Two LAPD officers watched over a man with a gunshot wound, handcuffed to a gurney. Colt heard a doctor tell them, "When the bullet hit his femur, it must have fragmented. He's got holes in his stomach and intestines."

From one of the examination rooms, Colt heard a woman cry out. Someone said, "Lie back, honey, we're gonna give you some medicine to make the pain go away."

A surgical team wheeled a critical patient, hooked up to several IVs and bleeding from the face and neck, down the hall.

Doctors moved from room to room, wearing gloves and masks.

Nurses consulted computer screens.

The phones rang.

The automatic doors opened with a hiss, and new patients were wheeled in.

Colt was already beginning to recognize many of the paramedics and some of the hospital staff. He approached one of the nurses, a muscular black man. "We sent a girl in yesterday from Malibu," Colt said. "Around 3:30 by AirSquad. Maybe 22 or 23. Severed foot."

"And?" the nurse asked.

"And I wanted to check on her."

The nurse raised his eyebrows. "I can't tell you anything, you know that."

"C'mon man," Colt insisted.

"You know the HIPAA rules. I could get canned."

"We couldn't find her foot. I want to tell her we tried."

The nurse scratched the stubble on his cheek and lowered his voice. "You didn't get this from me, bro."

"I understand," Colt said, moving closer to him.

"She didn't make it. Bled out and died on the helo. Cardiac arrest."

"No." Colt exhaled as though he had been punched in the stomach. Even though she was a complete stranger, Colt felt as though he knew her. He felt devastated. One minute she was enjoying a beautiful afternoon at the beach and the next minute some idiot hits a light pole, it cuts off her foot and she bleeds to death. No one deserved that.

"The body went to the morgue." The nurse looked around to see if anyone was listening. "Last I heard, they hadn't identified her."

"Her first name was Bibi." Colt remembered every detail of her pretty, tanned face, her ocean blue eyes and blond hair. He thought about the bleeding stump of her right leg. He hoped she had been unconscious on the AirSquad, but imagined her still awake, lying in the helicopter, terrified, surrounded by strangers and feeling her life draining away. Now her body was on a metal gurney in the basement of the L.A. County morgue. "What if someone's sitting around, waiting for her to show up?" Colt said to the nurse. "What if they still think she's alive?"

The nurse shrugged. "What if?"

"She must have a family or a boyfriend," Colt said. Someone would eventually have to retrieve a bag from the medical examiner containing her blue CALIFORNIA T-shirt and white shorts spattered with blood.

Colt needed fresh air. He always entered through the back end of the ER and had never exited through the front of the hospital. "How do I get out of here?" he asked.

"Straight down this hall." The nurse pointed. "You go through two sets of doors and come out in the front lobby by the elevators. Make a left."

"Thanks, I owe you." Colt clapped him on the shoulder.

He followed the nurse's directions and exited the front of the hospital into a courtyard filled with benches and tables formed by the surrounding buildings. He sat down and checked his watch. It was almost 7:00 p.m. The warm September evening still had another hour of daylight. Visitors entered and exited the hospital. Groups of doctors in white jackets, some with stethoscopes in their side pockets and pagers clipped to their belts, sat around drinking coffee. Healthcare staff in blue gowns and surgical assistants in green scrubs sat at other tables, talking and eating. Some checked text messages. A patient in a hospital gown, accompanied by a nurse's aide, pulled an aluminum rack with IVs toward the entrance. Students carrying bags filled with books walked through the square, using it as a shortcut to other destinations.

Everyone was with someone, drawing strength from companionship. Colt sat alone. A strong gust of wind blew dust through the hospital courtyard, caught loose newspapers, empty cups and napkins and swirled them into the air.

Another dust devil from another time twisted toward Colt from the far side of a corral while he sat on a split-rail fence and watched his father break a stallion.

"Damn you, you son of a bitch," his father cursed at the horse. He pulled at the reins and gouged its flanks with his spurs. The horse reared up and threw him out of the saddle. It had happened before, but this time his father's boot caught in the stirrup. He tried to kick free as the panicked animal dragged him across the dirt.

Colt was off the fence, running across the corral and screaming when the horse kicked his father on the side of the head. His foot came out of his boot and he fell to the ground. The stallion retreated to the fence at the far end of the corral, pawed the ground and watched. "Stay there, you fucker," Colt screamed.

Colt knelt down and rolled his father onto his back. His eyes were open and he was still breathing, but his temple was caved in. The right side of his skull looked as though a sledgehammer had hit it. One ear hung by a strip of flesh. Blood oozed out. Colt touched his father's head and looked at the red liquid on his fingers.

"Dad?" Tears welled up. "Dad?" A chill passed through Colt's body. His father's eyes were open. He moved his lips but made no sound. Colt left him lying on his back in the dirt and ran up to the house to call Fire and Rescue. It was a 20-minute trip out from Sheridan and he already knew his father wouldn't survive. When he returned to the corral, his father, eyes still open, was dead.

"Can we share the table?"

The corral dissolved and Colt looked up at two nurses holding green plastic trays. "All yours," he said. He stood up and ran his hands through his hair, as if to clear his head of the memories. Evening shadows stretched across the courtyard, climbing the buildings on the far side.

Colt walked out onto the campus, full of open plazas surrounded by brick and stone buildings. He had driven past California University and had brought patients into the ER, but he had never been on the campus. It went on forever. He followed the broad sidewalks past centers, halls and institutes surrounded by pine and eucalyptus. Jacaranda trees with delicate canopies of leaves grew on quadrangles of carefully manicured grass. Large black crows, perched in the trees, cried out. Gray squirrels ran across the ground in a final search for food before night set in. The sound of chimes from a clock tower, followed by seven low-pitched peals of the hour bell, echoed across the campus. Colt looked at his watch and found it was slow.

As he walked farther, Colt passed students sitting on benches, walking, riding bicycles and coasting on skateboards. They were conversing, texting, listening to iPods and talking on cell phones, all at the same time. He heard strange languages. Colt saw men with purple hair, ponytails and shaved heads. The female students wore everything from cut-off shorts and high leather boots to jeans that looked like they were spray painted on their bodies. One girl who walked past him had a small silver rod anchored through holes pierced in the top and bottom of her ear.

So many of the students were Asian. CU looked like the United Nations, completely different from anything in Wyoming, which was 99 percent Caucasian and the remainder American Indian. Where did they come from? China? Japan? Korea? What other countries? Colt wondered how often they connected with families half-way around the world. Did their parents know what they were studying, who they were dating, how they were feeling? Colt had no idea how a regular family worked.

As Colt continued on, a short, dark figure appeared, walking toward him on the sidewalk. A man, dressed in black, wearing dark glasses and a black hat, made his way along the sidewalk. Colt recognized him immediately—there was no doubt it was the person he saw standing in the parking lot at the Surfrider. He stepped aside. As the man walked past him, Colt saw white hair sticking out from under the hat. Colt waited a few seconds and started after him.

He trailed the man across the campus, trying to decide his next move. Colt tried to follow him without being detected. He closed the distance between them, fearful of losing the black figure in the impending darkness. They walked between buildings, across grass courtyards and down a sidewalk past a construction site. A forest of inch-thick black iron rebar grew from the cement foundations. Colt watched the figure in black cross in the middle of a street and followed him into a multi-story parking structure that covered a square block.

Inside, Colt looked in both directions. Rear bumpers and hoods of vehicles stretched in all directions, bathed in a metallic blue glow from sodium lights on the low ceiling. White arrows on the cement floor pointed in every direction—UP, DOWN, IN, EXIT, DO NOT ENTER. A group of vending machines created an island of contrasting fluorescent light near a stairwell at the center of the building. Colt heard the muffled sounds of automobile engines and tires squealing on cement. Somewhere the vibrations triggered the horn of a car alarm and the insistent sound bounced off the cement walls, echoing throughout the structure. At LEVEL 2-EXIT, Colt followed his quarry out over a row of sharp metal teeth embedded in the cement.

Standing in the street on the other side of the parking structure, Colt had no idea where he was. The sun was now gone and darkness was setting in. The man ascended a long steep flight of stairs and Colt followed him. When he reached the top, Colt saw the entrance to a modern glass and stainless steel building, unlike anything else he had seen on the campus. Letters over the entrance identified it as the Nano Research Center. The man stopped to remove his dark glasses, and in the glow from a nearby campus streetlight, searched for something in his pockets.

Colt made his move. "Hey," Colt said. "Hey, you."

The man looked up and stared at Colt.

Colt stared back. In the illumination of the streetlight, the man's irises reflected red. His skin was pale. He had white hair.

"You talking to me?" the man asked.

For crissake, Colt thought, he's an albino. No wonder he's all buttoned up and wears dark glasses. "Yes. I wanna ask you something."

"What are you, a campus cop?"

"No, I'm a paramedic. County Fire Department."

"What d'you want? I'm late for work."

"Were you at the Surfrider yesterday afternoon? At the beach? Didn't I see you there?"

"The Surfrider? What about it?"

"We responded to a call. A girl lost her foot."

"Oh yeah? Did she find it?" The albino had a nasty smile.

"This is no joke. There was an accident in the parking lot. Did you see anything?"

"Who said I was there?"

"I walked right past you."

The albino stared at Colt. His strange eyes were unnerving. "So?"

"The girl's foot was severed." And we lost her, Colt wanted to add. "We couldn't find it. Did you see anything?" Colt stepped toward the man.

The man stepped back. "Get out of my face."

"Someone may have picked it up."

"Not my problem. Why are you bothering me? I have to go to work." He withdrew a white plastic card from his pocket.

A wave of anger swept through Colt. He wondered why the albino was so hostile. "Did you take her foot?"

The albino stopped and stared at Colt with his red eyes. He was small and Colt was tempted to grab him, lift him up and shake the crap out of him.

"So long, fuckwit," the albino said. He walked to the entrance of the Nano Research Center and inserted a white ID card. The doors swung open.

Colt walked toward the entrance and called after him, "You can't keep it."

Once inside, Colt saw the albino turn and flip him the bird.

Colt found his way back to his pickup in the hospital parking area. He was certain he knew who had Bibi's foot.

# FIVE

O N MONDAY EVENING, A LI SAT with her class of PhD students around a conference table on the third floor of the new Nano Research Center. Hisao was finishing his pathology presentation with slides showing stained sections of mouse brains. While Dr. Murray studied the screen and nodded, A Li stared out the large window at the campus below. As the evening lights came on, she watched the strange man wearing black who worked in the center. He stood talking to someone wearing a uniform, then approached the entrance to the building and disappeared from view.

A Li turned her attention back to the slide presentation and the people in the room. Dr. Murray, a full professor at the center and one of the world leaders in research on reprogramming the DNA of stem cells, sat at the head of the table. He was the only American in the room. Six of the eight students in her research group were Asian and all but A Li were graduates of the top science universities in their countries. If A Li counted herself, there were three Chinese. The difference was, she was female and a member of the Zang ethnic minority in China, known to the rest of the world as Tibetan, and grew up in the TAR— the Tibetan Autonomous Region. A Li was taller than most Chinese women, not as delicate, had a ruddy complexion and wore her thick black hair in a single long braid. Like other successful Asian students, she had worked her way up through high-pressure schools, studying six days a week, 12 hours a day, sacrificing everything else in her life until she passed the *gaokao*—the Chinese college entrance examination. While most female Tibetan college graduates became teachers or minor government functionaries, A Li graduated at the top of her college class and went on for a master's degree in biochemistry. She felt she was as smart as the two Chinese men in her research group, but she had studied at Yunnan University in a remote southwest province of China.

A Li was not a member of the Communist Party, or part of any other influential group in China. Her parents were simple people and her father, her Pa Lags, was only a provincial science teacher who did not have the connections necessary to allow her to study at the best school, the University of Science and Technology of China. After working at a low-level job at a pharmaceutical company for a year, she received a loan from her provincial government to study for a PhD in America. California University had delayed her application for months while they verified her grades because another Chinese applying to bioscience studies had added phony courses to his transcript. After A Li arrived, she discovered the authentication policy did not apply to graduates of the top Chinese universities.

Hisao finished his presentation, turned off his laser pointer and hit the button to retract the screen into the ceiling.

"Excellent," Dr. Murray said. "No tumors after 12 weeks? This builds on David Zhao's findings. When do you dissect your next group of mice?"

"Eight more weeks," Hisao said. "Twenty weeks after transplantation." Hisao spoke perfect English, but had the habit of sometimes looking up at the ceiling when he spoke. He rarely made eye contact.

"Excellent," Dr. Murray said again and looked through his papers. "I have a note here to remind you all that this is the last chance to order mice from the Colony for next semester, so get your requirements to the lab manager by the end of the week." He sipped his coffee and swiveled his chair to face A Li.

She froze with fear.

"A Li, please update us on the progress of your work." He drummed his fingers on the table. "You are progressing?"

A Li was still struggling with English, but the impatience in his voice was unmistakable. As part of her PhD work, she was working on stem cells, the building blocks of the body. Dr. Murray's cutting-edge research focused on altering the DNA in a key gene that was capable of turning a stem cell into a blood cell. The investigation had progressed to the point that they were injecting and growing the altered cells in mice. If successful, Dr. Murray would eventually show the world that he could reprogram the existing DNA in blood cells to correct genetic defects in humans. It would also lead to the ability to change one blood type into another—a major breakthrough in the fields of blood transfusion and organ transplant rejection. Dr. Murray was competing against researchers at other universities and institutes around the world. The first group to successfully reprogram the DNA, document the process and recreate the results would find a place in medical history. If it happened in his lab, both Dr. Murray and CU would also reap incredible financial rewards.

When she arrived at CU, A Li was excited to be part of Dr. Murray's important research. She thought her work was going well, but sensed from the beginning that he lacked confidence in her. He seemed more critical of her than of the other students. Perhaps Dr. Murray would treat her with more respect if her family were more important.

"I ... uh ... plan to harvest the first mouse tonight," she said.

"Please start with a summary of your project." Dr. Murray looked at her with such intensity that his eyes seemed to bore into her head. "It's never too soon to learn to give a concise and informative overview of your research. You may have to do it for a grant review, or for a peer group evaluation."

"I am growing human blood cells in mice—"

Ignoring her, Dr. Murray continued on, "It's doubly important for those of you who are not yet proficient in English."

"Uh," she continued, "I am using SCID mice to—"

"No," Dr. Murray interrupted again. Now his impatience was tinged with anger. "You are using Severe Combined Immuno Deficiency mice."

"Yes, I am using Severe Combined Immuno Deficiency mice. ..."

"And?"

A Li paused. Now she was terrified. She hated speaking in front of a group, even people in her lab, without a detailed outline of what she wanted to say. Dr. Murray was right; she was not proficient in English. Mandarin was her second language. English was still a distant third. She glanced across the table at Tanay. He gave her an encouraging smile.

Dr. Murray drummed his fingers on the table and continued to stare at her. "You are using Severe Combined Immuno Deficiency mice that can accept human blood cells without rejection." He pushed his glasses up on top of his head. "Then," he gestured at A Li with his pen, "you are irradiating the mice to destroy their bone marrow ... yes?"

A Li nodded.

"And, finally," Dr. Murray made more stabbing motions with the pen, "you are injecting them with the altered human blood cells and tracing their migration to the various organs."

"Yes, yes." A Li looked down at her laptop. She felt humiliated in front of her classmates. "That is correct," she repeated softly.

"For next week, A Li," he went on, "please prepare a brief summary of your research and update us on your progress. Be prepared to discuss the alteration in the mechanisms that prevent the mouse from rejecting the human cells." He drained his coffee, pushed his chair back and stood up. "OK, have a good evening. I'm available for consultation on projects or grant applications if anyone needs help." On his way out, he picked up the paper platter of uneaten bagels and stale cream cheese left over from the morning and tossed it into the trash. The students closed their notebooks, turned off their laptops, filled their backpacks and followed Dr. Murray out.

A Li remained seated and held her head in her hands.

Tanay came back into the conference room after the others departed and put his hand on her shoulder. "Cheer up," he said. "Interested in some dinner? Italian? Ethiopian? Brazilian? Mexican? How about Chinese?"

"Thanks," A Li said and tried to smile. "I've got work to do." An Indian, Tanay was her only friend in the research group and, in fact, her only male friend in Los Angeles. She didn't know him very well, but liked him.

"You've always got work to do." He sat down and put his feet up on the conference table. "You have a life, too."

She had never noticed the size of his feet.

"How about takeout?" he said. "We could eat dinner here."

She gave him a look. "I don't like takeout. No one eats fresh vegetables in this country." At home, local produce still coated with dirt came to the market in wooden tubs, metal buckets and baskets. When A Li's host, Professor Chen, took her on her first shopping expedition to a supermarket near the campus, she was overwhelmed at the number of items and was amazed at the variety and quality of the fruits and vegetables. She was astounded to see several men standing around polishing each item before placing it on the counter for sale. With such abundance, she couldn't understand why everyone ate tacos and KFC.

"C'mon, you need a break," Tanay insisted.

"Not tonight." A Li was taking four hours a day of molecular biology, immunology and biological chemistry, working for Dr. Murray to earn her research stipend and attending English language classes. There was no free time for anything else.

"The old man getting to you?"

A Li nodded. "Dr. Murray doesn't like me."

"He does the English proficiency number on everyone and he's always critical until he gets to know you. Once you're past that, he's not a bad guy."

"How long does that take?"

"How long have you been here? Four months?"

"It seems like forever. I'm homesick."

"It hits everyone, but you'll get over it." Tanay looked at her. "Are you staying here after your studies, or are you going back to China?"

"I don't know, what does it matter?" A Li stared out at the dark campus again. Her home, Zhongdian, was a town with crooked cobblestone streets on a 9,000-foot plateau surrounded by mountain meadows and grazing yaks. Los Angeles might as well be on another planet. How could anyone be happy in a hot, crowded city where it hardly rained?

"Let's have dinner tomorrow night," Tanay said.

"Maybe." She wasn't sure what signals Tanay was sending about their relationship. Was his intention more than friendship? Did he want to be her boyfriend? Would he ever try to kiss her? She knew she was ordinary looking, nothing special. Most of her life had been devoted to studying and she never had a chance to date or go to parties. Her sexual experience was limited. When she came to Los Angeles, men stared at her and sometimes brushed by and touched her. Once, an older man, standing next to her on a street corner, whispered in her ear, "Hey honey, I love Asian girls." She knew little about the more subtle flirtations between men and women. Maybe Tanay wanted to get into bed with her. He was tall and good-looking and she felt attracted to him. She liked his coal black hair and the bronze color of his skin. It reminded her of the skin of the people in Zhongdian, the dark healthy hue they called "plateau blush" which came from the high altitude rays of the sun. She wished his sideburns were shorter but that was of little importance. A Li was unsure how to respond to Tanay and, anyhow, there was no room for him in her life. She was busy, there was so much to do and she had her sister.

"Do you own a car?" she asked.

"Yes."

"Could you drive me down to the Flower Mart?"

"Sure, I could take you down there sometime."

"It would have to be tomorrow."

"Why tomorrow?"

"I'm looking for iris flowers for my twin sister. It's her birthday."

"You have a twin sister? You never mentioned her. What's her name?"

"A Mei. Our names come from the Meili Snow Mountain Range."

"Where is she? Is she here in Los Angeles?"

A Li was silent for a moment. "She died when we were 7."

"What?"

"Twenty-two years ago. She was hit by a car. A black Mercedes."

"A hit and run?"

"Yes. It was a Party member. No one else had a car like that."

"Where did this happen?"

"At home, in Zhongdian. After the accident, the police drove us to the People's Hospital in Lijiang. It took three hours. I was so frightened for my sister."

"And she died on the way?"

"No, she died in the hospital." A Li took a tissue out of her pocket and dabbed her eyes. After all the years, she still became emotional when she spoke of her sister's death. "They transfused her with whatever blood they had. I don't know what type it was, but it didn't matter. I didn't understand it at the time, but she had a hemolytic reaction. Our family has Bombay Blood. Her body rejected the transfusion and shut down from organ failure."

"Bombay Blood, what's that?"

"We were so close. I still miss her. When she died, part of me died too." A Li rubbed her eyes and felt embarrassed in front of Tanay. "Her birthday is tomorrow. Every year, I have gone home to honor her, but for the first time it's impossible. I want to get some iris. It's her flower. They grow in Tibet."

"What's Bombay Blood?" Tanay asked again. "Should I know what that is?"

"I'll tell you about it tomorrow. Can you pick me up at 12:30?" She reached for a napkin left on the conference table and scribbled on it. "I live with a Chinese family on Canyon Avenue. Here's the address. I'll be waiting outside."

"I should be in the lab tomorrow," Tanay murmured. "Do you have a cell phone number in case I have to call you?"

"Yes." She wrote her number under her address on the napkin. A Li didn't use her cell phone often unless she was talking to another Chinese. She found it impossible to understand anything in English unless she was face to face with the person speaking.

"It's your birthday, too. Right?"

A Li nodded. "Yes." She gave Tanay a shy smile, gathered her things together and stuffed them into her backpack. She had several hours of work to do in the laboratory and then had to go to the Colony to retrieve one of her mice for dissection. It was going to be another long night.

# SIX

AFTER HE WALKED into the Nano Research Center and the glass doors closed behind him, Markus turned and looked back at the paramedic in his dumbass uniform, standing outside. Markus couldn't resist. He held his hand above his head and gave him the middle finger salute. "Up yours, mister crew cut," he whispered. "Finders keepers."

He walked past the security office inside the entrance and saw the two night guard retards through the glass window in the wall. The little one looked up from his computer screen, recognized Markus and nodded. The big one with no neck ignored him. Markus called them Dumb and Dumber. He had visited the security office once and stayed just long enough to pilfer a master key to all the doors in the building while he had a conversation with them.

The lobby was dim and Markus walked through what he was certain was the quietest place on earth. "The building's built on state-of-the-art springs and shock absorbers," the information technology manager told him during his job interview. "When you have experiments with particles one-thousandth the width of a hair, there can't be any noise or vibration, and I'm not just talking about an earthquake, I'm talking about a trash truck on the street a block away."

Markus took off his silver earring with the tiny skull for the interview. Software people are all strange, but Markus felt the earring might be too much. In the end, IT only cared whether Markus had the skills to convert old employment records on CU's system from dBASE 4 to SQL. No one cared how he looked or when he came to work. Markus was accomplishing his task faster than expected and using the rest of the allotted time for his own purposes. The pay was all right, but he wasn't getting rich. Markus was caught in a chicken-and-egg situation. The only way he could get some big bucks was by online hacking. To do that, he needed new software. To get the software, he needed money.

Markus pushed the elevator button. Why had he bothered with the paramedic? The guy was a moron with a short haircut and an idiot blue uniform. He looked like a doorman from one of the fancy condominiums on Wilshire Boulevard. Why had he even spoken to him? What if the asshole decided to investigate? That would be just what Markus didn't need—someone interfering with his life. He should have just kept his mouth shut. Tonight was important. He had to forget the conversation with the paramedic; they would never see each other again. It was time to collect blood from the China Doll and that required his complete concentration.

The elevator doors opened and closed without a sound. Markus descended into the bowels of the research center. On lower level 2, Markus heard the sound of his own heartbeat as he walked from the elevator to Office 3, one of the spare rooms in the building used for temporary workers. He swiped his ID card and the click of the electronic lock sounded like thunder.

Markus didn't bother to turn on the lights. A computer screen, flashing the CU logo, illuminated the space. He usually spent the first hour tending to his private business. He did some of his best hacking from this computer because it was much harder for anyone to penetrate CU's firewall and identify his IP address. He also played online games and connected with the Goth community. Markus also managed several e-mail accounts here, some of which he changed weekly. Most of the Goths were just kids going through teen-age rebellion. Others were suffering from depression or dysfunctional family lives, but would eventually grow up and be boring and normal like everyone else. The older ones had day jobs and some were just psy-vampires, not even interested in blood. They were all harmless and lame. They just wanted to dress up, look weird and see the shock on normal people's faces. Markus kept them at bay with his changing e-mail addresses and the CU firewall.

His true friends were another story. They were a small group devoted to blood-fetishism and the vampire way of life. They were the true vampires; the elite of the undead, and Markus considered himself at the pinnacle of the group. He had a special permanent e-mail address for them and he used the name BloodyFangs, his first and most treasured moniker. At the bottom of his e-mail, his original signature had been, BITE ME. Later he changed it to DARK ANGEL. Finally, he began using, IT IS BETTER TO RULE IN HELL THAN SERVE IN HEAVEN. Markus thought the phrase was awesome and was certain it was written by a fellow Goth. He was surprised to learn it was actually from Milton's *Paradise Lost*, but he continued to use it anyway.

Markus pulled the keyboard toward him and logged on to one of his favorite vampire websites.

"You don't think this is a fairy tale, do you?" The deep voice exploded from his computer speakers.

"No," Markus whispered, slipping into the reverie.

"You are a predator with a hunger."

"Yes." Markus thought about the China Doll and his plans for later in the evening.

"You are one of us!"

"Yes. Darkness rules."

"Seek out the blood of others. Drink your fill. Your blood will grow stronger."

Markus jumped up from his desk chair. "I will take her blood," he said in a louder voice.

"Your undead life has—"

Markus sat down again and disconnected. Much as he would have liked to continue to chant the ritual, he had to get the data conversion work out of the way before his date with the China Doll. He logged on to the CU virtual private network. When the system came up, he inserted his dongle—the electronic key—into the USB port to authenticate himself and gain access to the old records. When he started the work four months ago, the first thing Markus did was find out what other files were on the server he was using. It took him a week to hack into the list and two more weeks to find the 128-bit encryption code that gave him access to the current confidential information about personnel working at the Nano Research Center. Some nights, when he became bored with the job he was supposed to be doing, Markus played a game. He looked at ID pictures from the center's personnel files and tried to match them up with faces he had seen in the building. The center was full of individuals from Europe, South America and Asia. After a month, Markus recognized more than two dozen people. One of the first was a Chinese woman named A

Li Jian. He had seen her in the lobby several times in the evening. He rode up on the elevator with her once and found out she worked on the third floor. He decided to call her China Barbie Doll, then shortened it to China Doll.

When Markus tired of the ID picture game, he began to access and read individual personnel files. One night he scanned the China Doll's file: She was 29, born in Zhongdian, and part of her tuition came from some sort of a government scholarship. Her field of research was pluripotent stem cells, whatever that was. Blah, blah, blah—much of the information was of little interest to Markus. At the bottom of the file, however, there was a highlighted entry: Blood type – Bombay. Markus couldn't believe it. The first time he saw it, his pulse went through the roof and his hands trembled. He scrolled to the next page of the file and then went back. The words were still there; he wasn't imagining it. Blood type – Bombay.

What a killer discovery. The Great Markus, the kickass vampire, had found the Holy Grail. He deserved this reward. Over the years, he had visited every hematology website and had studied all the obscure blood types—*Le Pore, Saskatoon, Titusville, and Bombay.* Among them, Bombay was the rarest of the rare and this Chinese woman carried it in her veins. It occurred in one out of 250,000 people and only in those of East Indian or Chinese descent. Markus knew about the antigens, the phenotypes and the inherited recessive genes of Bombay Blood. A person with this rare blood type could donate to anyone, but would suffer an immune reaction unless a transfusion came from another person carrying the same blood.

When he first read about Bombay, Markus became obsessed with it. He fantasized about it for hours. It was the *uber* blood. He imagined a drop of it on his tongue. He would savor it, letting it linger on his taste buds. What would the flavor be? Salty? Metallic? Acidic? Whatever, the rarest blood in the world would taste awesome, insane, wicked. It would be like nothing else. He was certain it would also have the most exceptional color. Markus imagined it to be carmine, the rich silky deep red color of a rare ruby. Markus even found a Bollywood movie about a gangster in Mumbai who had Bombay Blood and needed an urgent heart transplant. In the film, his goons located a man with a healthy heart who also carried Bombay Blood. They made plans to cut him up and take the organ, but he escaped at the end of the movie by threatening to shoot himself in the heart before they could salvage it. Markus loved the story.

Now someone who carried the glorious liquid was in the Nano building, on the third floor! Markus thought about the China Doll day and night and developed a plan. He didn't need her heart, just a sample of her blood. It would be so easy to obtain. Outside of his office, at the end of the hallway on LL2, a fire stairwell led to the underground tunnels connecting much of the campus. On Mondays, the Chinese woman came into the building around 4 p.m. Around midnight, she came down the stairwell and went into the tunnel. Markus had watched her and followed her twice to the entrance of the building everyone called the Colony where they bred mice, rats and who knew what else for use in the university's research projects. The passageway was deserted at that hour. He decided that was the place to take her.

When he told his blood-sucking friends what he had in mind, they were rapturous and all agreed that this rare blood would have miraculous restorative powers. One wanted a sample for energy enhancement. Another wanted it for use during sex. A third felt it would strengthen his immune system. A female vamp thought it would take the edge off her menstrual cramps. Drakkar, one of the most powerful vampires on the West Coast, told him, "Man, just get some for me, *I want it!*"

What vampire wouldn't pay to sample Bombay Blood? Markus realized he might even sell it on eBay. Vampires everywhere would bid up the price. His mind ran wild with the idea. He imagined himself a Goth gangster-kingpin. He would kidnap the Chinese woman and keep her chained in the basement of his huge castle, surrounded by men with guns and vicious guard dogs. She would bargain, cry, plead and promise him sex, anything to go free, but Markus would make her his blood slave. He would stuff her with red meat and iron supplements and every day his men would strap her to a table and bleed her, collecting quarts, no, gallons of her Bombay Blood. He would sell it to the highest bidders. He would become a dealer of Bombay Blood, he would become *the* dealer of Bombay Blood. He would be famous, a gazillionaire. His power and fame would exceed that of Drakkar. He would become the extreme Bombay Goth Vampire.

Markus sat in the dark office and began to work on the SQL data conversion, but his heart wasn't in it this evening. He was too stoked to concentrate. Markus couldn't think about anything other than the China Doll and the elixir running in her veins. He turned on the small desk light and dug into his duffel, removing the bag containing a bottle of ether, a washcloth, two sterile syringes with needles capped in blue plastic and two blood collection tubes containing a few drops of heparin, an anticoagulant. He planned to splash the ether on the cloth, come up behind her in the tunnel and hold it to her face. If there was a struggle, he would overpower her. If she screamed, no one would be around to hear, not at that hour. Once she slumped to the ground, he could draw blood from her arm and collect it in the tubes. He would be gone before she regained consciousness. She would never even know what happened.

He checked his watch and wandered out into the hall to stretch his legs. He still had three hours before hiding in the stairwell on the fourth floor to wait for the China Doll to enter from the floor below. He looked up at the ceiling where capped wires protruded from an electrical conduit. Markus knew that the Nano Research Center was over budget when completed. While it had some state-of-the art security devices, no monitoring equipment was ever installed in the fire stairwell at the tunnel entrance. Markus wondered how the university could spend money on guards and security equipment throughout the building, monitor everyone coming in the front doors and embed each person's office address on the ID cards, but still allow an unobstructed entrance through the old campus passageway.

The China Doll was punctual. On Tuesday morning at 12:05 a.m., Markus crouched on the fourth floor landing. The stairwell was flooded with light and the glare burned his eyes. Markus had left his dark glasses at his desk and now there was no time to go back to get them. He squinted, followed her and watched her delicate hand slide down along the metal banister as she descended below him. His dream was about to come true. Soon he would taste Bombay Blood. He heard the heavy steel fire door scrape when she opened it and he shadowed her into the tunnel.

Once underground, Markus was in his own world. The glare of the fluorescent lighting in the center's stairwell gave way to half-light and the pain in his eyes disappeared. The air was dank and had a metallic odor. Markus heard a low-pitched hum from machinery running somewhere nearby. Pieces of plaster from the walls had fallen away where moisture had seeped through. A maze of electrical conduits, ducts and pipes wrapped with aluminum insulation ran along the ceiling.

Markus crept along behind her, trying to be as quiet as possible. He could barely contain his excitement. A wave of sexual arousal washed over him. This exotic woman excited him more than all the titty bars and more than any vampire fantasy. This was not a dream; the woman was real. Her blood was real. She had a long, beautiful neck—how many times had he thought of that tender spot above her shoulders where her carotid artery pulsed. Just for fun, he wanted to bite into her warm and fragrant skin. Tonight for the first time he wondered what her feet looked like. Would they be as delicate as the foot in his freezer?

He stopped in the tunnel to open the ether bottle and held his breath while he splashed some of the liquid onto the cloth. When he shoved the bottle back in his pocket and set off after her again, he realized she was walking faster and he had let her get away from him. She was already at the security door of the Colony.

Markus ran to catch the door before it swung shut. He had never been in the Colony. When he entered, the blinding light hit him. The floor was white vinyl, the walls white tile, the ceiling white plaster. The entire hallway looked like it had just been washed and polished—reflecting, bouncing, intensifying the glare. Markus squinted. He felt a wave of nausea and the beginning of a ginormous headache. Could he do her in the whiteout of the Colony?

He crept down the hall listening to the sound of the China Doll's rubber soles on the floor. A cool breeze from controlled-climate air conditioning blew in his face and the ether evaporated from the cloth in his hand. Markus trailed her past RATS and looked through a window set in the wall. He took an involuntary step back. He had seen gray and Norwegian rats, but had never seen these huge white laboratory rats. Behind the glass, the rats pushed and shoved in their cages, biting and climbing over each other. Hundreds of sets of glowing red eyes, the color of his own, gazed back at him. Did they see a similarity? Did they regard him as friend or foe? Would they rip him apart or make him their master? Markus imagined hundreds of the white monsters, teeth bared, running over the cement floor of an abandoned warehouse. In a frenzy, they circled a lifeless body. At his command, they swarmed over it, bit and tore the flesh, tasting the blood.

The China Doll disappeared through another doorway. Markus crept forward and stopped behind a dolly loaded with mouse cages. Like a peeping tom, he watched through another window as she washed her hands in a stainless steel sink, donned latex gloves and took a sterile blue gown, paper slippers, hair net and mask from a cabinet. She put the gown on over her clothes, smoothing it over her body with her hands. Watching her just touch herself, even through a layer of clothing, aroused Markus. She was so close, just on the other side of the glass. He could almost touch her. He imagined the texture of her exotic blood, the color and the taste. It was time—he could wait no longer. When she came out into the hallway, he would do it. Vlad Drackula Markus would claim the reward of her blood. He removed the bottle of ether again from his pocket.

"... *so in some cases the stem cell function declines with age and—*"

"*Yes, but the aging process can be reversed. We're working on that right now ...*"

Markus froze. At midnight, someone else was in the Colony. Two men, one with a full beard the color of his white lab coat, were walking down the hall toward him.

"... *the osteoblasts send out signals from the bone marrow and ...*"

His excitement evaporated. Markus ran from behind the stack of mouse cages and charged back down the hallway toward the tunnel.

# SEVEN

THE FIRST TIME A LI ENTERED the vast, dark underground tunnel complex, she was frightened even though Tanay was with her. "It's perfectly safe," he had told her. "There's no one down here but faculty and students."

A Li had not felt safe. The tunnels were dark, damp, ran off in all directions like a labyrinth and she wondered if she would ever learn her way around. The passages reminded her of one of the fables she and A Mei heard when they were children. According to Tibetan legend, there was an underground city of gold in a vast cavern in the Himalayas, guarded by wayward spirits and connected to the cellars of the monasteries by an ancient tunnel system. People who ventured in to search for the gold never returned.

Months after her first underground venture with Tanay, A Li had made the round trip between the Nano Research Center and the Colony enough times to know the route and feel secure, although she would still not venture through the maze to any of the other science buildings or to more distant destinations on the campus. Tonight after her humiliation by Dr. Murray, she walked to the Colony alone through the tunnel and had the strange sensation someone was following her. She moved faster and tried to distract herself with thoughts about her parents and her home.

In her religion, the family bond was sacred. Even if they were 8,000 miles and 15 hours away, her connection to A Ma and Pa Lags was unaffected. In Zhongdian, it would now be dinnertime. In the early fall evening, the sun would be setting on the green hillsides and pasture lands. The wind would blow, bamboo would rustle and birds would take flight. Her father would enter their modest tile-roofed home, drop his battered leather satchel filled with his student's papers and walk into the kitchen. Her mother would have set the table with steamed dumplings, yak cheese and ginger tea. After dinner, they might sit quietly and sip *Chang*, the Tibetan wine made from highland wheat. If they walked to the square to watch the singing and dancing, they would see the candle-lit windows of the Ganden Sumsteling monastery on the hillside. A Li imagined every detail with perfect clarity, but no image of her family would be complete without including A Mei. If her sister were still alive, she would be at the dinner table with a husband and two beautiful little twin girls of her own. If A Mei were alive, A Li would be at home at her sister's side, not walking through a subterranean web of damp tunnels half way around the world.

A Li was hungry and thought how nice it would have been to have dinner with Tanay. Six hours ago, she had washed down her meal of raw vegetables and a bowl of noodles with a bottle of cold green tea before hurrying off to listen to the presentations in Dr. Murray's lab. Now it was after midnight and she still had to retrieve one of her mice and do a dissection. There was always so much work.

She turned to look behind her, still certain someone was following her through the tunnel. She wasn't imagining it; she sensed another person in the darkness behind her. A Li quickly climbed the flight of stairs to the security door of the Colony. She swiped her ID card and when she opened the door, a current of cool dry air blew around her from the air filtration system.

As soon as she was inside under the bright light, she felt safe. The breeze followed her as she walked through the gleaming white hallway to the change room where she donned sterile clothing before she went "behind the barrier" to retrieve one of her mice. All the breeding of CU's genetically altered mice occurred inside the Colony, which housed thousands of the little creatures. Many of them were "knock-out mice," which meant they had been bred with certain genes eliminated or knocked out. The medical research depended on a mouse population free of outside contamination and every precaution was taken to keep them healthy and untainted.

A Li was excited and for the moment forgot about her anxiety in the tunnel as well as her problems with Dr. Murray. The previous week she had completed the mouse anatomy and surgery course. She had learned how to inject stem cells into the live animals through the veins in their tails and had learned to dissect mice under the supervision of her instructor. This would be her first solo dissection. After harvesting samples from the various mouse organs tonight, she would search for the altered stem cells in the tissue later in the week. At the next lab meeting, she hoped to report to Dr. Murray and the others that she had found the stem cells thriving in the organs. It would go a long way toward establishing her as a respected member of the research group.

A Li left the change room and went down the hall to the room that held the mice used in Dr. Murray's experiments. Tonight she planned to harvest the organs from PGL0101, a two-inch gray mouse. The room contained a solid wall of cages supported on shelves. She turned on the dim night light. Most of the cages contained two or three of the creatures. A Li bent down and disconnected a cage on a lower shelf. She placed it on the stainless steel bench and checked the numbers under the bar code against the information in her notebook. Satisfied that she had the correct mouse, she turned off the light and made sure the electronic lock sealed the door behind her.

Back in the change room, she discarded her sterile clothes and went into the hallway, taking the cage with her. On the way to the tunnel, she passed two researchers from another department. She thought she recognized the one with the full white beard. They were busy talking about their experiments and barely acknowledged her as she walked past.

# EIGHT

Aᴠᴛᴇʀ ᴛʜᴇ ᴀʟʙɪɴᴏ ɢᴀᴠᴇ him the finger from behind the glass doors of the Nano Research Center, Colt walked back to his truck and drove to Santa Monica to pick up Nicole, a girl he had met recently at a local coffee hangout. By the time they finished their hamburgers, Colt had lost interest in Nicole. She kept using the word "totally" and it was driving him crazy. Her friends were totally cool. Her summer had been totally great and school was totally boring. They went to a movie about a man and a woman marooned on an island and she thought it was totally romantic. By the time the film was over, Colt was totally certain he didn't want to see her again and couldn't wait to take her home. When they came out of the theater, a fog bank had drifted in from the ocean.

Colt dropped off his date, drove home to his apartment on Chautauqua Street and sat in his pickup watching the tiny drops of moisture collecting on the windshield. It was after midnight and the marine layer from the ocean had enveloped the neighborhood in a thick mist. In the darkness, Colt thought back over his day and the run-in with the insolent, hostile, smart-ass albino. He tried to remember the scenario at the Surfrider. The albino was standing at the edge of the crowd next to the girl with the tattoos on her upper body. He was holding a plastic takeout bag, probably with the remains of his lunch. There were at least 30 other people standing nearby. How could he pick up the foot with all those people around? Would anyone really take a severed body part home?

Colt got out of his pickup and stood in the middle of the street surrounded by the fog. He looked up into the gray mist and felt it settle on his face. Growing up in Wyoming, he never imagined he would end up living a block from a white sand beach in Southern California. When he arrived in Los Angeles almost six years ago, he was 18 and had $12,600 in his pocket after the sale of the ranch and payment of his father's debts and funeral expenses. Rising land prices in Wyoming had bailed him out. He was happy to leave the coal mines, gas wells and marginal ranches, but the first months in Los Angeles were difficult. The crowded Southern California sprawl was a shock and he missed the days when he could ride his horse Flash in the open spaces under the endless sky of the high plains. He was also lonely. In a city of almost 11 million people, he found it hard to meet anyone. No one walked anywhere—everyone drove, locked inside a vehicle. He had no friends, no support group and no family. His father had been a difficult, mean man who drank too much and cursed everyone. Even so, Colt knew his father had loved him and felt adrift without his presence. Sometimes Colt felt so alone that he even yearned for the quiet companionship of Bear Cloud, the old Cheyenne Indian who worked around the ranch and barely spoke English.

For two years, Colt lived in a cheap converted motel near the airport while he studied for his fire science degree. After graduation from the fire academy, he got a job with Los Angeles County. The fire department brotherhood became his family and his life changed. He moved from the smell of jet fuel to the smell of salt air; into a studio apartment in an old wood structure on Chautauqua Street in Santa Monica. The building was surrounded by vegetation never seen in Wyoming—banana plants, palm and eucalyptus trees that shed long brown strips of bark onto the sidewalk. Colt lived on the third floor in the back, looking out at a dirt hillside. He couldn't see the Pacific Ocean, but he could smell it.

On one side of his rooming house was a gay bar called The Hideout, which opened at noon. The Canyon Steakhouse and a liquor store were farther down Chautauqua. Across the street, Paddy's Roadhouse, a white and lime green building decorated with dark green shamrocks, attracted the volleyball players and other people from the beach. In the morning, the smell of bacon frying in Paddy's kitchen drifted through Colt's window and reminded him of crisp mornings in Wyoming. At night, raucous crowds at Paddy's—groups of men trying to hook up outside The Hideout and people arriving in expensive cars to eat at the steakhouse—all created a lively atmosphere.

Where Chautauqua ended and dumped traffic onto Pacific Coast Highway, a stairway led down into a short tunnel that ran underneath PCH and out onto the beach. A homeless man, Roy, spent each morning using a broom and a cardboard box to sweep sand from the sidewalk, the stairs and the underground passageway. He swept during the morning and the wind blew the sand back in the afternoon. Roy was a large man who wore filthy Army fatigues. He had long matted hair, rotten teeth and no one could understand anything he said. Swimmers, volleyball players and sunbathers using the tunnel tried to ignore him, but he still managed to collect a few bucks every day from the neighborhood residents who felt sorry for him, knew he was harmless, and actually appreciated his efforts to keep the area clean. After he ended his sweeping chores around noon, Roy spent the rest of the day scouring the beach as far north as Malibu for anything left on the sand or in the trashcans. He dragged with him a large nylon bag that he filled with flattened plastic bottles and aluminum cans and often brought back abandoned beach chairs, toys, towels, bottles of lotion, stray shoes, magazines and books. Roy kept his treasures where he slept—under the outside stairwell leading to the second floor of Colt's building.

As Colt stood in the fog, he saw blue light from the window of the fortuneteller who lived and worked on the ground floor. The sign on her door said:

*DOREEN'S AMAZING GRACE*
*Life Counseling*
*Inspired Visions of the Future –$5*

During the time he lived on Chautauqua, Colt had never seen Doreen, but suspected she did a good business. People often wandered out of the restaurants, stopped at her door, looked at the sign and went inside. This was one of the crazy things to do in California—stop in and consult a fortuneteller in the middle of the night. Colt wondered what she told them. "Inspired visions" sounded like bullshit, but he decided to go for it. Why not, Colt thought. Doreen was the local equivalent of a Cheyenne witch doctor and after his date with Nicole, he needed five bucks' worth of hocus-pocus.

Her door was partially open. Colt hesitated and then knocked. A small bell tinkled when he entered and a strange but pleasant scent filled the air inside. He looked around. It definitely wasn't an Indian meditation lodge.

Yellow stars and a blue moon, fashioned from neon lighting, glowed on one wall. Silver Christmas tree ornaments and larger disco balls covered with mirrors hung from the ceiling, turning slowly, reflecting blue and yellow splinters of light. A black cat sat motionless on a couch under the window. A small table and two folding chairs were the only other pieces of furniture. The table was covered with a white cloth decorated with more stars and planets.

Without making a sound, Doreen appeared like an apparition from the adjoining room. Colt looked up to see her standing in the shadows. "Hi," he said. "I live upstairs. I saw your light—"

"It's OK, I'm up all night." She was a tiny, wrinkled woman wearing a shapeless dress and a blue turban that hid her hair. Colt guessed she could be in her 70s. She lit a candle on the table and slid onto one of the folding chairs. "Please." She motioned to Colt and he sat down. Doreen stared at him with dark eyes surrounded by blue eye shadow. "I feel negative energy coming from you."

Negative energy, Colt thought. She probably said that to everyone.

"Are you in trouble?"

"No."

"Are you here for life counseling?"

"No." Colt thought for a moment about what he wanted from Doreen.

Her tiny hands reached across the table.

Colt pulled out a wad of dollar bills from his pocket.

"No," she said. "I want to touch you. Turn your palms up."

Colt peeled off five one-dollar bills anyway and handed them to her.

Doreen took the money and slipped it into her smock. She grasped his hands in her own and closed her eyes. She sat transfixed for a moment, then opened her eyes and pressed his hands gently down onto the table. She bent toward him. "What's your name?"

"Colt. Colt Lewis." He was beginning to feel ridiculous, sitting with this tiny old woman, and tried to think of something to say. "Uh, how's my lifeline?" he asked.

"That's an old wives' tale. No one can look at your palm and tell you how long you're going to live." She looked down at his hands. "Have you suffered a loss?"

"Yes." Colt had suffered more than one loss.

Doreen raised her eyebrows. "Is she dead?"

For a moment, he was confused. Who was Doreen asking about? His mother? Bibi?

"Are you mourning her?"

"Mourning her?" Colt nodded. "I guess so." Colt glanced over at the cat. Its eyes were open, head up, but it still hadn't moved.

"Death is just a graduation, it's—"

"I'm a firefighter, a paramedic. We responded to an accident on PCH. A girl's foot was cut off. I'm searching for it."

"You're searching for someone's foot?" Doreen stood up and walked around behind Colt. She placed her hands on the top of his head and closed her eyes again. "You have a troubled aura. Perhaps because of this girl. Who is she?"

"I don't know."

Doreen opened her eyes, walked around and sat down again across from Colt. "So you're looking for a dead girl's foot but you don't know who she is?"

"Right. That's the problem." Colt leaned back in his chair and glanced again at the cat. "No one knows who she is. All we have is a first name. And there's this guy dressed in black—"

"Are the police involved?"

"The Sheriff's Department … uh … maybe." Colt had to check out the cat, which still hadn't moved. He stood up and walked over to the couch. He looked more closely, then reached out and touched it. The fur seemed real, but the animal was hard as a rock.

"That's Angel. That was Angel," Doreen said.

Colt sat down again. "I promised her I would take care of her. Shouldn't I try to find her foot? I think I know who has it. What do you think?"

"Has she returned yet?"

"Returned? I said she's dead."

"Someone who expects to die may return sooner. People who die unexpectedly take longer to come back. Did she expect to die?"

"Huh?" What was this woman talking about?

"Mr. Lewis, what's your question? What do you want from me?"

"I just asked you. Do you think I should—?"

"Are you having emotional problems?"

"No, I'm not." Colt got up again. "Why do you say that? There's nothing wrong with me."

"You promised a dead girl you don't know that you would find her foot and—"

"She wasn't dead when I made the promise."

Doreen shook her head. "I'm not a psychiatrist, just a medium, but I think you have a problem. You should talk to someone. Have a heart-to-heart. How about your father? Let him help you. That's my advice. Have a father-son discussion." She smiled at Colt.

"My father's dead."

"Well then, get some counseling. I'm not the one to help you."

"There's nothing wrong with me," Colt repeated. He stood up and went to the door. "Thanks." Thanks for nothing, he thought.

"Her soul may be—"

Colt slammed the door and stood in the fog again. What a waste of time. Doreen wasn't even listening. He might as well have talked to the cat. The whole day was a disaster. The news about Bibi's death started things. The albino flipped him off and then he had a date with the most boring girl in the world. Now some old fortuneteller insisted he needed a psychiatrist.

Colt approached the wooden stairs at the side of his building and found Roy curled up in the fetal position, sleeping on his rubber mat surrounded by his bags of crushed cans and plastic bottles. "Hey buddy," Colt said. Roy didn't move. Colt shook him harder until Roy looked up with bloodshot eyes. Colt gave him the rest of the one-dollar bills from his pocket. "Go get something to eat." Roy rolled over on his back, held the money in his hand and stared at Colt.

Colt ascended the stairs, walked around the outside balcony to his room and inserted the key in the door. In the dark, he went to his small refrigerator, took out a can of beer, popped it open and took a long swig. The light from the refrigerator illuminated the only décor in the apartment—a poster from Sheridan Fire and Rescue showing a bunch of firefighters with their helmets off, covered with soot, standing with their hands on each other's shoulders. Colt's worn cowboy boots sat in the corner of the room collecting dust. He saddle-soaped them once a month to protect the leather from the arid climate, but rarely wore them anymore. His shearling jacket, too warm for Los Angeles, hung in his small closet along with the belt and large silver and gold buckle that his father had won for saddle bronc riding at a PRCA—Professional Rodeo Cowboys Association—rodeo. Colt had long ago replaced his ranch work shirts with blue fire department T-shirts. Only his worn Levi's fit into his new lifestyle.

He lay down on the unmade bed and placed his beer on the floor. He closed his eyes but couldn't go to sleep. From the time he was a child, Colt had been a poor sleeper. A doctor once told him that he had an "intermittent sleep pattern." Being a light sleeper was a good quality for a firefighter. When the tones went off, Colt was able to wake up and be fully alert and ready to function in a matter of seconds while most of his brothers were still stumbling around. Colt tossed on the bed and thought about his mother. His problems with sleep began after she deserted him. Even now, 16 years later, he longed for her. He still wondered why she left him. Her absence still haunted him.

Colt got up and went to his dresser, opened the bottom drawer, lifted up his sweatshirts and withdrew a photograph. He took his halogen fire flashlight from the floor and shined it on the picture. His mother and father stood holding hands by a silver pickup truck. His mother wore a blue T-shirt with CALIFORNIA in white letters across the chest. The picture was taken before Colt was born. He examined their faces, as he had done countless times, looking for some sign. At times, he thought he saw love, disappointment, anger or no emotion at all in their faces. In the end, the picture told him nothing, but he still treasured it. He had so few reminders of his family's history and it was the only image he had of his mother and father together.

Colt's paternal great-grandfather, a blacksmith, was traveling the Bozeman Trail to the gold fields in Montana when he stopped in Big Horn, Wyoming after an Indian attack. He never resumed his journey and started the ranch where Colt lived with his father a century later. Named after the "gun that won the West," Colt grew up helping his father breed horses for dude ranches and pack trips into the mountains. His mother came from Cheyenne but he knew almost nothing about her background or her family. He did know she hated Big Horn. In fact, she hated all of Wyoming and ran off when he was eight. The date was February 8, 1992 and Colt never forgot it. Every year when it came around, he remembered how hard it was snowing the day she abandoned him. On his ninth birthday, a package postmarked Dallas, TX, arrived at the ranch. It contained a cowboy shirt and a birthday card that promised, "I will always be your mother and I will always love you." She lied. She sent no address, no telephone number and Colt never heard from her again.

After his mother departed, Colt continued his life in Big Horn, a town of 200 residents. Colt rode the school bus 15 miles each day into Sheridan, a city of 16,000 whose most famous citizen was Buffalo Bill Cody. In the afternoon, he returned on the same bus and did the chores his mother would have done. When he was older and asked his father why she left, the only response was, "She's not coming back."

The ranch was in the vast Powder River Basin, just south of the Montana border. Where Crow and Shoshone Indians once roamed through shortgrass and scrub vegetation, geologists and land men working for oil companies now drove around in SUVs. Bighorn sheep, black bear, elk and deer still filled the nearby mountains. Trophy hunts, wild-turkey shoots and the annual prairie-dog slaughter were a part of life. Colt had a horse, but few human friends. At times, he had wished for a brother or even a sister, anyone he could call family. Most of all, he dreamed of becoming a firefighter and helping people. Sometimes his father grew exasperated and asked Colt, "What's wrong with being a rancher? Isn't that good enough for you?" If one of his father's friends was around, which was seldom, he would mutter, "I must have the only kid in Wyoming who grew up on a horse but wants to drive a fire truck."

During high school, Colt volunteered at Sheridan Fire and Rescue. He started sweeping out the station and washing the dishes and imagined becoming one of them. He loved the camaraderie at the station. The men were always joking, laughing, and slapping each other on the back. Firefighters were a team, a family of their own, always together. They were also dedicated to saving people. For the first time, he thought of becoming a paramedic.

His father had no dreams and couldn't comprehend Colt's ambitions. He expected his son to spend his life shoveling shit, carrying feed and mending fences. Colt wondered if his father would have lived a different life if he knew that he was going to die prematurely. He concluded no, his father would not have changed the course of his life in any way. He was a stubborn man who would have continued on forever, doing the same thing, scratching out his existence on a dirt ranch in Big Horn, Wyoming.

Colt watched the television shows about Southern California and tried to imagine what it would be like to go surfing. He had never seen the ocean and knew nothing about Los Angeles, but wanted to move there. After the death of his father, Colt decided not to waste any more time in Wyoming. He moved to California to follow his dreams. After he arrived, he noticed that every store near the beach sold the blue CALIFORNIA T-shirt with the white letters.

Six years later, Colt thought less frequently about Big Horn, but he never stopped thinking about his mother.

# NINE

O N Tuesday morning at 1:00 a.m., the silence in the Nano Research Center was deafening. While Colt lay in his bed thinking about his parents, A Li climbed five flights of stairs from the subbasement tunnel to Dr. Murray's lab on the third floor. All she heard were the faint squeaks from the soles of her shoes and the even softer squeaks from the tiny creature in the cage.

When she unlocked the door to the lab, the lights were on. This was not unusual; students entered and left the labs at all hours. She walked past the counters with microscopes, centrifuges, racks of bottles and the belly dancers—the moving platforms used to mix antibodies.

A Li had to eat something. Food wasn't allowed in the laboratories, but she kept a few granola bars in one of the drawers on her bench. She found one that was stale and rock hard, bit off a piece and washed it down half-chewed. It tasted like cardboard but would give her energy and kill her appetite for a couple of hours. The water from the bottle she carried in her backpack was warm, but pure. She never drank bottled water in China; most of it came from the tap and was polluted.

A Li placed the cage on her lab bench and sat down on the stool. The tiny mouse stood up on two legs, its front paws on the mesh of the cage and looked out with its little black eyes. A Li gazed back at the creature for a few seconds and wondered if it had any inkling of its impending fate. Like all researchers in America running experiments using mice, rats or any other animals, she was bound by the Institutional Animal Care and Use Committee protocol. It governed the handling and killing of all research animals and the university insisted that she follow the specific procedures to ensure her mice did not suffer in the few seconds before she put them to death. A Li followed the guidelines, but thought that the lab animals in America lived better lives than some humans in Yunnan. She had seen so much human suffering on the gritty streets in China, where hungry people lived in cardboard boxes and subsisted each day on a single bowl of rice and a steamed fish head.

She turned to organize the stainless steel dissection instruments—she was now proficient with the tiny tweezers, forceps and scissors suitable for cutting apart a two-inch mouse. She spilled several small plastic tubes out of a box and arranged them upright in a tray, each numbered to correspond to a piece of a particular organ or lymph node. She spread a white paper pad and tore off strips of white masking tape to hold the mouse in place once she cut it open.

A Li needed saline to wash each bit of mouse tissue. She took an unopened bottle from Tetsu's bench and poured some into a Petri dish. Tetsu was an unfriendly Japanese post doc who would have been furious if he had known A Li had touched anything on his lab bench, even a common bottle of saline solution. He worked in one of Dr. Murray's other research groups investigating B cells, which produce antibodies in the blood. In the rack above his bench, he kept several pipetting syringes with sharp tips, which he used to dispense precise amounts of an acid needed to preserve cell samples. Tetsu had only spoken to A Li once, on the day she watched him mix the liquid and fill his pipettes. Wearing his white lab coat, gloves and mask, he warned her that the acid, sodium azide, was highly toxic and a quick-acting poison if ingested. He told her never to touch anything on his bench. Tetsu sometimes ignored some of the safety protocols for the lab, including keeping syringes filled with sodium azide. He somehow got away with it, even though the rules were strictly enforced. A Li detested him. He was a brilliant researcher but arrogant and mean-spirited. Fortunately, he was never in the lab at night when she did most of her work.

She went to one of the drug cabinets, unlocked it and removed an ampoule of ketamine. An injection of the drug, an anesthetic, would render her mouse unconscious before she broke its neck. A Li pulled on her latex gloves and drew the ketamine into a small syringe. Her mouse surgery instructor said that the drug was called Special K and was a favorite with the kids in the nightclubs and raves around LA. Inhaling it in powder form gave a hallucinatory feeling. A Li had never been to a nightclub and wasn't sure what a rave was. All she had ever done was study, study, study. The Americans had so many other things to do besides study. In fact, it seemed they did everything except their home-work, which was why none of the people in the advanced research classes were from the United States. Even though the Asians were smarter, the Americans made them feel vaguely ashamed and ill at ease. She didn't understand it. Didn't they know Asia was about to bury them?

A Li was almost ready. She needed a container with N2—liquid nitrogen—to flash-freeze the organ samples. Later they would be thawed and prepared for microscopic analysis and DNA sequencing to determine where the stem cells had migrated. She went to the back of the lab past the bank of refrigerators, each a different size, each with a different warning: CAUTION RADIOACTIVE MATERIALS; NOT FOR FOOD STORAGE; UNSAFE FOR FLAMMABLE SOLVENTS. Next to the refrigerators, the liquid nitrogen tank that Dr. Murray referred to as Humpty Dumpty, sat on the floor like a giant gray egg. A Li had no idea what Humpty Dumpty was until she checked the Internet. She had expected something scientific and was surprised to find a reference to a nursery rhyme, much like one that Pa Lags had read to her and A Mei when they were very young. A Li couldn't imagine Dr. Murray reading a nursery rhyme to anyone. The digital readout on the tank showed -270 degrees Celsius. The lab manager had filled several metal thermos containers with the coolant and A Li took one back to her bench.

She opened PGL010's cage and grasped the tiny gray creature. It made tiny sounds while she held it by the back of the neck as her instructor had demonstrated. She stuck the needle into its abdomen and injected the ketamine. She watched the creature's whiskers twitch for a few seconds before it went limp. A Li followed the Bon religion, founded some 18,000 years ago by Shenrab Miwoche. In the early years of Bon, sheep, dogs, yaks and even horses were sacrificed to please the gods. She wondered if the death of this tiny mouse would please the ancient God of Medicine, Yeje Tutob Gyalpo.

She laid the mouse on its stomach, pressed a glass rod against its neck, pulled its tail and severed the spinal cord. She turned the creature over on its back and taped its legs to the white pad. The fur on its underside was snow white. A Li opened her notebook to the page that outlined the order of organ removal. She used the scissors to cut open the skin on the mouse's stomach and pulled it aside. A sour odor drifted into her nostrils as she used a cotton pad to absorb the blood accumulating in the tiny body cavity. She started with the most accessible organs—the pancreas, spleen, kidney and liver. She cut away a sample of each and washed it in the saline, leaving small clouds of blood in the liquid. She deposited each specimen in a marked plastic tube. Moving on to the stomach, she cut it open and cleaned it before taking a sample. She cut through the ribs with a stronger pair of scissors and removed the lungs and thymus from the chest cavity. A Li failed to squeeze the heart before she cut into it and a tiny explosion of blood covered the scissors, the tips of her gloves and ran out onto the absorbent pad. She dabbed it away and took her last sample.

When she finished, she sealed each of the tubes and opened the liquid nitrogen container. A cloud of vapor escaped as she inserted the tissue samples, which would freeze within seconds. She rolled the mouse carcass up in the absorbent pad and deposited it in a Stericycle medical waste container designated for dissected carcasses with viruses or foreign DNA. Early in the morning, the biohazard crew would come through each laboratory, collect the toxic waste, needles and animal remains and cart it all off to a disposal center.

After washing her instruments and leaving them in the sterilizer, A Li was finished. It was 2:10 a.m. For a moment, she paused and allowed herself to daydream. She imagined a campuswide assembly in Jarrow Hall, where an announcement was about to be made confirming that Dr. Murray and his research team were the first to successfully reprogram the DNA in stem cells. The chancellor of CU, the dean of the medical school, the governor of California and many other important people were on hand. The possibility of a Nobel Prize for Dr. Murray was rumored. He stepped to the podium. After thanking everyone and making a short speech, he invited the members of his research team to join him. A Li imagined Hisao, Tetsu, Tanay and the others crowding around Dr. Murray, basking in the glory of the announcement. In her mind's eye, A Li searched for herself. Was she part of the group?

She sighed and stood up. She picked up her backpack, went to the front of the lab and turned off the lights. Out in the hall, she started toward the elevator. It was already Tuesday, A Mei's birthday—and her own.

*Dear sister, I wish you peace and love. Today is your birthday. I won't be at home to honor you, but I have a ceremony planned for you here in the lab. You are always with me. I know you are happy about what I have learned in America.*

*I have gained knowledge of the most sophisticated methods of genetic programming. I have learned the secrets of using stem cells. I will learn to create Bombay Blood. I am doing this for you.*

# TEN

MARKUS RETURNED to his apartment and fell asleep on top of the bed without undressing. He woke up when he heard Audra at the front door. It was 4:00 a.m. Tuesday morning, almost four hours since his failed China Doll blood quest. It all came back to him—the night had been a horrible disaster. While the Chinese bitch was in the room with the mice, some nerdy scientists almost caught him in the hallway and he had to flee into the tunnel. They had ruined all his plans.

Markus listened to Audra in the other room. No matter when she came home from work, late at night or early in the morning, he knew exactly what time she arrived. She tried to enter the apartment without disturbing him, but he heard her every time. This was the latest she had ever come home. What the hell had she been doing until now? Didn't she realize he seriously needed a taste of her blood and some nasty sex?

"Audra?"

"In a minute," she answered from the kitchen. "I gotta eat something."

"Come get in bed." He took off his clothes and pulled back the bedspread. He lay on the cool sheets and waited. His anticipation grew as he thought of Audra's body next to him. Minutes passed and she was still in the kitchen. "Now," he shouted. Why did she have to fucking eat when she came home? She belonged in bed. "Audra, I said *now*. Get in here."

She stormed into the bedroom. "Shut up. I've told you, don't ever say that." She kicked off one of her high heels. It sailed over the bed and hit the far wall. "You sound just like my father." She stepped out of her other shoe. "'Audra honey, come to bed with daddy.' That's how he always started it." She moved around the room in the semidarkness, her voice rising. "Every time I heard it,

I cringed. When I got older, it got worse. He got more demanding and more impatient and then it was, 'Audra, NOW!'" She lit several red candles on the dresser, walked to the side of the bed and stood over him in the flickering light, hands on her hips. "You sound just like him. I don't ever want to hear that again. Not ever."

Audra was always blaming him for her own problems, and Markus was tired of it. Sometimes she was just too much trouble. He sat up and reached for her. "C'mon, get in bed."

She continued to glare at him for a moment and then relented. She slid down her pants and thong and stepped out of them. She pulled off her top and stood beside the bed, wearing only her spider-web dance stockings. Her long black hair cascaded down past her shoulders. Her body gave off a faint scent of perfume and cigarette smoke from the club. The candles cast distorted shadows of her long legs on the wall. Her tattoos were a canvas of red hues and shades of black and gray ink. Roses with thorns wound around her arms and neck. Mermaids with flowing red hair stretched up from her waist and reached for the stars on her breasts. More roses grew upward over her bare pubic area. One shoulder showed the tips of the wings of the angel on her back; the other shoulder showed the head of the snake that curled around the angel. Audra's ears and belly button, pierced with rings, gave a sharp metallic contrast to her tattoos.

Markus looked at her and forgot about everything else. "I'm in a wicked bad mood and I need you." He tugged on the ring in her belly button.

She sighed and lay down next to him.

Markus grabbed her hand, reached for a pin he kept on the wrought iron night table and pricked her little finger. He wasn't interested in a lot of blood play; he was in a hurry and jammed the needle in hard.

"Ow," she cried, and tried to pull her finger away.

He held her tight, squeezed the tip of her finger and then sucked it. When he tasted the first few drops of her blood, he got an intense rush, which swept through his body and jacked him up. It was better than amphetamine. "SWEEET," he said. Markus rolled on top of her, worked his way between her legs and thrust himself inside her, releasing all his anger, disappointment and frustration.

Later, they lay together and listened to the sounds of the day beginning outside. Doors slammed in other apartments and car engines started. A siren rose above the hum of the traffic on Albion. Audra pressed her body against his back and he felt the metal ring in her belly button.

"A little rough," she said, and yawned.

Markus always mellowed out after sex. This was the one time when he forgot about the dancing at the club and the men she entertained.

"Your skin is like white marble." She ran her dark red fingernail down the back of his neck.

"You mean white like a corpse."

"Well, if you wanna be a Goth vampire, it's perfect." She reached around and pulled at the white hair on his arm.

"Ever been to Fresno, the fucking raisin capital of California? D'you know what the light's like up there? They put all the grapes outside and the sun turns them into raisins. Try going out in that when you've got no pigment."

"I hate raisins," she said and rolled over on her back. "My mom gave me those stupid little boxes in my lunch. I threw them away as soon as I got on the school bus."

"I couldn't stand school. All the kids were such dorks."

"Boys were always trying to touch me." Audra reached for a tissue and wiped away some of her eyeliner. "I don't remember what I looked like in sixth grade, but that's when it all started."

"I didn't make it to sixth grade at school. I was too smart, so I quit and my mother home-schooled me. I stayed inside and didn't have to listen to anyone making fun of how I looked."

"I like the way you look. How many men have pure white hair around their cock?"

"How many have you seen?"

"What's that supposed to mean?"

"Just what I said."

Audra rolled away from him.

"If you like white skin so much, how come you covered yourself with tats?"

"Because my father's fingerprints were all over my body. It was like everyone could see what he did to me. As soon as I got off the bus in LA, I started checking out tattoos."

"Well, I'm not your father."

"That piece of shit. He'll never see me again."

Her anger excited Markus again. He moved closer to her and bit her nipple, but not hard enough to get any blood. He ran his finger over the stars tattooed on her breast. "This could be your hottest part."

"The guy at Tattoo Fest told me, 'Your tats will become a special part of your body.' He was right."

Markus kissed a rose on her stomach.

Audra pushed his head away. "I told him I was thinking about tats and he wanted to know how old I was. I lied and said I was 18. He looked at my arms and legs and said, 'What'ja have in mind?' I told him a full upper body. Then he stared at me again like he was looking right through my blouse. I just stood there and let him eye-fuck me. 'It's three or four years,' he said. 'And pain. Hours of pricks and jabs and nicks.' He wanted to know how I was with pain and I told him it was OK. The only places it ever really bothered me was when he worked on my boobs and the back of my neck."

Markus knew Audra was good with pain and she could handle any of the things he did to her. Years ago, he moved beyond just sucking at a girl's neck to draw blood through the skin and leave a hickey. Now he was big time into biting, piercing and sometimes cutting; anything to draw a few drops of blood.

His pulse was racing again. He squeezed the tip of her little finger and sucked at it where he had stuck her earlier. He got a faint taste of blood on the tip of his tongue.

Audra lay on her back. When Markus got on top of her, she wrapped her legs around him. She gave a small cry when he pushed inside of her again.

His excitement didn't last. A stronger taste of blood or a few drops spread across her tits might have helped. It had been a long night and all of a sudden, the vibes weren't so good. He imagined strangers fondling Audra at the Alley Kat, whispering in her ear and taking her upstairs to one of the rooms. He pictured someone doing her while she made phony sounds of rapture. He imagined her stuffing cash into her purse after some fat retard had flopped her. Markus pulled away from her and moved to his side of the bed. How did he know the sighs of pleasure she made when he was boning her were genuine? Wasn't it her job to make a man's fantasies come true? Maybe she was a lesbo and didn't even like men. Maybe she just needed a place to stay and wanted to make him think she enjoyed it when he jacked her. She was making all that dough and not even sharing expenses with him. At that moment, Markus hated her.

Audra sighed and slipped under the bedspread. Without a word, she pulled a pillow over her head and went to sleep.

Markus lay on his back, wallowing in his anger and staring at the ceiling for a few minutes, then got up and walked naked into the kitchen to look once more at the foot. When he opened the freezer door, ice crystals drifted down like snowflakes and melted on his bare feet.

*Snowflake. Bleach boy. Cream puff.*

A group of fifth-graders pursued him across the dusty playground. The Central California sun was relentless. His eyes burned from the light. Markus, younger and smaller than the others, was crying. He stopped and they circled around him, shouting, taunting.

*Snowflake. Snowflake.*

Fucking snowflake.

Long before he heard the word albino or understood the absence of the melanin that creates pigment in the skin and hair, he heard kids calling him snowflake.

Markus was surrounded, trapped. They closed in.

*Bleach boy. Cream puff. Snowflake. Snowflake.*

It went on and on and on.

Markus, barely able to see, picked up a rock and struck out. A girl in a yellow dress cried out and fell to the ground, a large gash on her head spewing blood. His tormentors were finally silent and backed away. He stood over the injured girl and watched the blood run down her forehead and onto her face. He knelt, reached out and dipped his fingers in her blood. It was Markus' last day at school.

Fucking snowflake.

By the time Markus was expelled from school, doctors and blood had become a part of his life.

"Are they ever gonna stop sticking needles into my Markey?"

He sat in the back seat of the car and listened to his mother's sweet voice.

"How many blood samples do they need?" she said.

"They have to do what they have to do," his father said. "Mark can handle it. He's a man. Men are brave." His father turned and looked back at him. "Right, son?"

When Markus heard the doctor say they wanted to test for Hermansky-Pudlak Syndrome, a fatal genetic illness related to albinism, he didn't know what it was, but it sounded frightening. He cried and thought he was going to die.

"My Markey. Everything will be all right." His mother comforted him. "Come here, let Mama hold you."

He climbed onto her lap. The trips to the doctor became bearable because she shared his pain and showered attention on him. Soon, he looked forward to visiting the doctor. The sting of the needle and the dark red liquid streaming out of his arm into the syringe brought his mother's loving touch.

"My poor Markey. My poor brave little boy."

At home, his mother pulled him to her, wrapped her arms around him and cuddled him. He pressed against her breasts. He smelled her skin. She stroked his arms, his legs, his body, trying to make everything better. It became a ritual. As soon as he left the doctor's office, Markus tore off the bandage, pinched his arm and put his tongue to the puncture, hoping to taste a drop of his blood. Then he waited for his mother's touch. Sometimes, he even tried to scratch or bite himself just to draw blood and gain her attention. For almost a year, his father tied his hands together at night so that Markus couldn't tear at his flesh.

By puberty, he had substituted the agony of his infirmity for an obsession with blood and a raw sexuality. He had fantasies about drinking the blood of young women and ravishing them. At 14, Markus drifted away from his home-school lessons to spend hours in the basement surfing the Internet, dividing his time between studying hematology websites, searching for pictures of nude women and frequenting chat rooms like Blud Sukkers.

He also learned the art of computer hacking and soon became an expert at playing *Vampire: The Masquerade-Bloodlines*, an online role-playing game. Markus was a loner in real life and he played alone in the world of electronic games. Instead of aligning himself with one of the vampire clans or religious covens in *Vampire*, he sided with no one and rampaged as a lone blood-drinking monster.

The game played out in a virtual Santa Monica—at the Santa Monica Pier and in clubs and residences on rundown streets and alleys. Someday he knew he would live in Southern California and visit the real places.

Mark became Markus, took on the screen name BloodyFangs and began to search the Internet for a blood donor.

*BloodyFangs: Me – male - 6' 2" – handsome. lookin for a blood donor near Fresno. I need a gurl's blood.*

*CookieBitch: so ur a vampire???*

*GutterSlut: everbody wants 2 b a vampire.*

*BloodyFangs: I suk blud – real blud. I am a wicked, badass vampyre.*

*Violent Eyes: drinking a lot of blood can make you sick.*

Markus wanted to find out.

*Sinister Vamp: lol I luv real men U can bite me. I wud like it if u suk MY blud.*

A donor!

*BloodyFangs: Give me your maiden blood. Cum to Fresno!!*

*Sinister Vamp: I am a simple layback mello gurl in LA. Hahaha. R u a real vampire?*

*BloodyFangs: When I taste yur blud.*

*Sinister Vamp: how old r u? U cum to LA?*

Markus had a problem—he lived in the basement of his parents' home and was still two years away from even having a driver's license. How could he go to Los Angeles?

*Sinister Vamp: I wanna see what u look lik. Webcam? Need 2 see u.*

No way would he show himself on a webcam.

Later, Sinister Vamp published a letter on the Carnival of Hell chat board: *BloodyFangs is a fake. He's not a vampire, he's a predator hunting innocent pepl. Die a thousand deaths BF!*

The bitch.

Markus hacked into the web page and took down her letter. He left her his own message: *If I ever find you, Sinister Vamp, I'll drink my fill of your blood and let the rest run into the gutter.*

Ten years later, he still thought of Sinister Vamp and her comments still angered him.

Fucking snowflake.

The cold air from the freezer blew on Markus' naked body. During the 36 hours since he placed the foot in the freezer, the gray-blue color had faded. Through the plastic, the skin now looked pale—almost white, returning to its original color. Markus put the foot away and went to check his e-mail. He had several messages and someone had sent him a link to a website in India where some new hacking software was available. Markus had no money and deleted it before he saw something he wanted. He rubbed his eyes, returned to the bedroom and got back into bed.

He looked at Audra, her breasts rising and falling in the slow breathing rhythm of deep sleep. Just a month ago, she had fulfilled one of his great desires. They had become partners in a blood-bonding ceremony. The act of cutting open their fingers, dropping the blood into a glass of wine, drinking it and then making love, had been very erotic. That thrill was long past now, and he was getting tired of Audra. He needed something new to juice up his fantasies. He needed the elixir that flowed in the China Doll's veins. He knew it would taste so much better than Audra's ordinary type AB blood.

Markus closed his eyes. He needed sleep. After lunch, he had to go out to Gates of Heaven and face Alexei and Grisha.

# ELEVEN

On Tuesday morning, the squad was toned out for a car that had gone over the side of Malibu Canyon Road, an eight-mile asphalt ribbon winding up and down through deep gorges between Pacific Coast Highway and the 101 Freeway. Brian and Colt were on a quick run to the supermarket when the call came in. Instead of stopping to pick up food for dinner, Brian hit the lights and siren, and sped through the traffic up PCH.

A Code 3—lights and siren, immediate response—was the next report they heard through their headsets: "Car over. Vehicle entrapment. Dispatching 88's engine and Sheriff's Search and Rescue."

"What is it out here with people and their cars?" Brian said. "Last year a guy in a Ferrari hit a phone pole doing 110."

"Dead?" Colt asked.

Brian nodded. "It was really ugly. Driver and passenger ripped apart. PCH was covered with body parts and pieces of carbon fiber." He sounded the air horn, rolled through a red light and turned right onto Malibu Canyon Road.

Before he came to Los Angeles, Colt imagined that Southern California was flat. He didn't expect to see steep mountains running down to strips of white sand along the ocean. As they climbed up through Malibu Canyon, he watched the blind curves. Speeding vehicles often missed a bend, shot off the road and plunged hundreds of feet into the canyons below. "They need more guardrails out here," he said.

"Tell me about it," Brian said.

Command and Control now requested an engine from station 125.

"We're gonna be sliding into the canyon on our asses," Brian said.

Colt glanced at the speedometer. The squad was only doing 25.

Malibu Canyon was a two-lane highway with no room for traffic to move to the right and it was impossible to pass. "Someone might be out there dying and we're just creeping along," he said, chewing on his lip. The trip to the scene of an incident was always the worst part for Colt. After five weeks in the field, his initial panic had dropped to mere anxiety, but he still rode along thinking of all the possible injuries he might see and all the procedures and treatments he might be called on to utilize. He'd had a year of instruction and hands-on training, taken dozens of written exams and was certified by both the State of California and the County Fire Department. He was now a paramedic and was supposed to be able to take care of any injury situation. He had learned so much, but worried that he might only have seconds to make an assessment and decide on a course of action. What if he made the wrong decision when someone was lying injured at the scene of an accident, relying on him for help? Sometimes when he thought about the responsibility, it almost overwhelmed him. Fortunately Brian had years of experience and was there to back him up.

Brian looked at him and seemed to read his mind. "It's OK. You never get over the apprehension. When you get to the scene, your training kicks in and you'll know exactly what to do."

Colt nodded and hoped Brian was right. A car over the edge usually meant trapped bodies and a difficult rescue. Sometimes there was no rescue at all. A month earlier, a surveyor counting fish for the Department of Agriculture discovered two skeletons in a car at the bottom of a deep canyon near Malibu. The husband and wife were still strapped into their seatbelts. The couple had disappeared three years earlier and Search and Rescue never found them.

The squad ascended the second hill in the canyon. On the way down the backside, they saw the flashing red and blue lights.

"Here we go," Brian said. He slowed and pulled onto a dirt turnout, stopping next to the empty sheriff's car with the driver's-side door still open.

Colt jumped out and ran to the edge of the embankment. Four hundred feet below, he saw a deputy standing on a ledge of rock looking into the side window of a red sports car. From above, the vehicle looked like a crushed Coke can. Colt thought it must have rolled several times before coming to a rest, right side up, next to a boulder jutting out from the side of the canyon.

Brian joined him and looked over the edge. "Oh baby, look at that car," he said.

"Hey," Colt shouted and waved. His voice echoed in the silent canyon. The deputy looked up and waved back. "How the hell did he get down there without a rope?" Colt said.

They ran back to the squad. "I hope the driver was wearing a seatbelt," Brian said. "This isn't gonna be pleasant." There were no trees or guardrail on the turnout to use as an anchor point for the descent lines. Brian moved the squad up to the edge of the canyon, set the emergency brake and placed chocks under the rear wheels.

Colt uncoiled the nylon ropes and secured them to the front bumper. He pulled at each to make sure they were secure, and then tossed them over the side directly above the car. Colt tried to imagine what they would find below.

Brian took out the over-the-side medical bag and clipped on a small fire extinguisher.

Colt buckled a descent harness across his chest and around his waist. He pulled on his gloves.

"Go easy, don't rush it," Brian warned. "We don't want to have to rescue a rescuer." He buckled his own harness. "And try to avoid the poison oak." He slung the medical bag over his shoulder, clipped onto one of the descent ropes and backed over the edge.

Colt was right behind him with the KED – the Kendrick Extraction Device—used for spinal immobilization in place of a backboard. It was less than three feet long and lightweight, but felt like a surfboard hanging from the webbing on the back of his harness. Colt began to rappel down, looking over his shoulder as he hung onto his descent line. Most of the ground was exposed bedrock covered in places with decomposed granite, gravel and small stones. Clumps of vegetation and chaparral dotted the slope, but were brittle and useless for a handhold.

Colt dislodged a rock and slipped backward. "Damn it," he cursed. "I hate doing this." He tightened his grip on the line and regained his balance. His all-purpose firefighter boots were useful for everything but this.

Brian was already 10 feet ahead of him. As they made their way down, small stones and pebbles dislodged from the canyon's wall, cascaded past them and bounced off the damaged car below. The deputy, struck by some of the debris, moved aside and watched them descend. It took several minutes for Colt and Brian to reach the car.

The deputy recognized Brian. "Hey Brian," he said. "Glad you guys are here. We've got a trapped kid, and a dash bow."

Colt looked at the red Corvette. It was a disaster. What wasn't crushed, was shattered. The parts of the body made from carbon fiber were split and broken, and red pieces littered the side of the mountain. It looked as though the car had gone over nose first and the front of the vehicle took the first impact before it rolled down sideways. "How'd you get down here without a rope?" he asked the deputy.

"Wasn't easy. I traversed on all fours." He held up his forearm to show a torn shirtsleeve and a bloody patch of skin. "Nearly lost it."

Brian dropped his pack and tried to open the driver's-side door, but the frame of the car was twisted. He bent to look in through the space that had once been the side window. "Sir, can you hear me?" he said. "I'm a paramedic. I'm here to help you."

"Yeah, I'm fine," the kid inside said in a normal tone of voice. "I'm OK, just get me out."

"What's your name?" Brian asked.

"Tyler."

"Do you know what day it is?"

"It's Tuesday. I told you, I'm OK." He sounded calm.

Colt joined Brian at the window and saw Tyler, who looked like a teenager, pressed back against the expensive black leather seat with the seatbelt still around him. A deflated airbag hung over the steering wheel. The dashboard was pushed down and inward against his legs, obscuring his body from the waist down. He was bleeding from a large cut on his forehead, but Colt thought his upper body looked remarkably good.

"What happened, Tyler?" Brian asked.

"I guess I lost control."

The deputy interrupted. "Hey guys, we've got a gas leak." He pointed to the rear of the car.

Colt detached the fire extinguisher from Brian's pack and tossed it to the deputy. "Keep an eye on it. Our engine should be here in a minute."

"I'm OK," Tyler repeated. "I just need to get out."

Colt doubted if Tyler was "OK," although he probably wasn't feeling any pain yet.

"It's gonna take some time," Brian said. He reached inside the car and put his fingers on the boy's wrist, then turned to Colt. "Steady pulse, 110. He's got a strong heartbeat."

Colt's training did kick in. There were so many things to do, all at once. First, they had to stabilize their patient. He opened Brian's pack and pulled out the IVs. When he leaned into the car, he said, "You a football player?"

"Basketball," Tyler said. "Can I use a cell phone? I have to tell my folks I'll be late."

"Just take it easy," Colt said. It was important to talk to the patient and reassure him. "We're going to insert an IV in your arm." He reached in and tied a rubber strap around the boy's biceps. Colt patted, then slapped the boy's arm, found a vein and inserted the needle. Colt looked for an indication of desanguination—massive blood loss—on the floor of the Corvette, but the crushed dashboard obstructed his view.

Brian attached the IV tube to the saline bag and managed to suspend it from the bent doorframe.

Colt heard 88's engine above him. In the midst of everything, he realized he had learned to discern the different siren sounds of the engines, squads, ambulances and police cruisers. Colt pulled out his radio and called Captain Ames. "Cap, it's a high-angle descent and we need the extrication equipment. We've got a trapped driver down here. We have to do a dash push. We're gonna need the AirSquad and an ambulance."

"My dad'll be pissed," Tyler said. "This is a new car."

Brian checked the saline line to make sure it was flowing. "Please don't talk now," he said. "Try to relax and save your strength."

Colt looked at Brian. For the first time since Colt had been working with him, he saw an expression he had never seen before.

"Get the C-collar on him," Brian said. "I'll start a Bicarb IV. He's gonna have crush syndrome."

Colt took the collar out of the pack. He was able to reach in, slip it around Tyler's neck and secure it under his chin. Colt had learned about the severity of crush syndrome, but had never seen it. During an extrication, once the compression on a part of the body was released, acid and other metabolic waste from damaged cells flooded the bloodstream, causing heart fibrillation and possible death. Colt wondered again about Tyler's condition under the dashboard and how much blood he might have lost. He looked stable, but that might be because he was an athlete and in good physical condition. An adult body had five quarts of blood. One quart could be on the floor of the Corvette and Tyler could still look normal. A loss of any more would be a major problem—three quarts of blood was the minimum amount for the IV fluid to maintain blood pressure and allow the heart to pump to vital organs. Sometimes the legs were amputated on impact but the dashboard acted like a tourniquet until it was pushed back. Colt had heard stories about situations when arms and legs were finally freed and were found attached to the body only by pieces of skin. Colt wondered if Tyler would play basketball again.

Colt took Tyler's pulse again. "His heart rate's up to 127," said Brian.

"Search and Rescue just arrived," the deputy announced. "Equipment's coming down in the Stokes."

Colt was thankful for S and R. They were pros at high-angle rapelling with heavy equipment. Without them, the paramedics would need a helicopter to lower the ram, the Jaws of Life and the gas-powered hydraulic generator. Bringing the AirSquad into the narrow canyons was difficult and dangerous.

Brian finished inserting the Bicarb IV in Tyler's arm. He stepped back from the Corvette, looked at Colt and shook his head. "I'm sure he's bleeding," he said. "I don't know if he's gonna have a 'golden hour.'"

Colt tried to reconcile Tyler's matter-of-fact attitude with the severity of his situation. He heard another siren echo through the canyon and thought it must be the engine from 125s. When he looked up toward the road again, he saw four S and R members on the side of the canyon. They were attached to steel cables, walking face forward, two on each side of a Stokes basket held by a larger cable. When Tyler was freed, they would wrap the KED around him, load him into the Stokes and winch him back up. Then he would get his golden hour—and a chance for survival. The ambulance would take him the short distance back to the helicopter pad at Pepperdine University and the AirSquad could pick him up and rush him to CU's hospital.

As Colt watched, he saw Captain Ames and Moose, in harnesses, come over the side and start down on the ropes he and Brian had used.

"Do we need to crib the car?" Brian asked Colt.

Colt went to the side of the Corvette and tried to rock it. It was solid against the boulder and didn't move. "We're good," he said, and looked up again at the S and R men. They were moving fast, already halfway down the side of the canyon. Captain Ames and Moose were above them, coming more slowly. Higher up, above the edge of the turnout, Colt saw the last vestiges of the coastal fog disappearing from the tops of the Santa Monica Mountains. The late-morning sun would soon burn through and begin to bake the landscape. In another hour, the canyon would be like an oven. There was not a breath of wind. A flock of boisterous wild parrots flew by overhead.

Brian put a patch on Tyler's forehead to stop the bleeding.

Tyler still wanted to call his father about the damage to the car.

Brian told him again to relax and keep quiet.

Colt checked Tyler's pulse again. It had climbed to 136.

S and R arrived, unhooked from their descent cables and began to unload the Stokes. They looked like military commandos in gray form-fitting body suits and black helmets. One of the team members carried the Jaws compressor over to the Corvette and uncoiled the hydraulic hoses. He glanced inside the damaged car, looked at Tyler, then at Colt. He said nothing.

A familiar sick feeling began to well up inside Colt. He thought of his father lying in the corral looking up at him. He thought of Bibi, unable to speak, staring straight ahead with unfocused eyes. He saw paramedics wheeling injured patients with glazed eyes into the ER at CU. Colt knew Death was on the side of the mountain with them, waiting to take charge. He wondered if he was the only one who thought Tyler might not survive. No, Colt decided, Brian knew. The deputy probably knew as well. If the S and R men didn't know now, they would soon.

The three remaining S and R men dragged the basket filled with the tools over to the car. One of them set up the compressor and started it while another hooked up the hydraulic hoses to the cutter.

Brian told Colt, "When the cutting starts, be sure to cover the kid."

By the time Moose and Captain Ames arrived, the compressor had built up maximum hydraulic pressure. Moose went to work. He surveyed the damage to the front and sides of the car and looked inside. "Hello, sir," he said to Tyler. "We're gonna start this piece of equipment. It'll make some noise and take a while, but we'll work as fast as we can to get you out of here."

Tyler's eyes were open. "Hurry." His voice sounded weaker and more urgent.

Colt checked his pulse again. "145," he announced. Tyler's heart was pumping faster to compensate for a loss of blood. He put his hand on Tyler's forehead. It was cool and damp. Colt told Brian in a low voice, "He's losing blood and he's going into shock. What if we have to give him CPR?"

Brian shook his head. "We can't do it while he's trapped in the car." He turned to Moose and said, "Make it quick."

Moose nodded.

Colt looked at his watch. It was 10:55 a.m. They were toned out at 10:15 a.m. Tyler had been trapped in the car for almost an hour.

A second deputy came down on one of the S and R cables. Colt listened to him tell the first officer, "Looks like he came through the canyon too fast. Tire marks show his rear end started to come out. He steered into the skid like a big deal race-car driver, regained traction and the over-steer took him across the turnout and over the side."

The first deputy had his pad out and was already writing parts of his report.

"We ready to go?" Moose asked. "I'll spread the front quarter panel first and cut through the door hinge."

Yeah, Colt thought, Dad's definitely going to be unhappy about the damage to the Vette.

"Once I cut the A Post," Moose continued, "I think we can lift the dash without peeling the roof."

Colt took a blanket out of the Stokes basket, reached into the car and did his best to cover Tyler's upper body, leaving only his head exposed.

"The minute you get the door off, we have to try to get tourniquets on him," Brian said to Moose. "I don't know what's going on under the dash, but it can't be good."

Moose picked up the spreader tool and signaled to the S and R man, who throttled up the generator. It sounded like a lawnmower engine, but generated enough hydraulic pressure to cut and tear the structural steel parts of an automobile.

Another noise mixed with the sound of the generator. Colt recognized the distinctive clatter of the AirSquad and looked up to see the Blackhawk pass over the canyon, heading to the landing pad at Pepperdine University.

Colt prayed Tyler had enough strength to survive the next part of his rescue. The incident seemed like it had been dragging on for hours. He checked Tyler's pulse again. "165," he shouted to Brian. Now Tyler looked pale. Colt pulled the blanket away from his upper body and watched Tyler's chest rising and falling. His respiration and heart rate were accelerating. He was in shock.

Moose worked at fast as he could to pry the metal away from the front wheel well and gain access to the doorframe, but automobiles were not made to be taken apart quickly.

Colt tried to will Moose to work even faster. He tugged the blanket back up over Tyler's chest and saw him close his eyes. Colt let go of the blanket and searched for Tyler's pulse. "His heartbeat's down to 120," he called out to Brian over the sound of the compressor.

Colt watched Moose methodically work at the side of the Corvette, change the tool head from the spreader to a cutter and wait for the pressure to build up again. Thank God for Moose. He handled the heavy tools as if they were toys. Colt wondered how anyone did extrication before the invention of the Jaws of Life.

Captain Ames talked on the radio with the captain from 125s, waiting above.

Brian pointed up the slope, describing to the S and R team where the car had come down.

The first deputy wrote more of his report.

The second deputy talked on his radio.

Colt stayed at the window of the car, holding the blanket in place. Tyler's eyes remained closed. Colt was certain he would be the last to see the kid alive.

Moose started on the toughest cut, the "A post" that held the door in place. He was an expert, but it was taking too long.

Colt looked at his watch again. Now it was 11:20 a.m. Twenty-five minutes had passed since he last checked the time. Tyler had been trapped in the Corvette for almost 90 minutes.

Suddenly, Tyler opened his eyes and stared at Colt, inches away on the other side of the window frame. Colt's heart sank. He knew the look. The light in Tyler's eyes was dying out.

"We're losing him," Colt shouted. "Cut faster, Moose." Tyler's head was immobile in the C-collar and couldn't fall forward. Colt saw the muscles in his face go slack. He searched for a heartbeat, but there was nothing. He tried again. "He's in full arrest," Colt said to Brian, and began pressing Tyler's chest as best he could through the window.

Brian pushed Colt aside and gave Tyler shots of epinephrine and atropine, then stepped back. Tyler's face was white.

Colt leaned in and again tried CPR. "Don't die," he whispered. Colt pumped Tyler's chest. Nothing happened, the stimulants had no effect.

"Again?" Colt asked.

"Yeah," Brian said, and administered another round.

Colt began CPR again, but after a minute, Brian stopped him and shook his head. "He's bled out. It won't help. It's over."

Colt stepped back. He clenched his fists and looked up—as though he were looking for Tyler's soul rising from his body. A tear ran from Colt's eye. He shook his head, walked a few steps away and stood looking down into the canyon, his back to the others. He took a couple of deep breaths and swallowed the urge to scream.

Brian leaned into the car and checked Tyler's pulse one last time. "He's gone," he confirmed and looked at his watch. He pulled out his radio and contacted the MICN—the mobile intensive care nurse—their base connection at the hospital at CU. When he reached her, Brian identified himself and said, "We have a vehicle entrapment and cardiopulmonary failure. Two rounds of epi and atropine were unsuccessful. Another round would have no effect. Patient is still trapped in his vehicle and has bled out." Brian looked at his watch. "I determine the time of death to be 11:23 a.m." He listened while the nurse repeated the information back to him, then said, "That's correct, thank you."

The first deputy stopped writing his report.

The second deputy stopped talking on his radio.

Captain Ames stood next to Brian. Neither of them said anything.

The S and R men stood around the Stokes basket. One made a quick sign of the cross on his chest.

Only Moose continued to work. He licked a drop of sweat off his upper lip, glanced toward the motionless body covered with the rescue blanket and kept cutting.

Colt stood looking down into the canyon and felt empty. There was no golden hour. There was no miracle. No angels descended from heaven to save Tyler's life. The look in Tyler's eyes had sent Colt the goodbye message. Tyler was alive and then he was dead—that was it. Colt wondered if Tyler knew he was about to die. Was he thinking about his family? The damage to his car? His basketball team? Did Tyler see anything? Did he disappear into a tunnel of light? A circle of darkness?

Colt kicked at the loose shale and sent a rock bouncing down into the canyon, starting a small rockslide. As a teenager, his time at Sheridan Fire and Rescue had stoked his desire to help people. The first five weeks of his service as a paramedic weren't working out as he expected.

# TWELVE

WHILE THE 88s WATCHED the oversized tow truck drag the damaged red Corvette up out of Malibu Canyon late Tuesday morning, Markus spent half an hour driving eight miles north on the 405. Traffic in both directions on the five-lane freeway always moved at a crawl. Even though he was in no hurry to see Alexei for the third time, Markus insisted on driving as fast as possible. People were such retards. They were such slow drivers, poking along in the left-hand lanes doing less than 60. At the Victory Boulevard exit, Markus took the ramp too fast, jammed on his brakes and almost rear-ended a man in a BMW. When Markus pulled up at the red light, the man put down his window, shook his fist at Markus and yelled, "You moron." Before Markus could respond, the light turned green and the BMW took off. Markus turned right and headed east toward the Gates of Heaven in Burbank.

Although he had a confrontation or a near miss every time he drove, Markus had been involved in only one serious incident, in San Pedro, the port city south of Los Angeles. When he moved to Los Angeles and found a job, one of the first things Markus did was search for a custom set of vampire teeth. He found Dr. Damian, the premier vampire dentist, located in San Pedro. On his first trip down to see him, Markus was so excited that he changed lanes on the freeway without looking and sideswiped another car. It happened in the middle of the day and the freakin' CHP officer kept him out in the searing sunlight for almost an hour. By the time Markus arrived at Dr. Damian's office, he had one of his humongous sunlight headaches.

During the consultation, Dr. Damian told Markus that he made all the fangs for the vampire movies. He explained, "It's an art to design something that's strong and fits in the mouth. You want something that looks good."

The good doctor recommended his trademarked Damian's Dental Daggers. He assured Markus they would be both realistic and comfortable.

On the first visit, he took molds of Markus' upper and lower jaw. On the second visit, Markus saw a wax model of his upper teeth with the new cuspids. Markus studied the mold. "I like it," he said, "but the fangs are too short, they need to be a little longer," The doctor took another mold of the roof of his mouth. Two weeks later, after a $950 charge to his credit card, Dr. Damian presented Markus with a set of Dental Daggers that fit over his real upper eyeteeth. The porcelain fangs were bonded to gold, which in turn was fused to a paper-thin titanium plate that rested against the roof of his mouth.

"This is state of the art," the doctor said. "The plate won't interfere with your speech and you can pop it in or out in a second. If you really want to bite into flesh, this'll do the job. The teeth won't move." He inserted the Daggers into Markus' mouth and held up an oval mirror.

Markus lifted his upper lip and said, "Badass!" as he gazed at his frightening image with red eyes and vicious teeth. "Ahhh, I will drink your blood," he growled in his best Transylvanian accent.

He only wore his Dental Daggers a few times before he realized it was foolish to have spent money on vampire teeth. They looked good at Goth clubs, but were otherwise useless. Only wannabees wore them. No one of Markus' stature, who really wanted human blood, would try to rip open someone's neck with vampire teeth. That was a movie stunt. A needle or knife was the only way to go. Markus realized he was beyond vampire teeth; he was into the real thing. He put his Dental Daggers away in a drawer and never wore them again. It was a complete waste of money, but the encounter eventually led Markus to Alexei.

Markus had seen conversations in chat rooms about funeral parlors secretly carving up bodies scheduled for cremation. There were rumors that brokers bought body parts, patches of skin, teeth, corneas and arteries for resale to surgeons, medical and research laboratories, even to medical schools. A fresh corpse in good condition was supposed to be worth thousands of dollars.

Markus thought about how sweet it would be to show up at a bloodsucker's gathering and flaunt a human hand. It was the kind of thing the others would expect from him. He mentioned the stories about body parts to Dr. Damian, who gave a sly smile and said, "Who knows what happens to a body before cremation? If you're interested, I know a Russian named Alexei. He runs Heaven's Gate in Burbank. Just be careful around him."

Heading east from the 405 to Alexei's funeral parlor, Markus drove through neighborhoods of small homes with metal grates on the windows and front yards full of dirt and weeds. Check-cashing businesses, liquor and convenience stores with bulletproof glass, and even a marijuana dispensary, clustered on the street corners. The scenery didn't change in Burbank.

Heaven's Gate Funeral Parlor was one block from the entrance to Valhalla Memorial Park Cemetery. On the far side of Valhalla lay the Burbank Airport. At regular intervals, red and blue Southwest Airlines jets thundered in on the glide path, shaking the ground and rattling the gravestones. There was no rest for the dead in Valhalla.

Markus drove into a parking lot occupied by a black Cadillac hearse and a beat-up van. White flowers lined the front walk. The mortuary was a shabby gray Victorian house that needed a fresh coat of paint. The steep roof had two third-story attic rooms with tiny windows. If the house was haunted, the attic would be where the ghosts lived. White shutters framed large bay windows on the main floor. A deep porch with a sagging wooden balustrade ran along the front of the house and connected with a gazebo on one side. White gingerbread wood trim, broken away in places, bordered the top of the porch.

Markus climbed the wooden steps, walked across the porch to the front door and paused. He looked around and imagined a crowd of mourners, dressed in black, standing outside and consoling each other after a memorial service. While they wiped away their tears, the staff inside dismembered the deceased. They carved up the corpse with a chainsaw, probably a small quiet electric model, and placed the body parts in an ice chest destined for a medical lab.

Markus pushed the door open. Inside, the dim light was a relief and he removed his sunglasses. In the entrance, a vase of roses and a leather bound memorial book from the last funeral greeted him. Markus added his name to the list of mourners, and wrote in large ornate letters, "HAVE A NICE TRIP." A sharp, sweet smell, stronger than the scent of flowers, filled the air. A dark red carpet covered the floor and the short hall leading into the chapel. Markus looked around for Alexei.

On his first visit, Markus had found the Russian standing in the hallway. He was a large, corpulent man with a shiny bald head, dressed in a dark suit. Markus immediately mentioned Dr. Damian's name.

Alexei cut him off and launched into a discussion of caskets. "Steel is cheapest," he said. "Wood is nice, but even expensive wood casket eventually rots. Copper-bronze model is best and lasts forever. Famous statues everywhere made from bronze for that reason. Prices from $750 to $15,000. What kind of casket you want?" Alexei paused and stared at Markus. "You are albinos?"

"Cremation is the least expensive," Markus responded, ignoring the question and using the exact words Dr. Damian had laid out for him. "I'm interested in a cremation."

"*Da nu.* Yes, cremation is best," Alexei agreed, still eyeing him.

"Just ashes and maybe a hand left over."

Alexei gave him a how-do-I-know-you're-not-a-cop look and walked to the front entrance.

"What's the price range?" Markus asked, trailing Alexei.

"Cremation service comes with urn. You have memorial service with choice of scented candles." Alexei held the front door for Markus.

"The cost?" Markus persisted.

Alexei scratched his nose and said, "*Ya zanyat.* I am busy now. Come back next Monday. Bring $1,200 cash and we discuss. In meantime, I check with Dr. Damian. You are really albinos?" Alexei came closer to Markus and looked at him from head to toe. "Albinos," he repeated.

Markus had emptied his bank account, took a $700 advance on his credit card and returned the following week.

Alexei wasn't any friendlier on the second visit, and got right down to business. "We sell doctors and medical laboratories. I never have request from … ah … private person like you."

Markus handed Alexei the manila envelope with the cash. "I want a hand, a woman's hand," and imagined all the things he could do with it. He thought of his mother and felt her soft, fleshy hands caressing him.

"Is not so simple." Alexei opened the envelope and looked inside. "I cannot run downstairs and get hand. I match supply and demand for whole body. You choose left or right, but not man or woman."

"Is a left hand cheaper?"

"Yes, left is cheaper. Is still another $1,200, payment on delivery. You take male or female, whatever comes. People don't die so often in summer. Everybody outside, having fun, no time for death. I give you couple day's notice."

On his third visit, after Alexei called to say the "item" was available, Markus had already maxed out his credit cards and arrived without the second payment. Alexei was actually friendly and said, "Go ahead, take treasure. Do what you do with it." He handed Markus a small styrofoam container.

Markus removed the top and saw a left hand, neatly severed at the wrist, nestled in shaved ice. Markus was disappointed big time. It was a skinny, almost emaciated hand of an old man. The skin was brown and blemished. What a bummer. Who wanted an old geezer's hand? It wouldn't work; there was nothing erotic about it. How had he let himself be forced into paying so much for such a lame, crappy piece of flesh? Alexei had screwed him. He wanted to tell fucking Alexei the Russian that this was not what he had in mind.

Before Markus could speak, Alexei looked at him and smiled in a way that was not a smile. "You have one week. Come back Tuesday with money."

Now, on Tuesday, a week later, Markus was back at Heaven's Gate for the fourth time. A blue suit met him at the entrance to the chapel, but it wasn't Alexei.

"He's busy."

"Who're you?" Markus asked.

"I am Grisha."

Markus looked at Grisha and immediately disliked him. He was big, and his suit was a size too small. He wore a white shirt, a thin black tie and scuffed black dress shoes. Grisha's hands had bruises and cuts and his nails were filthy. He needed a shave. All the people Markus hated in his life, which was just about everyone, were bigger than he was. Grisha fit right in. "It's important. Tell him Markus is here."

"I know who you are. Wait." Grisha walked into the chapel and disappeared through a doorway at the far end.

Markus paced back and forth. He knew his measly $175 wouldn't impress Alexei.

Grisha came back through the door and left it open. He brought with him an odor that Markus could smell from the other end of the chapel. "Alexei's working in the basement. Go on down." Grisha went to a large vase at the side of the chapel and began arranging a bouquet of white flowers.

Markus thought Grisha resembled a gorilla foraging for something to eat. "Nice flowers," he said. Markus had no interest in flowers. They grew in the sun.

"Gladiolus Iridaceae," Grisha growled.

Markus walked to the door at the back of the chapel. As he started down the stairs, an overpowering chemical stench assaulted him. He opened his mouth and tried not to breathe through his nose, but the odor was too strong, Markus could almost taste it. At the bottom of the stairs, he saw fluorescent light and a white tile floor. He thought of the reflected light in the Colony at CU and put on his sunglasses. When he reached the basement, the temperature felt like 50 degrees. He started to shiver as he entered a prep room for embalming bodies. The first thing he heard was the chugging sound of a small pump. Pans of stainless steel instruments were lined up on a table. The tools were all oversized, and were made for sawing, slicing and puncturing. Curved needles, the size of large fishhooks, were threaded with white filament.

Alexei looked up. Today he wore a long-sleeve white gown that buttoned at the back, a paper cap over his shiny head, a mask over his nose and mouth, blue latex gloves and clear plastic glasses. The body of a naked old man lay on a porcelain table, his clothing neatly folded on a countertop. It could have been a wax figure. The pallor of the skin was pale, almost translucent. The body was clean, the hair trimmed, the face smooth. Markus glanced at the hands. Even this old fart on the embalming table had better-looking hands than the one Alexei had sold him. Again, Markus wanted to complain to Alexei about the crappy hand.

Two tubes protruded from an ugly red gash on the right side of the cadaver's neck. Markus watched as the noisy pump sucked pink embalming fluid from a small tank and forced it into the man's neck through one of the tubes. A mixture of fluid, blood and dark red clots came out through the second tube, spread across the floor and emptied into a drain. Alexei wore ankle-high gray plastic boots, which were covered with flecks of the same dark red color. The odor of formaldehyde hung in the air and began to make Markus sick.

Alexei turned to adjust the pressure of the pump. "How you like?"

he asked. "This is embalming for public display of body. Fluid in carotid, blood out jugular." His voice was muffled behind his mask. He tapped the corpse's chest. "No parts here for you. Family come tomorrow for open casket viewing. We provide nice picture."

Markus gagged. "I have to talk to you about the hand."

"*Shto?* What about hand?"

Markus gagged again, his stomach heaved and sour fluid rose in the back of his throat. Markus wanted to tell Alexei what he thought of the lame hand, but settled for, "I need more time to pay you." He reached into his pocket, withdrew a roll of bills and handed it to Alexei.

Alexei pushed the clear plastic glasses up on top of his paper cap. He took the wad of money, placed it on a counter and spread out eight $20s, a $10 and a $5. "*Babki.* You are kidding. Where is rest?"

"I need more time."

Alexei glared at Markus and picked up a small pistol from the counter. A needle protruded from the barrel. He pointed it at Markus and walked toward him.

Markus backed away. "Alexei, no," he cried.

Alexei held the gun up to Markus' forehead, then laughed and turned to the cadaver. He tilted the head back and opened the mouth. It was stuffed with cotton. He lifted the upper lip and pointed the gun at a spot above the teeth on the gum. It made a small popping sound when he fired, and the needle wedged in the upper jaw. "I run business," Alexei said. "I don't know what you do with hand, but you buy it and you pay for it." He went back to the counter, reloaded the pistol, waved it at Markus again, then returned to the cadaver and shot another needle into the lower gum. "Pay, or I send Grisha to do mayhem on you. Understand? Not a happy visit." Alexei took a wire, wrapped it around the two needles and tied the mouth of the cadaver shut. When he finished, he cut off the ends of the needles with a wire cutter and smoothed the lips. He stepped back, looked at his handiwork and smiled. "So peaceful. Today is Tuesday. You are back next Monday by six in evening with rest of money."

Markus watched Alexei lift the cadaver's eyelids. Underneath, the eye sockets were empty. Alexei took two wads of cotton and stuffed them into the hollows. He took two half-round pieces of plastic the size of bottle caps and placed them on top of the cotton. Each piece had tiny barbs. Alexei pulled the eyelids down over the spikes and pressed them in place.

The pump continued. Markus looked again at the blood and body fluids running into the floor drain. The odor of the formaldehyde became overpowering. It filled Markus' nose. It was in his mouth, on his tongue. His eyes burned.

Alexei looked at Markus, waved his hand and glared. "*Vsyoh.* That is all, albinos." He took a two-foot long metal tube attached to a plastic hose, and shoved the pointed end into the corpse's body just above the belly button.

Markus saw yellow liquid start to flow out of the corpse through the hose. His stomach convulsed, this time delivering a mouthful of bile. He stumbled up the stairs out of the basement and past Grisha who was still arranging flowers in the chapel. Markus ran to the front door, flung it open and nearly fell down the front stairs as his half-digested lunch filled his mouth and washed over his tongue. Markus bent over the flowers lining the side of the walk, clutched his stomach and threw up.

As he dribbled the last of his vomit on the tiny white petals, he felt a staggering pain in his tailbone and saw a white flash of light before his eyes. Markus fell forward onto the flowers and the contents of his stomach. He looked up and realized Grisha had kicked him.

"Hey albino." Grisha stood over him in his white shirt and too-small blue suit. "Don't heave in my *Brassicaceae.*"

"What?" Markus wiped his mouth and tried to brush the vomit off his shirt. He tried to stand up, but could only groan when he tried to move.

"You threw up all over my alyssum." Grisha stood over him for a moment, then walked across the mortuary's small parking lot and got into the van.

Markus rolled over onto the grass, choked back another surge of vomit and felt the pain in his lower back spread through his body.

Grisha rolled down the window of the van. Over the idle of the old engine, he said, "Bring our money, albino."

The odor of the formaldehyde in Markus' nostrils dissipated, but the smell of vomit and fear replaced it.

# THIRTEEN

While Markus sat on the grass at Heaven's Gate watching Grisha drive away in the van, A Li stood on the sidewalk in Brentwood waiting for Tanay to pick her up for their trip to the Flower Mart. After countless hours under fluorescent lights, the daylight seemed unnatural. She checked the time again. It was 12:45 p.m., and no sign of Tanay. She looked at her cell phone. No messages. She hoped he hadn't changed his mind. A Mei would not be pleased if she failed to obtain the iris. A Li walked to the corner, turned and walked back. She glanced again at the directions to the Flower Mart, which she had printed out from Mapquest.

Five minutes later, Tanay arrived driving a filthy, old Honda with a crumpled rear fender. He jumped out, ran around the car and opened the passenger side door for A Li. He pressed his hands together in front of his chest, fingers pointed upward and said, "Welcome to the royal carriage."

A Li swept a pile of crumbs off the front seat and got in. Tanay's car was a mess. The back seat was filled with newspapers, biomedical research magazines and an old suitcase. A layer of dust covered everything and the windshield was grimy. Tanay was such a neat and organized person. A Li wondered how his car could be such a disaster.

"Sorry I'm late," he said. "I had to get air in the tires. I don't drive much; it's so hard driving on the right-hand side." Tanay shifted into gear, popped the clutch, and the car lurched forward. "Happy birthday," he said.

"Thank you," A Li said. "What's important is A Mei's birthday." She buckled her seat belt. "Do you know how to get to the 10 Freeway?" Her own knowledge of the city and its highway system was limited. The longest trip she had taken in Los Angeles was the bus ride from the airport to the university. "Here."

"What's this?"

"Directions." A Li gave Tanay the Mapquest sheet. "From the Flower Mart to Chinatown, it says you just stay on Broadway."

Tanay held the sheet in one hand without looking at it. "Chinatown?"

A Li looked at Tanay. "Please? It's nearby and it won't take long."

"What are we doing in Chinatown?" Tanay looked at the map and the Honda veered into the oncoming lane.

"Oh," A Li exclaimed.

Tanay steered back into the right-hand lane.

"I have to pick up something else. … I was hoping … "

"I thought we could have a birthday lunch," Tanay said. He looked at his watch. "But I have to be back by three." Tanay sped down Santa Monica Boulevard. After a few minutes he said, "How did the mouse dissection go?"

"It was slow, but I didn't make any mistakes."

"Pretty soon you'll be able to do it in your sleep. Want to hear a mouse joke?"

"Yes." A Li wasn't proficient enough in English to understand most of the jokes she heard.

"Scientists can cure any disease known to mice." Tanay laughed and looked to see if she understood.

A Li didn't get it, but she smiled and changed the subject. "Did you hear about the hematology seminar last week?"

"What about it?" Tanay sped up at an intersection just as the light turned red.

A Li shifted in her seat and braced herself with a hand on the dashboard. "They had a presentation on artificial blood. There's a new substitute with fluorocarbons. It's a clear liquid that looks like water, but it holds dissolved oxygen. They showed a mouse submerged in it."

"Submerged in it?" Tanay turned to look at her.

"Watch the road, please. It was alive and breathing this fluid that had oxygen in it. It was like having regular blood going through its lungs. It lived underwater for an hour."

"Speaking of blood, I researched Bombay Blood last night. One out of every 250,000 people? That makes you special."

"It's a curse."

"It should be called Mumbai Blood now."

"Most people who have it are of East Indian descent."

"Are you part Indian?" Tanay reached out to touch her arm. "We could be related."

A Li felt the warm touch of his fingertips. "My ancestors were from Tibet."

"There are Indian bloodlines in the Tibetans. Way back."

"No," A Li said, shaking her head. "We're not related."

"Just a thought," Tanay murmured.

"We're what are called para-Bombay individuals."

"What's that?"

"True Bombay have no antigens at all in their blood. Para-Bombay's are closer to Type O, but not close enough to accept it in a transfusion." A Li looked out the window at downtown Los Angeles. From the freeway, she saw construction cranes towering over building sites and thought of Beijing, where construction was spreading like a tidal wave, destroying whole neighborhoods, crushing and pushing aside the homes of thousands of people.

"Does Dr. Murray know about it?" Tanay asked.

"About what?"

"Your blood."

"Yes, he knows. He's never mentioned it, but I think he wants samples for research. In fact, that may be the reason I'm in the program."

"No, I'm sure you're in the program because you're smart."

A Li ignored his comment. "It's almost impossible to get Bombay Blood for use in lab work."

"Do you think he's planning to reprogram bone marrow stem cells to make Bombay Blood?"

"Yes, you have it."

"I have it?"

"You have it."

"I think you mean, 'you got it.' It's slang."

"Yes, you got it, that's correct," A Li said. "Maybe I should bottle my blood and sell it for research. How much do you think a liter is worth?"

"Don't be ridiculous."

"I could use the money. I'm still paying back the state grant program for the tuition money at Yunnan University. I haven't even started to pay back the provincial government for my CU loan."

"You don't have enough blood in your body to pay all those loans. Forget it."
He held up the map again and glanced at it.

When Tanay turned off the 10 Freeway at San Pedro Street, A Li saw signs
pointing in different directions for the Toy District, the Fashion District and
the Flower Mart. Tanay proceeded several blocks into an area filled with stores
selling cut flowers, wreaths, bouquets, ribbons, glassware and balloons.
Everything was displayed out on the sidewalks. It reminded A Li of marketplaces
at home. Farther on, delivery vans with open doors were parked in the middle
of the street, along the curb and even on the sidewalks. Merchants loaded them
with boxed flowers and bouquets wrapped in cellophane and paper. Instead of
the usual urban litter of old newspapers and plastic bags, the breeze blew colorful piles of flower petals and leaves into the corners of doorways.

"The Flower Mart," A Li said, "is supposed to be a big building."

They drove further. The sidewalks were filled with Americans, Japanese
and Latinos, a new word A Li had learned since coming to Los Angeles. A
group of young schoolchildren walked, danced and skipped as their teachers
herded them along. The boys wore red T-shirts, the girls wore white. Each
clutched a carnation.

"There it is." Tanay pointed to a pale yellow building that ran the length
of an entire block. He scanned the street. "There's no place to park." He pulled
in to a spot in front of a fire hydrant. "I'll wait for you here."

"Thank you, I won't be long."

After she got out of Tanay's filthy car, A Li brushed herself off. When she
entered the Flower Mart, the air was moist and heavy with fragrance. The scent
was so thick it smelled as if someone had spilled perfume. A kaleidoscope of
colors greeted her. Red, pink, yellow, purple, orange, and white blooms filled
the building. As A Li started down the center aisle, she saw sunlight shining
in from the far entrance on the next street. The activity was frantic. Men opened
refrigeration units and pulled out flowers. Trucks were loaded and unloaded
along an indoor dock. At tables, men and women sprayed, trimmed, arranged
and bundled bouquets, piling them on flatbed dollies. One man stood at a table
piled high with long-stem roses. He worked quickly, stripping thorns and pulling the outer petals off each bud, creating a blood-red ocean at his feet. Everyone
in the warehouse was busy.

A Li wandered through the building, too shy to ask anyone where to find the iris, she saw a man in the middle of an aisle with a cart full of lilies, gladiolas and other white flowers. She thought he might be some sort of official because he was wearing a blue suit, a white shirt and black tie, while everyone around her wore jeans and T-shirts. "Excuse me," she said. "Do you know where the iris are?"

"Iris? What kind of iris do you want?" he said. *"Germanica? Sibirica? Pseudacorus?"*

"I don't know. Just iris."

The man looked at her. "Where are you from?"

"China. Tibetan Autonomous Region."

"Iris *Latistyla*. But you won't find anything like that here. What they do have would be over there." He pointed to the other side of the building.

"Thank you."

"Are you bereaved?"

"Bereaved?"

"Have you lost someone?"

"Oh yes, my sister." A Li lowered her eyes.

The man unbuttoned his blue suit jacket. He had a big, strong body and his clothes were too small. He pulled out his wallet and withdrew a card. "I work for the Gates of Heaven Funeral Parlor. We specialize in memorial services and cremations." He gave her the card. His hands were bruised and he had dirt under his fingernails.

"Crema …?" A Li studied the card.

"Cre-may-shuns. The body is burned up. Flames? Smoke?" He fluttered his big hands upward. "You understand?"

A Li nodded. "Oh yes. We do that at home with the bones of the dead." She put the card in her pocket. She looked at him closely. "Are you American?"

"I am Russian." He thumped his chest with his fist.

"Thank you," A Li said. She gave him a polite nod and set off for the iris on the other side of the Flower Mart.

As she wound her way through the building, she passed a group of vendors who sold moss, ferns, leaves and branches used for flower arrangements. She stopped and purchased several juniper twigs. When she finally found the vendors selling iris, she was pleased to see that the ones growing in America resembled those found on the high plateau of her home. She selected a small bouquet, paid and made her way back to Tanay's car.

When she opened the door, Tanay started the engine immediately. "Get what you wanted?"

"Yes," A Li said, "my sister will be pleased."

"I was sure I was going to get a ticket."

A Li took the sheet with the directions off the dashboard and looked at it. "You turn left on Ninth Street." She pointed to the intersection in front of them. "Go four blocks and you come to Broadway. We stay on Broadway all the way to Chinatown."

Tanay took the directions from her. "How far is that? You didn't print out the mileage."

"I don't know," A Li said. "Just turn right and keep going."

Tanay drove through open 12-foot-high steel gates topped with barbed wire, passed a barricade of shipping containers with a sign warning BIO SECURE AREA and parked in front of the China Sun Fresh Market. The moment he turned off the engine, the sound of hundreds of chickens filled the air. "What is this?" he said.

"It's supposed to be the closest you can get to a real Chinese market in Los Angeles," A Li said. As soon as she opened her door, the odor filled the car. It was a disgusting smell from a mixture of chicken droppings, poultry intestines, animal offal, and fish.

"*Yech*," Tanay exclaimed, "this makes the rat room at the Colony smell good."

"I'll just be a minute."

"I'm not coming in."

A Li walked into the market and instantly felt at home. The odor was even stronger inside, although the cement floor had just been hosed down and was still wet. China Sun sold only a few kinds of fish and meat; the poultry was killed on the premises. Chinese men and women carrying ragged shopping bags lined up at the counter. Several stood in the fish line for *Ca Ro Bien*—red Tapia; *Con Hao Song*—Oysters; and *So Mong*—clams. A Li waited at the meat counter. Behind it, she could see through a doorway where men scurried back and forth holding live chickens upside down by their legs. The birds flapped their wings, cackled and struggled to get free. In the background, A Li could hear the difference between the ordinary sounds of chickens and roosters and the shrieks of the animals whose necks were about to be broken.

"Can I help you?" a woman behind the counter asked. She was old, her gray hair covered by a hairnet. Her face was fat and puffy and she looked at A Li through thick round eyeglasses with wire frames.

"Yes, I came to pick up a special order for Jian."

"Just a minute," the woman said and disappeared into the back.

A Li waited and looked at the items in the glass cases in front of her. Hundreds of pink and yellow chicken feet filled several metal pans. Pig's feet, with the skin removed but the hooves intact, were also available. Ground meat, stuffed into large plastic bags, filled the end of the refrigeration case.

The woman returned and handed A Li a small package wrapped in white butcher paper. A Li unwrapped it, checked the contents and shoved it into her purse. "How much is it?"

"Twelve dollars."

"Twelve dollars?"

"Special order, short notice. You wanted today." The woman smiled, resembling a Buddha.

A Li withdrew a ten-dollar bill and two ones from her wallet. Americans had the cleanest money of any nation. In China, the paper money was torn and filthy. She handed the crisp bills to the woman and went out into the parking lot. A forklift carrying a pallet-load of live chickens in small metal cages nearly crushed her feet as it rolled past.

Tanay was resting his head against the back of the seat with his eyes closed. When A Li opened the door, he snapped forward.

"Asleep?" she asked.

"No, I was meditating and trying to block out the smell. It didn't work. I'm about to throw up." Tanay looked at his watch. "It's 2:20, too late for lunch, but I couldn't eat now anyway."

"Thank you for doing this for me."

"I have a present for you." Tanay reached into the rubble on the back seat and pulled out a white paper bag, which he handed to A Li. "Happy birthday."

A Li was surprised at its weight. She reached inside and withdrew something wrapped in brown paper. She unwrapped a small brass elephant, perhaps 4 inches long, inlaid with glass jewels and decorated in exquisite detail. She turned to Tanay. "Thank you, how beautiful. I wasn't … I didn't expect you to give me a gift."

Tanay blushed under his tan skin. "I didn't expect to either, but I did. I hope you like it."

A Li thought of kissing him on the cheek, but before she could do it, Tanay put the car into gear and shot out onto the street without looking. An oncoming car swerved and sounded its horn.

On the way back, she looked at Tanay out of the corner of her eye and thought about inviting him to accompany her to the Moon Festival Celebration sponsored by the Chinese Students and Scholars Association. Planned for September 25 on the University of Southern California campus, it promised to be a wonderful night. A Li was looking forward to it because the dances, music and singing would remind her of home. It was certain to draw people from the entire Los Angeles area. Even the Consul General of China and his family were supposed to attend. For a moment, she imagined how proud she would be if everyone saw Tanay at her side.

"I want to ask you something," she said.

"Yes?"

"Do you like women with blond hair? There are so many here."

"Blond hair? No, no one in India has blond hair. I like black hair."

A Li wondered what it would be like if Tanay were her boyfriend. She tried to imagine what they would do with the little free time they might have together. She didn't even know where he lived. Would she leave Professor Chen's home on Canyon Avenue and move in with him? Would they make love when she came home from Dr. Murray's lab in the early morning? What did Tanay look like naked? Would he like the way she looked? She had once seen a movie in which a man came up behind his girlfriend, reached under her sweater and cupped her breasts. Would Tanay ever do that? Unlike most American girls, she was thin and had small breasts.

A Li was shocked—and excited—by her thoughts. She thought of A Mei, ever-present, and gave a small sigh. Would A Mei approve of Tanay? She had her twin and that had always been enough. A Li decided not to mention the festival to Tanay.

# FOURTEEN

AGONY! SHARP, STABBING, SEARING PAIN. On the way home from the Gates of Heaven, Markus twisted around in the driver's seat of his PT Cruiser, trying to find a comfortable position. He couldn't move without feeling the effect of Grisha's assault on his tailbone. His spinal cord was sending one signal to his brain: PAIN! Every nerve in his lower back radiated the aching message from the spot where Grisha had kicked him. He stopped in Burbank and hobbled into a drugstore to buy aspirin, but knew he needed something much stronger.

Back on the 405, he had visions of Grisha creeping … no … stomping up the stairs to his apartment in the middle of the night. Dressed in his shiny blue suit, white shirt and skinny tie, he carried a pistol in his belt. Instead of his scuffed black funeral shoes, Grisha wore heavy military boots, which he used to pulverize the front door of the apartment. Once inside, he smashed the bedroom door with his ham-sized fist, held the gun to Markus' forehead and demanded payment.

Pain and panic competed for control of Markus' brain.

By the time he pulled into the carport at 4:00 p.m., Markus wanted to die. His stomach was still churning; the taste of vomit lingered on his tongue and bits of regurgitated food stuck to his shirt. The aspirin wasn't helping his back. Grisha had kicked him so hard that Markus thought a bone might be broken. He opened the door of the PT Cruiser and eased out of the driver's seat. Pain shot up his spine. He climbed the stairs to his apartment one at a time, stopping on each step to let the stabbing sensations subside.

Markus unlocked the door, stepped into the gloom and without going to his computer to check incoming e-mail, went directly into the bathroom. He stood with his back to the mirror, pulled off his shirt and dropped his pants. In the reflection, he saw an ugly bruise starting to form above his butt. It wasn't black and blue yet, but he could see the spot where the tip of Grisha's shoe hit him and scraped away a large patch of skin. It looked like the surface of a giant raspberry and for once, the sight of his own blood did nothing to excite Markus. He pulled up his pants, opened the medicine chest and went through a dozen plastic bottles of prescription medications until he found the Vicodin. He shook three of the white football shaped tablets into his hand, tossed them into his mouth and slowly bent down to suck cold water from the tap.

Markus hobbled out to his desk. He could barely sit down. What had Grisha done to him? Markus googled TAILBONE PAIN. Several entries came up, including BROKEN COCCYX. Markus skimmed the pages and became more alarmed. His tailbone might be broken, chipped, cracked or even shattered. Markus saw no references to a kick in the ass from an angry Russian but every medical page focused on the acute and long-lasting deep body pain that came from trauma to the tailbone. He went to the webpage of Coccyx.org and discovered that in the worst injuries, surgeons performed a coccygectomy, the removal of the tailbone. His pain intensified with every word Markus read. The fucking Russians, how could they do this to him? How could Dr. Damian have gotten him into this mess?

He struggled out of his chair and went into the kitchen. He had six days to come up with the money and was afraid to think of what would happen if Grisha really tried to hurt him. Markus figured he might draw as much as $100 from his credit card. Next week he would receive a paycheck for $800, but not until Wednesday, and that still wasn't enough. He thought about calling his parents. His mother would be hysterical. He could cope with her meltdown if she had any money to send him, but his jackass father controlled the family wallet. Markus knew all he would get was tears from his mother and a lecture from his father.

Did Audra have any green stashed away? He knew she had no checking or savings accounts, not even a credit card. She lived a marginal existence and spent everything on her tats. Markus had never seen her spend a nickel on anything else. She must have hidden some money in the apartment. He thought of her at the Alley Kat, taking hundred dollar bills after doing tricks. She was living with him for free, sucking up his food, his water, even his electricity, like a sponge, without contributing a penny. She probably had thousands hidden away for herself, while he couldn't even get together enough money to save his life. She owed him! He slammed his fist down on the counter and the impact sent a wave of pain through his lower back.

Markus opened the freezer and took out the plastic baggies containing his treasures. He took the hand out and put it on the counter. The fingers were now contracted and bent. It looked as if it came from a body that had been clinging to a windowsill on the thirtieth story of a building. Could he return the hand to Alexei and call it even? Markus dismissed that idea as soon as he thought of it. He took out the foot and placed it next to the hand. The foot was so delicate, the skin spotless, the second toe so sexy.

How quickly things soured and turned to shit. Just last Sunday, he found the foot and everything was insane. Since then, the Chinese bitch got away from him, he owed Alexei money for an ugly hand and Grisha was coming to beat the crap out of him. To top it all off, he might need a coccygectomy. How would he pay for that? How could all this be happening to Markus, the uber vampire?

Markus put the hand and foot back in the freezer and went into the bedroom. The first warm feelings from 1,500 milligrams of Vicodin began to wash over him. He eased into bed and pulled the covers over his head. Soon he was floating in a deep, dark, warm ocean. The gentle waves rocked him back and forth, as his mother had done.

# FIFTEEN

"COLT." SOMEONE CALLED to him several times. It might have been his mother, but he no longer knew what her voice sounded like. It might have been Bibi, but he had heard her whisper only a couple of words. It might have been Tyler, trapped in his crushed car on Malibu Canyon.

The rumble of a truck on Pacific Coast Highway interrupted his dream, leaving a residue of sadness. It was after two in the morning. Out of habit, Colt reached for his old girlfriend, Ginny. For a split second, he expected her to be there next to him, but he was alone. Colt rolled over onto his back and stared at the ceiling in the dark apartment. He thought about the failed rescue in Malibu Canyon and retraced every step, wondering what would have happened if they had arrived minutes earlier, or if they had been able to get down the side of the mountain sooner or if Moose could have done the extrication faster.

Colt got out of bed. Barefoot and wearing only shorts and a T-shirt, he went outside and down the stairs to the street. Roy lay curled up asleep on the piece of cardboard that served as his mattress, surrounded by his bags of junk. The restaurants, the gay bar and Doreen's parlor were all dark. Pacific Coast Highway was empty. Colt walked to the underpass. The sand Roy had painstakingly swept away during the day had blown back in from the beach, along with newspapers and discarded plastic bags.

As he descended into the passageway, Colt smelled a strong odor of piss. The tunnel was lined with white tile, but the shifting earth and the passage of time had left the walls cracked. In many places, whole patches of bare cement showed. Graffiti was everywhere. Most of the overhead fluorescent lights, built into the ceiling, were burnt out or missing. Colt saw a pile of feathers, blood and the scattered bones of a pigeon. The homeless people who went into the tunnel to pee and smoke crack often killed the birds.

Once out on the beach, it was cool and Colt felt a chill pass through him. He took a deep breath and tasted the salt air. He felt the fine sand under his bare feet. During the day, he sometimes sat at the base of the lifeguard tower painted in psychedelic colors, surrounded by seagulls and pigeons clustered together in tight groups on the sand. He watched the waves and the water, a changing mixture of blue, silver, gray and green. On a clear day, he could see the coastline stretching a dozen miles north past 88's station in Malibu, where the Santa Monica Mountains sloped down to the beach.

At this hour, Colt couldn't see any birds and he could only hear the waves. He wandered through the thick fog, shivering and feeling like the only person on the planet. Clouds of luminous mist surrounded him. It was so thick he thought he could grasp some in his hand, but when he reached out, it seeped through his fingers. He remembered a late afternoon in Big Horn, when he was returning home after riding his horse to the Sheridan Airport to look at the planes on display for the annual Flying Cowboys Show. He had stayed late and had to make his way back through frozen rain and snow. Colt could barely see a thing, but Flash knew the way and was anxious to get home for his supper. Tonight, Wyoming was a million miles away.

Pinpoints of water touched Colt's face. Moisture seeped through the thin fabric of his T-shirt. The orange streetlights along PCH cast an eerie glow. Maybe, he thought, death was neither a tunnel of light nor a circle of darkness. Maybe it was like this colorless vapor—it just surrounds you, blurs your vision and clouds your mind before it carries you away. He listened to the waves and thought he could hear the ocean sigh, its currents pushing one way, then another. He shouted once, but the mist swallowed the sound of his voice. He wandered on, blind, and thought he heard women's voices singing or crying out. Bibi called to him from the depths of the fog, pleading with him to find her foot, telling him that she must have it, that she could not move on without it. Yes, he assured her, he would recover it. Colt remembered his first day at the fire academy when Chief Bresnahan asked each man why he wanted to become a firefighter. The responses were divided roughly between those who were adrenaline junkies and those who wanted to help people. Colt counted himself in the second group; he wanted to help people. He was committed to helping Bibi, and there would be no closure until her foot was located. That was part of his job.

For a moment, Colt became disoriented and walked into the surf. When he felt the cold water on his bare feet, he realized he was headed in the wrong direction and turned around.

An hour later, he lay in bed, still wide-awake, still thinking about Bibi. He tried to imagine her life and decided she worked in one of the fancy boutiques in Malibu. She sold expensive clothes to wealthy women who had summer homes at the beach. She was the favored sales person because she was charming and friendly and she selected only the most beautiful clothes for her customers. Bibi had a boyfriend who was an F-35 fighter pilot. She planned to marry him next year when he finished his stint in the Air Force. While she waited for him, she lived with her parents in one of the big houses with glass walls looking out onto the Pacific Ocean from the bluffs of Malibu. Her father was an executive at a Hollywood studio who attended meetings with film stars. Her mother, who was also beautiful and had the same ocean blue eyes, painted watercolor pictures. Colt tried to imagine what this happy family talked about at the dinner table. He wondered whether Bibi had a brother, but couldn't decide. Colt fell into a dreamless sleep. He had four days off. His next duty was on Sunday.

# SIXTEEN

I N THE EARLY HOURS of Wednesday morning, while Colt lay in bed imagining Bibi's life, A Li held her ID card up to the scanner and entered the Nano Research Center. She walked across the lobby, past the security office and stopped to look at the brass plaque on the wall.

*"You, your joys and your sorrows, your memories and your ambitions, your sense of personal identity and free will, are in fact no more than the behavior of a vast assembly of nerve cells and their associated molecules."*
*— Francis Crick, co-discoverer of DNA*

It was a small, superstitious ritual. A Li knew Crick's words by heart, but read them each time she went to the elevator. She believed in the power of science and understood it could unlock great secrets, but Francis Crick was wrong. The spiritual world was something apart. Her own Bon religion was based on life forces that lived in the mountains, trees, rivers and even in the sky. Both could exist in parallel universes and A Li had no problem reconciling the two. Each time she read the inscription, she sent Dr. Crick a mental rebuttal: There is more to life than science.

Riding up in the elevator to the third floor, A Li felt something was wrong. When Tanay dropped her off late in the afternoon after their trip downtown, she had been in a good mood. Her own birthday was of little matter, but A Mei's birthday was always a joyous time when she felt particularly close to her twin. By evening, her happy feeling had given way to a vague sense of anxiety and trepidation. She had never felt this way on A Mei's birthday and searched her mind for the cause. She was anxious about

Dr. Murray and the progress of her research, but that was a continual worry. This was a new and different feeling.

She walked down the hall to the laboratory and unlocked the door. Tonight it was dark inside and she swiped her hand over a half dozen switches. Light erupted across the ceiling. A Li went to her workspace, laid out the bouquet of iris and the juniper branches and withdrew a plastic baggie from her pocket. She dumped the contents—rice grass from a natural foods market—on the counter next to the juniper.

A Li sat down on her stool, hooked her feet around the back legs and listened to the pulse of the lab. The insulation in the center had the effect of trapping sound within each laboratory and conference room. She heard the air conditioning, the rumble of the refrigerators and the whistle from a fan left running in a fume hood. She also heard A Mei's heartbeat, a memory from the time when they shared their mother's womb. A Li remembered how it felt when her twin's tiny hand touched her own as they floated in their warm amniotic fluid. Their DNA was identical. They were identical, but A Li was born two minutes later. A Mei was older and stronger. A Li was the follower. What fate, what command from the spiritual world, had guided A Mei to the left, closer to the road, the day the Mercedes sped by, hitting her and missing A Li?

*Droonkher tashi delek.* Happy birthday, sister.

A Li sat with her memories for a moment longer and then went to the back of the lab. She opened her refrigerator filled with beakers of reagents and other chemicals and a box of microscope slides with cross sections of mouse organs. She withdrew the package wrapped in butcher paper from the China Sun Market. It had been in the refrigerator since Tanay dropped her off several hours ago, and was cold to the touch. She took it to her workbench and opened it.

The goat's leg, or what was left of it, was four inches long, weighed a few ounces and might have fit inside one of the large test tubes in the lab. A meat cleaver had made two clean cuts through the bone, one below the knee and one above the hoof, leaving a shank covered with white hair. A Li took one of the scalpels she used for dissections and cut away the hide and flesh until only the bone remained. She inspected it carefully. According to the ritual, not even the slightest bit of flesh could remain. She placed the juniper sprigs and the bare bone on a large ceramic dish and emptied the bag of rice grass on top.

If she were home in the TAR, and the *Awu Gungba* was performing this ceremony, he would use the flint grass from the high plateaus, but rice grass was as close as A Li could get and it would have to suffice.

She wondered what Dr. Murray's reaction would be if he knew what she was doing. She wondered what Master Shenrab Miwoche, the founder of the Bon religion, would think. What would they say to each other if she could have arranged for them to meet in the conference room?

A Li carried the ceramic dish and the bouquet of iris into the room with the fume hoods, raised one of the protective shields and placed the dish inside. She pulled a stool up in front of the fume hood, sat down and stared at the dish.

A Mei, I love you.

They knew each other as they knew themselves. As children, A Mei and A Li were devoted to each other. They were indistinguishable and spoke with the same voice. If one of them called out from another room, neither A Ma nor Pa Lags knew which twin was speaking. They had their own language—not Tibetan and not Mandarin. They whispered to each other, "Sister, I love you," in the secret words no one else could understand. They saw things with the same eyes and loved the same colors and flowers. They ate and rejected the same foods. Neighbors could not tell them apart and sometimes they played a wicked game of exchanging identities. Their dresses, shoes and coats—every piece of clothing—were identical. Everywhere they went, they looked the same. Until the accident, A Li could not remember a time when she was not with A Mei. After the accident, A Li had twice as many clothes and until she outgrew everything, she never knew whose clothing she was wearing.

We've been through so much together.

A Mei granted her complete acceptance and unqualified love.

I am so glad I have someone who understands me. You give me strength because you are always with me. We are still one.

A Li thought of the day they sat in the courtyard in front of their white-washed home built of stone and clay. The night before, A Ma had given them identical yak bone pendants carved with OM, the first of the six syllables of the mantra of compassion. They drank buttered tea and admired their new adornments. Soon they exchanged them, and then again. Later, they strung beads of glass, bone and *naga* shell on silk thread and when they became bored, A Ma helped them arrange bright colored pieces of cloth in the shape of a rainbow. A Li remembered the warmth and happiness of that time—the feeling of contentment and security they had together.

A tear ran down her cheek. She brushed it away with her hand. What A Li remembered most clearly from all their time together was the ride to the hospital in the police van. A Mei lay on the back seat with her head resting on A Ma's lap. A Li sat in the front and kept looking back at her sister. A Mei was badly injured and by the time they arrived in Lijiang, blood was everywhere—on her mother's dress, on the seat and all over the floor of the van. A Li felt like she too was bleeding. She felt weak, as if it were her own blood spilling out. She knew her sister was dying and felt as though she was about to accompany A Mei on the journey to the next world.

A life for a life—that was the rule of law in China. Everyone knew whose car killed her twin; there was only one black Mercedes in the entire Province and it belonged to a high-ranking official. Everyone knew, but no one would investigate. The authorities ignored A Mei's death. It was an injustice A Li would never forgive.

My sister, we are still together and I live for you. I will never leave you and I will never forget you.

She switched on the exhaust fan in the fume hood and lowered the protective cover. She put her hands into the gloves, which allowed her to work inside the chamber. She ignited the Bunsen burner and pointed the long blue flame at the goat's bone. Under the intense heat, it began to darken and turn to ash.

A Li switched off the exhaust fan and directed the Bunsen flame at the juniper sprigs and the rice grass. Thick gray smoke swirled inside the hood as the vegetation vaporized. She thought of A Mei's sky burial, so many years ago. Three days after A Mei's body was wrapped in a white cloth and placed in a corner of their house, the Daodeng came to take her corpse to the burial site in the mountains, far from Zhongdian. The ritual required him to slice her small body, sever her limbs and scatter the pieces on the ground. He burned juniper and the scent attracted the sacred vultures, the birds that sensed death. Coming from miles away, gliding on 10-foot wingspans, the majestic birds arrived to peck at her sister's flesh with strong, razor sharp beaks. When they finished, they took A Mei's soul up to heaven. Later, the Daodeng collected the bare bones and brought them back to the village where they were cremated to prevent another soul from taking over her twin's body. Afterward, A Li spread a handful of the ashes on a bed of Chinese iris growing near their farmhouse. She licked the dusty residue remaining on her hands and remembered the sharp, bitter taste of the ash on her tongue.

A Li recited the sutra for passing from one existence to another.

*Phags pa srid pa pho ba zhes bya ba I mdo.*

She pulled her hands out of the gloves and lifted the protective hood. She stuck her head inside the chamber and took a deep breath of the fragrant scent of juniper and rice grass mixed with the acrid smell of the burnt goat's leg. She coughed as the smoke entered her lungs. She held her breath and felt the warmth spreading first through her chest, and then her entire body. When it reached her brain, she felt lightheaded. A Li looked into the smoke trapped inside the hood and saw her twin looking back at her. It was not A Mei the child. The face looking back was that of a very old woman. Her skin was loose and gray, her eyelids sagged, but her eyes flashed anger. It was a frightening face. A Mei's lips were moving; she was saying something. A Li strained to hear what her sister was telling her. Her sister was unhappy; her words were sharp. The fluorescent lights in the ceiling of the lab flickered. A Li's head spun and she fell off her stool. The room went dark.

When A Li opened her eyes, her cheek was resting on the dirty floor. She could see dust balls under the fume hood counters. The side of her head hurt and A Li realized she had blacked out and fallen. She had no idea how long she had been unconscious. She sat up and used the counter for support as she struggled to regain her balance. She touched the tender spot on her head and thought she must have hit the sharp corner of the counter when she fainted. A trace of her Bombay Blood showed on her fingertips. When she looked inside the fume hood, she saw traces of smoke. She remembered the fragrance of the juniper and the odor from the burning goat's foot when she stuck her head inside. Her head was still spinning. Had she dreamed of her sister's anger?

It was time to go home. She raised the fume hood again, dipped her fingertips in the ash and touched her tongue.

May the hundreds of thousands of suns of happiness and peace be upon you, A Mei. Happy birthday, my sister.

A Li swept the remaining ash into the plastic baggie. She sprayed an alcohol disinfectant inside the fume hood and wiped it with a damp paper towel, then dropped everything in the trash. She was hungry and exhausted. On her way out, before she turned off the lights, A Li stopped to survey the empty lab once more. She felt a distinct foreboding. Were the 21st century gods of stem cell science angry because she had performed an ancient ritual from a religion of demigods, spirits, hungry ghosts and beings from hell?

# SEVENTEEN

H E SWAM UPWARD to the surface. What day was it? Where was he? Who was he? A noise had summoned him back to the real world from a Vicodin-induced sleep. His brain began to function—slowly. Markus remembered his own name. He recognized where he was. He looked at the clock—it was 11:30 p.m. The Vicodin had knocked him out. He had slept for almost six hours and missed work. He thought he heard someone at the front door. It was too early for Audra to be returning from the club.

GRISHA! The gorilla had come to beat him to a pulp. Why had Grisha come now?

Markus was confused; he couldn't think straight. In a panic, he tried to get out of bed. Pain shot up his spine and he collapsed on the floor. He lay motionless until the agony died down and he regained his senses. The apartment was quiet. No one was at the door.

Markus stood up and walked unsteadily into the bathroom. He swallowed two more Vicodin and washed the pills down with tap water. He needed something stronger to kill the pain in his back. He also needed enough money to pay the Russians. Only one person could help him with both—Marty the medicine man.

During the 30-minute drive to Hollywood, he thought he might be driving too fast, or maybe too slow. Markus wasn't sure which, but he didn't want one of the cops who patrolled Sunset Boulevard to stop him. He took a left off Sunset, making certain he used the turn signal, went down Highland, then turned left again down a dark residential street. Tucked away in an alley, Club Cyanide, or C2, as the regulars called it, didn't even register on a GPS. Markus drove slowly, looking for the entrance to the narrow cul-de-sac. He drove past it, hit the brakes, backed up and turned into the alley. At the far end, he could see the glow of the small blue bulb over an unmarked door. Markus parked in the darkness and slowly walked to the entrance.

At the door, the security guard was busy on his cell phone. He recognized Markus and motioned him inside. It was early and the action didn't start until around 1:00 a.m. The club could be empty, but Markus didn't care. He didn't want to talk to anyone; he just wanted to find Marty.

Markus started up the steep stairs, grimacing as he climbed. From above, he heard the beat, beat, beat of industrial Goth music and it made him feel better. Halfway up, the vibrations from the bass speakers shook the stairs. At the top, Markus paused and looked at the scene. There was a bigger crowd than he expected. In the low light, he watched the Goth crowd dance. People floated around the room. Couples rubbed their bodies together. Several men danced behind their women with hairy hands cupping and squeezing their breasts.

Everyone wore black. The women had lace draped across their upper bodies. Some wore black feathers; others dressed in tight corsets and short black vinyl skirts. Mesh stockings and platform boots covered their legs. Black chokers, bondage belts, tattoos and piercings were standard. Their eyes were black holes surrounded by heavy eye shadow and white face powder. The men were more simply dressed in tight black stretch jeans, black undershirts and studded belts. In this group, Markus was an uber Goth. Even the most extreme makeup couldn't match his red eyes and natural white skin, hair and eyelashes.

He moved slowly through the crowd and sucked in the atmosphere as an antidote to the noise of the Vicodin in his brain. He scanned the crowd for Marty, who always wore jeans, a black pullover and a sleeveless vest with dozens of pockets, each containing a different drug. Across the dance floor, Markus caught sight of a girl he thought he knew. Her real name was Alyssa or Alana; he couldn't remember which, but she called herself Goth Girl and everyone else called her Gigi. When he first arrived in Los Angeles, she let him crash at her place in Venice for three days. She looked heavier now and her hair was metallic blue instead of red. It was too dim to see the scars on her shoulders, but he was certain they were there. She was his first introduction to real blood play. She told him she was a member of Cirque de Sade and he thought he had finally met the right girl when she said, "Blood is the most erotic thing I can think of." On his first night with her, they stood naked in her bathroom and she cut tiny nicks on her shoulder with a razor. After the blood covered her skin, she pulled his face to her flesh and smeared the red liquid on his lips. The experience was new and exciting to Markus, something he had only dreamed about. After tasting her blood, he was in his own private ecstasy. He felt a rush he had never felt before, followed by an insane hard-on. They made love for the rest of the night. She threw him out two days later.

Markus wandered past the booths that lined the wall. In the shadows, he saw Marty, standing motionless, like a statue. Markus approached him. "Hey Marty," he said.

The statue moved. "What's up, Markus? How come you're walking funny?"

"I hurt my back. Bad. I'm taking Vicodin, but it still hurts. I need something. Got any K?"

"Just picked up a batch from the vet in Tijuana." Marty fished in his vest pockets and pulled out a tiny plastic envelope with white powder. He handed it to Markus. "This'll help for a while."

"Thanks, man." Markus took the envelope and emptied the powder on the back of his hand. He closed one nostril with his finger and sucked the powder in through the other. "Ooh yeah," he said, as the ketamine flooded his body with a warm feeling and increased his heart rate and blood pressure. For the first time since Grisha kicked him, Markus felt some relief.

"It'll only last a couple of hours. I haven't got anything for long term."

"How about some X?"

"That won't do anything for pain."

"I know, but it might help me get through the next couple of days. I got a lot going on. I'll take a couple."

"Suit yourself." Marty fished out two ecstasy capsules and handed them to Markus. "That do it?" he said, and scanned the crowd to determine if anyone was watching. "It's a hundred fifty."

"Listen Marty," Markus said. "I have a problem. I need to borrow a grand."

"What?"

"I need to borrow a thousand dollars. You know I'll pay you back."

Marty glared at Markus. "I'm not a bank, asshole. No way am I lending you a penny. You owe me one fifty."

"Well, I haven't got it."

"Gimme back the X." Marty moved toward Markus. Marty wasn't much taller than Markus, but he was strong. When he wasn't dealing drugs, he was lifting weights.

"No." Markus stepped back and popped the two ecstasy pills into his mouth.

"Damn you," Marty said, and grabbed Markus by the throat. "Pay me."

Markus shook loose and managed to swallow the pills. "Thanks for helping out a friend, Marty. I'll pay you next week."

"Friend? I'll beat the crap out of you if I you don't pay me."

"Get in line." Markus started toward the stairs leading up to the bondage play stations without looking back. He hoped Marty wasn't following him. By the time he reached the top of the stairs, Markus was beginning to sweat from the effect of the drugs.

There wasn't much bondage action going on. One girl was bent over, bound to the spanking station. Her skirt and black underwear were down around her knees. An older woman with fake dreadlocks of neon blue hair punished her with a short black leather riding crop. The concave-convex mirrors on the ceiling reflected back distorted images of the red welts on the slave's bare buttocks, which looked like flesh-colored beach balls.

The bare flesh reminded Markus of Audra. He imagined her at the Alley Kat. Some retard was caressing her elegant, long legs. She was bent over and the retard was doing her. She was enjoying it. She was crying out with pleasure. She was stuffing hundreds of dollars into her purse. Some of the bills were spilling out onto the floor but she didn't bother to pick them up.

Markus tried to focus on the slave bound to the spanking station, but the China Doll bitch, Alexei and Grisha were standing nearby, laughing at him. Marty came up the stairs and joined them. He whispered "Snowflake" to the others, and they all looked at Markus and laughed again. It was a conspiracy to make his life unbearable.

Markus fled the club. It was almost 2:00 a.m. when he walked outside. The light over the door was out. His head was spinning and the ecstasy was surging through his bloodstream as he searched for his car.

Lying in bed, Markus heard Audra open the front door and walk into the kitchen. She was talking on her cell phone.

"Sorry, I had to cut it short, wasn't feeling well. We'll do it again another night."

Markus tried to clear his head while he waited for Audra to come into the bedroom. The combined effects of the ketamine and ecstasy, added to the Vicodin, had driven his heart rate to an unbearable level. Each beat pulsed through his brain. He was drenched in sweat. His mouth overflowed with saliva.

"Ohh," Audra sighed when she finally came in. "I really feel crappy." She dropped her bag on the floor and collapsed on the bed next to Markus. "I feel like I could sleep for a week."

"Hard night?" Markus said.

"Very."

"Harder than other nights? Too much wear and tear on the body?" Markus' brain was vibrating like a tuning fork.

"What's that supposed to mean? Are you starting up again?" Audra sat up and looked at him. "What's wrong with you? You look terrible."

"Want to hear what kind of day I had?"

"Do I have a choice?"

"A terrible day. The worst. A total disaster."

"Too bad." She lay down again and closed her eyes.

"I said, I had a horrible day."

"I heard you."

"And I have an epic problem. I need some dinero."

The bitch didn't say anything.

"Hey, are you listening?" Markus shook her. "Did you hear me?"

Grisha was standing at the end of the bed, watching and smirking.

"Leave me alone," Audra said.

"Where's all the dough you've been collecting from turning tricks?"

Audra opened her eyes and looked at Markus. "Fuck off," she said and pulled a pillow over her head.

"No, you fuck off." Audra didn't respond and Markus stared at her, feeling his fury build. Who was this hooker skank who entertained men all night and then came home to sleep in his apartment? It was time to throw her out. Too bad she wasn't an online opponent. A few keystrokes and a flick of the delete button would put an end to her.

Fucking Grisha was still standing in the bedroom. Alexei had joined him.

Markus got up. His lower back throbbed and his mouth was sour. He went into the bathroom, closed the door and turned on the light. He looked at his lower back in the mirror. Now he had an enormous purple bruise and the area above his butt was swollen. He rinsed his mouth and looked at his face. Red irises stared back. Audra was right about one thing; he did look terrible.

Markus reached into the medicine chest and took out the ether. The China Doll stood next to him by the bathroom sink. He watched her reflection in the mirror as she stared back at him. He loosened the top of the bottle, took a green washcloth from the towel rack, turned off the light and opened the bathroom door. He heard the sound of Audra's deep breathing under the pillow. Grisha and Alexei were gone, but hundred dollar bills covered the bedroom floor.

Markus came around to Audra's side of the bed and poured some of the anesthetic on the washcloth. He held his breath, straddled her, lifted her pillow and placed the washcloth over her nose. Markus squeezed his eyes shut, trying to stop the throbbing in his head.

Audra went from sleep to sedation without moving. It was so easy—easier than fighting off a bunch of Anarchs online.

Markus eased himself off the bed. He turned on the small night-table light and waited again for the pain in his back to subside. Audra's breathing was slower now. He lit one of the black candles and kneeled on the floor by her side. The hundred dollar bills had disappeared. He held the candle close to her inert body and looked at her tattoos. His face was inches from her skin and he struggled to focus his weak eyes. He could see the black and red ink underneath the pores. Audra looked like an avatar, an online digital image with mega-pixel resolution. Markus blew out the candle and tossed it on the bed. A small amount of molten wax ran off onto the sheet.

The drugs and Markus decided it was time to delete Audra and send her into cyberspace. Markus climbed back on the bed and straddled her again. As he held the pillow above her face, he saw Alexei standing next to the bed wearing his embalming clothes. A white surgical mask covered the lower part of his face. "Go ahead, Snowflake," Alexei said. He spoke in Russian, but Markus understood him.

Markus felt drug-fucked. Audra made no movement when he lowered the pillow and held it tight over her face. "Lights out," he said. He turned to see if Alexei had anything else to say, but Alexei was gone. Markus had no idea how long it took to smother someone. He pressed the pillow against Audra's face until the pain in his back became unbearable, then tossed the pillow onto the floor and leaned forward to check her breathing. Audra's mouth was closed. No air came from her nose. He raised her arm and held his fingers against her wrist in search of a pulse. Nothing. He dropped her limp arm and it hung over the side of the bed. Audra looked so peaceful.

Markus went back into the bathroom. In the bottom of the cabinet, he found the razor he had used for their blood bonding ceremony. Blade in hand, he went into the bedroom and sat on the bed next to Audra. His hands shook as he cut the tip of her index finger and the blade went much deeper than he intended. When he squeezed, several drops of blood dripped out onto the bedsheet. Markus lifted her finger to his mouth and sucked at the cut. He let the blood lie on his tongue, then swirled it around and swallowed. It did nothing for him; it didn't even taste good. His head throbbed.

He took her purse from the floor and dug through it. He found nine $20 bills and a handful of change. Where was the roll of hundreds? Audra had no wallet and no credit or debit cards. She had an expired Ohio driver's license, several Alley Kat business cards imprinted with her name and a small address book. Markus opened it and saw the names and telephone numbers of men written in Audra's childlike hand. He placed the money on the nightstand. He cut up her license, took it into the bathroom and flushed it down the toilet. He tossed the address book and business cards into the wastebasket.

Markus dragged himself back into the bedroom, seized Audra's big canvas bag from the dresser and emptied it out on the floor. A tattoo magazine, hairbrush, three colors of lip gloss, breath spray, red high-heel shoes, six dollar bills, another handful of change, and one of her prepaid cell phones fell to the floor. He hadn't realized how few possessions Audra had. She barely existed.

Markus started to go through the Victorian dresser. The first drawer held her dance costumes—brassieres, wide leather belts, stockings, thongs and see-through blouses. The second drawer contained shorts, jeans, T-shirts and socks. Markus looked through her pockets, inside her socks, anywhere he thought she might have hidden cash. He found nothing. The bottom drawer had sandals, an Italian cookbook and a book of tattoo designs. When he found the box of Real Feel condoms, he flung it across the room, spreading the rubbers over the floor.

Markus went out to his desk. In the darkness, he shoved the chair aside and picked up the coroner's body bag from the floor. He took it into the bedroom, laid it out on the bed next to Audra and unzipped it. He looked at Audra for the last time. Her beautiful body was the same, but her life force was gone; whatever made her erotic and sexy had evaporated. She was a cadaver just like the body in Alexei's basement, no longer human. He knew he was supposed to feel emotion, something more than the sizzle of the drug, but the Vicodin told him, "Not to worry, it doesn't matter."

When Markus rolled her into the body bag and zipped it up, he saw that Audra's blood was already beginning to pool in her back, butt and the backsides of her legs. He lifted the bag from the bed and the pain in his body came alive, shooting up his back. Markus grunted and managed to get Audra over his shoulder. Her dead weight pressed down on him. He staggered and took small steps to the door, wondering if he could make it down to his car. Outside on the stairs, he descended with one hand on the handrail, struggling to bear the pain in his back and to keep his balance.

In the carport, he opened the door of the PT Cruiser, and somehow managed to place the body bag upright on the back seat, with Audra inside in the sitting position. The chemical change in Audra's muscles had just begun the process of rigor mortis and she would soon be frozen in that position.

Markus returned to the bedroom and looked at the blood on his sheet. He'd removed bloodstains before, using cold water and powdered meat tenderizer, but not now. He ripped the sheet off the bed and left it on the floor. He lay down on the bare mattress for a few minutes and tried to doze off, but too much was going on in his head, and the China Doll, Grisha and Alexei kept appearing and disappearing. Sleep was not an option. He got up and wandered through the apartment.

# EIGHTEEN

"**D**ON'T LET THE CORONER BECOME your designated driver," admonished the public service television ads. Colt had heard the message many times. On Wednesday morning, he drove through a part of East Los Angeles he had never seen before. On one side of Mission Road, a rail yard went on forever. Trucks pulling shipping containers filled the oncoming lane and lumbered past him spewing diesel exhaust. Above, he saw the gray cement underside of the freeway he had just exited. Ahead, past a string of fast-food restaurants, he spotted the large white sign:

*Los Angeles County Coroner*
*Medical Examiner*
*Forensic Laboratories*
*Law and Science Serving the Community*

When Colt became a paramedic, he realized the time would come when he would have to visit a morgue. That day had now arrived. He felt he could deal with any medical situation that required a response in the squad, but he dreaded going into a morgue—he knew it would bring back all the painful thoughts of his mother's death.

Soon after the sale of the ranch, Colt spent an afternoon cleaning out the office where his father worked every Sunday, managing their precarious finances. Thirty years of his father's life was jammed into the drawers of the desk. Colt dumped everything out on the Indian rug, sat on the floor and began to sort through the remains. A decade of Sheridan Bank statements and cancelled checks went into a box that Colt later discarded. He saved a couple of pictures of horses long gone and the rodeo belt with the beautiful silver and gold buckle that his father had won for bronco riding. Most of the documents and correspondence no longer had any significance. Letters from packhorse buyers, animal health and feed articles, a $575 invoice for his father's Savage Model 110 30-06 deer rifle and a Wyoming registration for an old trailer went directly into the trash.

Amid the jumble of paper, Colt found his own birth certificate, dated June 2, 1985, and the picture of his mother wearing the blue CALIFORNIA T-shirt, holding hands with his father next to the pickup truck. He also found an envelope containing a certified letter addressed to his father, dated September 14, 1994, from the Texas Department of Public Safety. Colt read it once, stood up and walked to the window. He looked out at the high plains grassland and rocked slowly back and forth. When his emotions subsided, he took a deep breath and rubbed the tears from his eyes. He reread the letter several times, hoping for more information than the sterile sentences contained.

*Dear Mr. Lewis:*

*The Texas Highway Patrol in Dallas County has tried without success to contact you on several recent occasions. Our investigation shows that you are the spouse of Carol Lewis, D.O.B. 5/12/57.*

*We are sorry to advise you that Mrs. Lewis died on the night of September 2, 1994. The vehicle she was driving was involved in a head-on collision with a semi trailer on U.S. Highway 30, approximately 10 miles west of Dallas, near the city of Grand Prairie.*

*The Texas Department of Public Safety extends its condolences to you and your family. We request that you contact the undersigned immediately. The Department needs instructions concerning the disposition of Carol Lewis' remains.*

*Sincerely,*
*Wesley Dawkins*
*Texas Department of Public Safety*
*Austin, TX 78701*

Colt laid the letter on his father's desk and went back to the window. It looked like it might rain. Black storm clouds were pushing across the sky, ending the day.

For years, Colt believed his mother had divorced his father and found another husband. He thought she might even have more children—half brothers or sisters he would never know. The letter shook all his assumptions. His mother had died just after his ninth birthday. For more than half his life, Colt bore the pain of what he thought was her rejection. Now he realized that what he thought to be real was untrue. His mother might have still loved him when she died. She might have had plans to see him. She could have even been thinking of him that night, at the time of the accident.

Colt wanted to know why she was in Dallas. Did his father ever respond to the letter? Did he go to Dallas in 1994 to arrange for the burial of his wife, or did he ignore the letter and leave it in his desk drawer? Why hadn't he said anything? Colt was entitled to know; she was his mother. Was there no one in Texas to claim her body? Did she ever have a funeral, or a memorial service?

Colt didn't sleep the night he discovered the letter. He lay awake going over the same unanswered questions, and felt guilty for his unkind thoughts about his mother. The next morning, he called Texas and spent two hours in voice mail hell, switched from one extension to another at the Department of Public Safety. When he finally spoke to a human, she referred him to the Highway Patrol in Dallas. They told him only criminal records were kept indefinitely; files concerning automobile accidents were destroyed after seven years. They had nothing. The following day, he checked with the morgue in Dallas, but there was no record of Carol Lewis. Grand Prairie didn't even have a morgue. Colt agonized that his mother's body might have been left unclaimed somewhere in Texas. He would never know; his father took the information with him to his grave.

Until he discovered the envelope in his father's desk, Colt lived with the hope that someday he would see his mother again and ask why she left him. Once he realized she was dead and there was no further information beyond the three-paragraph form letter from the Texas Department of Public Safety, he plunged into a depression that lasted several months. He was left to decide which was worse—wondering if his mother would ever return or knowing she would not. Both hurt. He thought of driving to Dallas to try to find out more information about what happened to his mother's body. He decided it was useless.

When he moved to California and began studying for his fire science degree, some of the sadness dissipated, but Colt still wondered what happened to his mother. Was she cremated? Was she buried somewhere? Was there an urn with her remains or a grave he could visit? The reason she left her family in Big Horn was never explained, and her departure left a wound that never healed. Colt grew up with an empty spot in his heart, which only her love could fill.

Colt parked next to a dozen white cars marked CORONER. A red brick building surrounded by old streetlights with glass globes stood at the end of the parking lot. Carved granite decorated the front façade and lined the wide stairway leading up to the entrance. Colt had once seen something similar on a horse-buying trip with his father—the Cheyenne City Hall, built in 1889.

He ascended the steps two at a time. Inside, the floor of the lobby consisted of thousands of small black and white six-sided tiles. Slabs of gray marble reached halfway up the walls. A light fixture with one large globe, surrounded by several smaller globes, hung from the center of an ornate ceiling. Plastic trees covered with dust surrounded the entrance to the restrooms.

Colt was wearing his County Fire Department blues and tried to look official when he approached the front desk. A receptionist in a tan uniform was busy talking on the telephone. "No ma'am ... no, the body would not be here ... what? No ... no, it would still be at the hospital ... thank you." She hung up and looked at Colt.

"Good morning," he said.

The phone rang again, and again. The clerk held up her hand to silence him. "Los Angeles County Coroner's Office, may I put you on hold? ... Los Angeles County Coroner's Office, how may I help you?"

Colt gave up and walked past the receptionist toward several doors with frosted glass. He opened the first, marked NOTIFICATION SECTION. Inside, several clerks worked at computer screens. One looked up and asked, "Can I help you?"

"I'm here to find out about a body that was sent from the CU trauma center on Sunday afternoon."

The woman stood up and came to the counter. "Do you have the name, or a case number?"

"No, there was no ID other than a first name."

"You're in the wrong place. This is for death certificates. You want the medical examiner's office. Behind this building."

"Thanks," Colt said, already halfway to the door.

Colt descended the outside steps and walked around the building. Behind it, he saw a two-story rectangle cement structure. It had tiny square windows, a nest of radio antennae sticking up from the roof and looked like it could survive a direct hit from a nuclear bomb.

When he entered, a blast of ice-cold air hit him. Behind a pane of security glass, a man wearing a shirt with the Los Angeles County logo and a photo ID hanging around his neck was finishing a telephone conversation. Colt wondered how many people died each day in Los Angeles and how many calls came in to the coroner.

Colt spoke through the hole in the glass. "I'm a county fire paramedic. I came to get some information on an accident victim."

"What day did the body arrive?"

"Sunday."

"Name?"

Colt shook his head.

"Hold on, I have to call an investigator. Have a seat."

Colt remained standing and looked around the bleak reception area. It was inhospitable and clearly not intended for visitors. A security door on one wall announced AUTHORIZED PERSONNEL ONLY. The bare walls were a tan color. The cement floor, also bare, was a darker color, almost brown. A row of off-color blue chairs lined one wall. That was it; there weren't even any dusty plastic trees.

Colt waited for a few minutes until the door opened and a man came out. He had a law enforcement haircut — shaved close and flat on top — but not the body to match. He was short, had no ass, and a middle-aged belly protruded over the front of his pants. A silver carabiner with a cluster of keys hung off a belt loop.

"Nate Petruno," he said. When he stuck out his hand, Colt saw short, muscular arms and enormous hands.

"Colt Lewis."

"What can I do for you?" Petruno cracked his knuckles.

"Sunday afternoon we responded to an accident in Malibu. The victim was a female. She died on the way to the CU hospital. I need some information."

"You don't have a name?"

"Just her first name. Bibi. Does that help?"

Petruno cracked his knuckles again. "We get 350 bodies a day in here and—" His cell phone rang. He pulled it out of his pocket, glanced at it and silenced the ringer.

"She came in without her right foot," Colt said. "We never recovered it."

"Oh yeah, I know that one. A Jane."

"Jane?"

"She's a Jane Doe. Unidentified."

Colt frowned. "You'll find out who she is? How many 'Bibi's' can there be?"

"She didn't give you a last name?"

"No, she was in shock. She was in such bad shape, all alone when it happened. She could only whisper a couple of words."

"Well, she was two months pregnant."

"Pregnant?"

"Yeah."

"Jesus," Colt exclaimed. "She was gonna have a kid?" He paused and thought about it for a moment. "Maybe she whispered 'baby' to me."

Petruno looked at Colt. "What's your interest in this?"

"I wanted to tell her family what happened, and how we tried to find the foot. They should know."

"Sooner or later we'll ID her, but until then she's a Jane Doe." Petruno's phone rang again. He looked at it again and stopped the ringer. "Dead people have parents, friends, and lovers. Eventually they start asking questions. If it's a recent death, they usually call us. We ID more than half the Janes and Johns. It's just a matter of time."

"Can you believe someone walked off with her foot after the accident?"

"People pick up all sorts of body parts. We get a lot of skulls. Someone finds one, takes it home, leaves it in a closet for years and then drops it off at the sheriff's department. They bring it to us. Those are the tough cases."

"This is different. The foot might have been reattached."

Petruno shrugged. "Must be something in the water out here. I come from Indiana. No one back there would pick up a severed foot." Petruno looked at his watch. "I have to be somewhere in 45 minutes. Want a quick look around?"

"Yeah, sure," Colt said without enthusiasm. "Why not?" During two years as a firefighter and five weeks as a paramedic, he had avoided the morgue. It was time to complete his education.

Petruno went to the security door and waited to be buzzed in. "C'mon," he motioned to Colt. "This place is the end of the line. When you leave here, you're goin' on someone's mantel or into the ground."

Colt followed Petruno through the door and down a hallway. A woman came out of one of the small offices and handed Petruno some papers on a clipboard. "Each morning we do a printout of everyone who arrived in the last 24 hours." Petruno looked at the last page. "No Janes or Johns yesterday. We're supposed to determine the cause of death and identify every body that passes through here. Most are easy and we take care of them in a couple of hours. Some take months or years and there's a few where it just doesn't happen."

"So what happens if you can't ID ... uh ... Jane?"

"Her body'll be cremated after 60 days. We'll keep tissue samples and prints." Petruno stopped and punched an elevator button. "We'll skip the labs. It's just a bunch of guys running blood and tissue samples through chromatographs." The elevator door opened and Petruno nodded to a group of men wearing green medical scrubs. "I'll show you the morgue." He held the elevator door for Colt and then hit the button for the basement.

The hydraulic elevator groaned and moved at a snail's pace. When it bumped to a stop and the doors opened, cold air blasted Colt again, this time carrying a slight odor like a veterinarian's office. He followed Petruno out into the hall.

"Here, you have to wear this." Petruno paused at a cart with a box of surgical masks. "Put it over your nose and mouth and pinch the little metal band over the bridge of your nose. It'll keep it from sliding off." Petruno handed Colt a white mask with elastic bands and took another for himself. He pulled on flesh-colored latex gloves. "Don't touch anything, OK? And breathe through your mouth." Petruno laughed. "You know, we tell visiting VIPs that the purpose of the mask is to catch their vomit. You'd be amazed how many people believe that."

Colt slipped on his mask and thought of the day he and his classmates practiced intubation on a cadaver. They had been so nervous, their masks were soaked with sweat. He followed Petruno around a corner and the first thing he saw were three naked bodies, two men and a woman, lying face up on stainless steel carts along a wall. One of the men had filthy, calloused feet. Colt thought he must have been homeless, wandering the streets without shoes. The second man had more hair than Colt had ever seen on a human body. The woman looked young.

Petruno turned to him. "I know what you're thinking, but there's no modesty down here. We're about to cut them open to find out why they died. No reason to cover them up."

Colt checked the woman more closely. Her skin was starting to turn gray, but it was unblemished. Her eyes were open, gazing up at the ceiling, seeing nothing. They were human eyes, but void of life, empty and glass-like. Her mouth was also open, as if she were about to say something. The hair on her head and her pubis was jet black. He guessed she might be 35. She appeared to be healthy.

Petruno looked at the woman. "Here's a bit of trivia for you. If the eyes are open when rigor mortis sets in, you can't close the lids. Way back when, people were superstitious about a corpse with open eyes, so they covered them with coins." Petruno paused for a few seconds. "Of course, we've got a budget crisis, so the county cut off our supply of pennies."

Petruno turned and led Colt down the hall and into an enormous tiled room where several autopsies were underway. Colt counted ten bodies stretched out on marble tables with grooves at the edges to catch and drain fluids. Each cadaver was undergoing a full or partial autopsy. The first three had the classic "Y" incision, starting at the shoulders, meeting at the breastbone and descending down past the stomach. A doctor had just finished cutting off the top of a man's skull. Colt watched him peel part of the scalp down over the face, then remove the furrowed pink-gray mass of the brain and drop it into a metal bowl. One technician used an overhead hose to wash body debris off a table, pushing it across the floor into a drain.

Everyone in the room wore green scrubs, gloves that reached to the elbows and full plastic facemasks connected to air filtration units hung on their backs. Colt thought it looked like a scene out of an alien abduction movie.

Strange green life forms from another planet were bent over their victims, using saws, cutters, clippers and unfamiliar instruments to slice, carve, probe and dissect, searching for secrets about the human race. The nearest body was open from neck to waist. Colt watched someone remove a spleen, set it aside, then turn back to the cadaver and begin to cut again. Another doctor reached into a chest cavity, lifted out a lung and walked to another part of the room cupping it in his hand and dripping liquid across the floor. He deposited it in a plastic container containing a clear solution. As soon as the organ was submerged, the fluid became red with blood. The doctor sealed the container and added it to dozens of others.

"Just like on TV," Colt said to Petruno. He tried to sound casual, but the sight of the lifeless, dissected bodies was more disturbing than any injuries he had dealt with as a paramedic.

"On TV you just see one cadaver," Petruno said. "And it's all squeaky clean. Here we process ten at a time, 24/7, and it's anything but spotless. Everything on TV's a full postmortem. We do a limited autopsy whenever possible. We have to be fast and efficient."

As Colt turned to walk out of the autopsy room, he saw a carved wooden mask mounted above the door. It was 2 feet tall and adorned with a crest of black, red and white feathers, which reached almost to the ceiling. The face was white with the red marks of a warrior. The mouth was an open grimace, displaying two even rows of carved wooden teeth. The nose was sharp and strong; the eyes were empty semicircles below a furrowed forehead. Colt had never seen anything like it. "Is that the official mascot?" he asked.

Petruno smiled. "It's actually a Polynesian war mask that one of the docs brought back from vacation. It's here to scare off any spirits or lingering life forces."

"Life forces?"

"A couple of years ago, there was a TV series about a group of angels who retrieved souls from the bodies of people just after death. Well, in one episode, an angel screwed up and forgot to get the soul of a person about to go through an autopsy. We were all creeped out after that one. So we got Martin." Petruno pointed up at the mask. "It's his job to make sure the souls clear out before the autopsies start."

"His name's Martin?"

"What? He doesn't look like a 'Martin'?" Petruno tugged at Colt's shirtsleeve and led him back down the hall. "Do you want to see Jane?"

Before Colt could say no, Petruno stopped in front of a large stainless steel door and slid it open.

"She's in here," Petruno said.

Colt had always assumed that bodies in the morgue were stored separately, each resting under a sheet on a shelf. What Colt saw was a mass of bodies packed in plastic bags, stacked up floor to ceiling in a walk-in meat locker.

"I think that's her." Petruno pointed to one of the bags in the middle of the pile.

"Oh no," Colt said. "I don't want to see her. Not in a cooler." He turned away. A chill rippled up his spine. It could have been his mother, folded up in a bag, sandwiched in between the other cadavers.

"We call it a refrigeration crypt; it's one of three," Petruno said. "Slaughterhouses have meat coolers."

Colt stood motionless, trying to sort out his emotions. This was exactly the scene he did not want to see.

Petruno slid the door closed and led Colt back to the elevator. "Sorry, I didn't think you'd mind." He removed Colt's mask and his own mask and gloves and dropped them in the trash. He cracked his knuckles again and said, "If you want to give me your number, I can let you know when we find out who she is."

They stepped into the elevator and Colt pulled a fire department card out of his wallet and handed it to Petruno.

Petruno glanced at it and put it in his shirt pocket. He took out his own card and gave it to Colt.

"Do you take any of this home with you at night?" Colt asked.

"I try not to. When I first started, I had to sit in my car for 15 minutes every time I went home. I couldn't be with my family until I decompressed. I don't have to do that any more. There is one thing that still bothers me." Petruno stared down at the floor of the elevator for a few seconds. "I see all these people, all different ages, at the end of their lives, and it reminds me how close death is to everyone. You just never know when it's coming for you, and when it does, that's it, over and out. All the things you planned to do, or hoped to do." Petruno shook his head.

The elevator lurched to a stop and the doors opened. Colt stepped out first and shook Petruno's hand. "Thanks, Nate. Find the girl's family, OK? While you're doing that, I'll find her foot."

"We'll find the family before you find the foot." Petruno turned and started down the hall.

"Nate?" Colt said.

"Yeah?"

"What do you think? Do people have souls? Are there spirits lingering around?"

"I don't know." Petruno cracked his knuckles. "With all the stuff I see, I kinda hope they don't."

Outside, sitting in his truck in the parking lot, Colt rolled down the windows and let the dry September air fill his nostrils. Even the smell of diesel exhaust from the street was better than the air in the morgue. Colt pictured his mother, years ago, in a morgue in Texas, folded up in a plastic bag. The thought, the image, was too terrible to consider. He knocked his head twice against the steering wheel, as if to clear his mind.

In place of his mother, the image of Bibi's body appeared, stuffed into a plastic bag. Colt couldn't bear to think she ended up like this either. He wanted to remember her while she was alive. He wanted the vision of the pretty blonde with the eyes that matched her blue CALIFORNIA T-Shirt. The girl from Malibu he might have dated if she wasn't engaged to a fighter pilot. The girl he promised to save. The girl who was going to have a baby. In his mind, she would remain "Bibi" until her real name was discovered.

Colt wondered whether anyone would ever come to identify and claim her body. Where were her friends, her family, or anyone who knew her? They should be searching for her right now. Wouldn't someone have already contacted the police or called the morgue? Wasn't there a missing-person's list? How could someone not come forward to claim Bibi?

Colt couldn't think of anything worse than ending his life as an unclaimed body in a refrigeration crypt, in the hands of uncaring strangers. If he suddenly died, who would miss him? Who would search for him? Not his mother. Not his father. He had no siblings, and his grandparents were long gone. He was a county firefighter and paramedic—it would be left to his firefighter family to find him. They would not forget him.

Colt drove across Los Angeles and listened to the Wednesday midday weather forecast. A red-flag warning was in effect for the next 72 hours. The Santa Ana winds sweeping in from the east were bringing low humidity and high fire danger.

# NINETEEN

THE HOT, DRY SANTA ANA WIND BLEW through the campus, across Los Angeles and over all of Southern California. In China, it would signal the beginning of a sandstorm, bringing stinging eyes and a nose and mouth full of grit. A Li sat outside in the heat and wind, on the patio of a restaurant at the edge of campus. She ate rice, vegetables and boiled chicken with clumsy pink plastic chopsticks. Instead of drinking tea, she sipped an iced cappuccino, something she had come to love in America. She touched the side of her head and felt the lump from her fall the previous night.

A Li had little time or money to waste, but Wednesday was the one day of the week when she indulged herself. When her biochemistry class ended at noon, she walked across campus to eat lunch. She had two hours before her next class and she reserved the time to enjoy the fresh air, have a good meal and clear her mind. By the end of lunch, she usually felt relaxed and focused. Today she found it difficult to achieve any tranquility. The smoky image of her angry sister from the night before disturbed her. Sitting on the patio of the restaurant, she wondered why A Mei was angry. She should have been happy and felt honored by the birthday ceremony. Could she be jealous of Tanay?

A Li looked around. She was the only one sitting alone. Every couple seemed to come together at lunchtime. She watched undergrads and graduate students, unkempt engineering students and researchers in white lab coats, football players and cheerleaders and even a few homosexual couples—all walking the sidewalks hand in hand or sitting on the café patios looking into each other's eyes.

Today, in the bright sunlight, A Li felt especially alone and even thoughts of her sister could not dispel her solitary feeling. Yesterday she turned 28, and if she were Han Chinese, she would be regarded as unmatchable. In China, most women her age had already married and started families. Even today in Beijing, she knew that white-collar Chinese parents gathered in Zhongshan Park, bringing their children's information and lists of requirements for marriage, hoping to arrange meetings for their sons or daughters at teahouses. She knew that A Ma and Pa Lags were anxious about her marriage prospects even though they rarely mentioned it. Her parents were willing to let her pursue her research, but she sometimes felt she was missing something in life. She remembered the Tibetan weddings she had seen as a child. Would she ever have such a ceremony, with singing and dancing, with white flour worn on the foreheads of her family members and holy water sprinkled on the ground to worship heaven, earth and the mountain gods? She thought about Tanay, their trip to the Flower Mart and his gift of the brass elephant, and wondered again if A Mei disapproved of him.

The wind carried a cloud of sickly sweet smoke over from the next patio, interrupting her thoughts. Strings of tiny white lights, like frosting dripping from a cake, hung from the awning at Shakkar's, where the Middle Eastern students gathered to smoke their hookahs. Half a dozen of them sat around a table, each with three day's stubble of dark whiskers, conversing in loud voices, gesturing with their hands, sucking smoke into their lungs and blowing it into the air. Each of their ornate water pipes had a marble bowl at the top that held burning coals and pressed cubes of flavored tobacco. The pipe bodies of silver or gold contained a tube that channeled the smoke down into cut-glass water bowls. The smoke bubbled up through the water and the men drew it in through slender flexible hoses. A Li once looked at Shakkar's menu, which offered only tobacco—dozens of fruit and flower flavors and a selection of specialties like Sex on the Beach and Code 69. A few American students went there to smoke, but most of them congregated at the coffee shops. The Asians shunned Shakkar's and went to the noodle restaurants.

A Li grew restless and anxious sitting on the patio. She paid her check and started back to the campus. On the corner, the movie theater was about to open its doors for an afternoon matinee of the newest vampire movie. Dozens of teenagers were already lined up. A Li couldn't understand the interest in vampires. They were featured around the world—in books, movies and on television. Half the people in the United States, adults included, were obsessed with vampires and seemed to believe they actually existed.

She knew every culture had its vampire stories, but that was all they were, stories. The Tibetan Book of the Dead told tales of the Wrathful Deities, also called the Blood Drinking Deities. These spirits stole blood from sleeping people and drank it from cups made of human skulls. Some of them had blue-green bodies, others had three blood-shot eyes and flames in their eyebrows and still others had canine teeth. Even the Chinese had *Ch'ing Shih,* the vampire with poisonous breath, which could be stopped only by spilling rice in its path. These old tales were wonderful and entertaining, but they were only fables of Buddhist lore, used to teach lessons of morality. The fact that the vampire stories in America took place in the present made them even more ridiculous. Who would believe that the bloodsuckers actually existed and moved among the population wreaking havoc? Maybe a group of them attended CU and snuck through the tunnels at night—A Li wondered whether they would be undergraduates or graduate students. She smiled at the thought of something with a blue-green body and three bloodshot eyes coming in the middle of the night to suck her Bombay Blood. She would have to make a decision in a nano-second about which eye to stab. She might be laughing too hard to defend herself. The amusement over the blue-green vampires distracted her temporarily from the growing sense of foreboding that was lurking in her mind.

# TWENTY

WHILE A LI THOUGHT about three-eyed vampires, Markus drove up the 405 and glanced in his rearview mirror. He wasn't checking the midday traffic or searching for the highway patrol. He was looking at the black bag that held Audra's body. It still rested against the back of the seat, held in place by the seat belt. Markus was certain he saw movement inside the bag. Was Audra about to unzip it from the inside? Would he look back and suddenly see her sitting there, as though nothing had happened? Would she smile, climb into the front seat next to him?

He pulled off the freeway, parked on the shoulder and reached back to unzip Audra's cocoon. When he opened it, he saw that her skin had turned a faint purple color and looked waxy. Her sensual lips, as well as her fingernails and toenails, had faded to white as her blood had drained away. Her dark eyes were receding into her skull. The stiffness of death had progressed from her eyelids, neck and jaw to all of her other muscles. Whatever Markus thought he had seen, Audra had not moved. Her days of supple erotic dancing were over.

He zipped up the bag and drove back onto the 405. The K and the X had worn off, leaving only the overload of Vicodin in Markus' body. The drug was upsetting his stomach. His skin felt clammy and his heartbeat was so slow, it seemed to pulse only once a minute.

The night before seemed like a dream.

He had actually killed someone—it had been so easy, just like an online game.

Maybe it was an online game.

Was it a mistake?

Audra was just a hooker.

Would he be caught?

No one cared about her.

Was she worth more dead than alive?

*Yes.* In the early hours of the morning, Markus had come up with a brilliant idea.

When Markus drove into the parking lot at Gates of Heaven, he saw Grisha the thug, in his blue suit, watering the alyssum. As Markus opened his door, Grisha turned the hose toward him, but was too far away.

"Hey, you little creep," Grisha shouted. "I'm still washing your vomit off my flowers."

"Screw you, retard," Markus said, but not loud enough for Grisha to hear him.

Grisha turned off the water and approached the car. "Got our money?"

Markus tried to stand up straight and present a strong front to Grisha. "I've got something better," he said. He pushed his sunglasses up the bridge of his nose, closer to his eyes. The sunlight was deadly.

"Oh yeah, what?" Grisha said.

"I'll discuss it with Alexei." Markus said, and walked around to the other side of the car. He opened the door and pushed the front seat forward. He struggled to pull the body bag out of the back, choosing to bear the pain in his back rather than ask Grisha for help. Audra's body seemed even heavier than the previous night. After much effort, Markus laid the bag on the parking lot cement.

Alexei came out of the funeral parlor and down the stairs. Today, he wore jeans and a white T-shirt. Even though he was big and fleshy, Markus could see that Alexei had a lot of muscle. He had tattoos on his bare arms and under the thin material of the T-shirt, Markus made out stars on Alexei's shoulders and an elaborate design that looked like religious figures on his chest. He recognized them as the Russian prison tattoos that Audra had once described. "Every prisoner's life history is tattooed on his body," she had told him. "If he has barbed wire on his arms, the number of barbs will tell you how many years he spent in prison."

*"Da nu,"* Alexei said. "What is this?" He touched the body bag with the toe of his shoe.

"It's the money I owe you. In fact, now you owe me money." Markus bent down slowly, unzipped the top of the bag and opened it far enough so that

Alexei and Grisha could see Audra's head and neck.

Grisha unzipped the bag farther and took a closer look.

"It's a body," Markus said, "a beautiful body with a lot of valuable parts."

Alexei ignored the bag and glared at Markus. "You brought us a body?"

"That's right. And the parts are worth more than the whole." Markus smiled at his clever joke.

Now Alexei bent down to look inside. *"Prid'urok*, you idiot," Alexei hissed. "How long she has been dead?"

Markus counted. "About eight hours, give or take."

"She will start to rot soon. Her face will be gone by tonight. She will turn green, and she will stink. What are we supposed to do with her?" Alexei slapped the side of Markus' head, knocking his dark glasses onto the cement. "Do you think you can just bring us dead body? You think we are criminals?"

"Alexei, I—" Markus' face stung.

Alexei grabbed him by the shirt and shoved him with such force that Markus stumbled backward and fell. When he hit the cement walk, his back erupted in pain. "Oww!" he cried out.

Alexei ignored his exclamation. "What do you think happens to organs? You think we can take heart that has stopped for eight hours, put in freezer and use later? Idiot."

Grisha unzipped the bag farther and looked at Audra's upper body. "Nice tattoos," he said.

"You are an idiot too," Alexei said to Grisha. "Close bag. Who can use graft of green skin with tattoo on it?" Alexei glanced at the tattoos on his own arms, and gave Grisha an angry stare.

Grisha zipped up the bag.

"Who is woman?" Alexei asked.

"My bitch." Markus stood up, grimaced from the pain in his back and rubbed his shoulder. He picked up his sunglasses. One of the lenses was cracked and the frame was bent. He put them on anyway. The light was killing him.

"Who's gonna be looking for her?" Grisha asked.

"No one," Markus said. "She ran away from home. In Ohio. Six years ago."

"Get her out of here," Alexei said to Markus.

"What am I supposed to do with her?" Markus whined. "I brought the body for you. Take it. We'll call it even. You don't have to pay me anything. You keep all the profits."

Alexei turned and whispered something in Grisha's ear. Grisha nodded and smiled. "So," Alexei said. "You are good friend and we are going to help. We will give her AAS." Alexei smiled.

"What?" Markus said. "Ass?"

"AAS. Aerial ash scattering," Alexei said. "A cremation and release of ashes into ocean, out near Catalina. She will share container with another lady."

"You'll take care of this?" Markus smiled. "Thanks comrade." He thought maybe Alexei wasn't such a bad fuck after all. Markus started for his car, anxious to be done with the Russians.

Grisha stepped in front of him. "Cremains," Grisha said. "Skin and hair go first. Soft tissue, guts and other organs burn next. The brain is the slowest to fry. Do you want us to save your girlfriend's brain? Does she have one?"

"We will take care of problem," Alexei said. "*Tseluyu.*" Alexei walked over to Markus, grabbed his head with both hands and kissed his forehead. "I am sorry for your loss. I am sure you want to pay for ash scattering. Yes?" He turned to Grisha. "What does premium AAS cost? Special prayers, fancy container, flower drop?"

"What kind of flowers?" Grisha asked.

"I think $1,500 cost," Alexei said, answering his own question. He turned to Markus. "You want best for your girlfriend, no?"

"I—"

"So, now you owe $3,900."

"I—"

"No. Mistake. You paid already $175. We are honest, we don't cheat. You owe $3,725."

Markus saw Alexei's smile that was not a smile.

"We are like bank," Alexei continued. "You owe money. We charge interest. Today is September 15. If you don't pay us end of week, is $3,925. At end of two weeks, amount is $4,125. *Ponimaju?* Understand?"

Grisha approached Markus, but not to kiss him. He put his arm around Markus' throat and tightened his grip. Markus saw the blue sleeve of Grisha's suit jacket under his chin. He couldn't breathe and he knew what was about to happen.

It happened.

Grisha jerked him backwards and pain shot up his back.

Markus cried out.

Grisha still held him.

"Stick out tongue," Alexei said.

"What?" Markus sputtered. He could barely speak with Grisha's arm around his throat.

"Stick out tongue," Alexei repeated.

Markus showed the tip of his tongue.

"You are precious person," Alexei said. "In Africa, albinos body parts very valuable. Full set bring $75,000."

Grisha released Markus. Pain shot up his back. "Full set?" Markus said.

"Arms, legs, ears, nose, tongue and genitals," Alexei said. "You have nice genitals?"

Markus was silent.

"Fishermen tie arm to fishnet, get bigger fish. Miner put ear and tongue outside hole. Find big jewels. Shepherds take genitals and—"

"No!" Markus shouted.

"Yes," Grisha said.

"You don't pay us, we ship you in ice chest to Tanzania. Albinos big prize and big money, even after cost of air freight."

Markus stood, stunned, imagining his body parts, his cock, in an ice chest on the way to Tanzania. Where was Tanzania?

"See you soon," Grisha said. He picked up the body bag with Audra still in the sitting position, slung it over his shoulder as if it were a small sack of potatoes and carried it up the steps into the funeral parlor.

"So," Alexei said. "*Ischezni! Get lost.*"

Markus' eyes hurt as he drove home. He was having difficulty seeing through the broken right lens of his sunglasses. He twisted and shifted in his seat, trying to ease the pressure on his lower back. It didn't work. He thumbed open the plastic medicine bottle and emptied two Vicodin into his mouth. He had no water and swallowed them dry. The pills left a strong, bitter taste and lodged in his throat.

Life seriously sucked. How could this be happening? The fucking Russians were threatening to chop him up! He pulled out his cell phone and tried to find Drakkar's number in San Diego and drive at the same time. It was the middle of the afternoon and the Big D was probably still sleeping in his coffin. Markus knew he couldn't reach him until the sun went down, but wanted to leave a message. Now.

He pulled to the side of the freeway, found Drakkar's number in his cell phone memory and called. "Hey, how are ya?" Markus said, trying to sound jovial on the voice mail. "It's Markus. I'm sure you're asleep, but call me tonight. As soon as possible. It's important." Markus sent a text message as well, put his phone away and looked at the digital clock in his car. It was just after 2:00 p.m. He felt terrible and needed some sleep. First, he had to go home, gather all of Audra's stuff and find a place to dump it.

Before he could get back on the 405, Markus' cell phone rang. He looked at the ID and saw that Drakkar was already returning his call. "Hey Drak," Markus said, pressing the phone to his ear. "What're you doing up and around at this hour?"

"I might ask you the same. What's up?"

"I have a *dinero* problem."

"What's new?"

"I owe somebody big time. There's gonna be epic trouble if I don't pay him. I could be dead."

"That's about as serious as it gets. What about the Bombay Blood?"

"What about it?"

"Can you get it?"

"I think so. Uh, yeah, sure, definitely."

"How much?"

"What?"

"How much can you get?"

"How much do you want?"

"I'm coming up to L.A. tonight. Let's talk about it. Can you meet me at the Santa Monica Pier, at the very end past the harbor office? Seven-thirty?"

"The Pier? Ha. Last time I was there I was online in a scene from *The Masquerade*, after I found the mummy in the sarcophagus."

"Get serious."

"I'll be there. Thanks man." Markus felt better. Drak was a true friend, always ready to help. He pulled out onto the 405, narrowly missing another car.

Markus thought about it. How much blood could he get from the China Doll?

# TWENTY-ONE

RETURNING FROM THE CORONER'S OFFICE, Colt looked at the back of his hand on the steering wheel and tried to imagine something smaller than the width of a single hair. When he used 88's computer to check the Internet, he learned that Nanoscience was "the study of matter at the atomic scale; a billionth of a meter." A description of some of the scientific applications followed, but the information was beyond his understanding. An insect virus? A cloned gene inserted into an insect virus to produce a protein? A protein used as a nanocapsule to deliver genetic material to human cells inside the body? Colt read it twice and it gave him a headache. It might have all been in a foreign language. He still had no idea what nanoscience was. Learning to be a paramedic had been hard enough. He couldn't imagine sitting in a laboratory, day after day, studying something you couldn't even see.

By the time he reached the Westside, it was early Wednesday afternoon. Colt stopped for a hamburger and thought about the missing foot. He felt a rising sense of outrage. It belonged to Bibi; it was part of her body and the albino had no right to it. The foot had to be retrieved.

After lunch, Colt drove to CU and parked in the short-term parking lot behind the hospital. He got out of his truck and glanced at his face in the side-view mirror. Did he look official? Could he pull this off? He smoothed his blues and checked the firefighter badge on his shirt. No, he decided, the badge would be better inside his wallet. He could pull it out quickly, flash it like cops do on TV and then put it back in his pocket before anyone got a good look at it. Colt didn't want to cut through the ER and run into someone he knew.

He walked around the outside of the massive hospital building and set off across the campus to find the Nano Research Center. He looked for anything familiar and thought about Bibi. Why would such a classy girl like Bibi be with someone like the albino? Maybe she went out with him a couple of times because she was fascinated with his white skin and hair. Maybe they did something stupid and he got her pregnant. Then, on Sunday, the day of the accident, she told him she was going to have a baby. She said she loved her Air Force pilot, the man she intended to marry. While they ate lunch, she burst into tears. She was afraid to tell her parents—what would they think? She told the albino she was planning on an abortion. The albino didn't know what to do. Outside, after lunch, the accident intervened, like the hand of fate. The cowardly albino left her there to die, but at the last minute, on an impulse, he took her foot. If he couldn't have her, he could keep a part of her. Colt was certain that was the way it happened.

Deep in thought, Colt wandered and became lost on the vast campus. It took almost half an hour before he found himself at the bottom of the stairway where he had followed the albino. He bounded up two stairs at a time. At the top, he paused, tucked in his shirt and approached the entrance to the Nano Research Center.

The thick glass doors were locked and an arrow pointed to a red button on the wall. Colt pressed the button twice and stood waiting, hands on his hips, trying to look important. A security guard in a gray uniform appeared behind the glass doors. He was small, with a thin black mustache that might have been drawn on his upper lip with an eyebrow pencil.

"County Fire Department," Colt said, lowering his voice and trying to sound authoritative. "Arson investigation." Colt pulled out his wallet, flipped it open and flashed his badge. He thought it was a good performance. He had the wallet back in his pocket before the guard could get a good look.

"Hold on," the guard said. He waved to someone inside, and Colt heard the electronic signal that released the lock. The little mustache swung one door open and motioned Colt inside. "What can I do for you?" he asked.

Colt walked into an enormous lobby. The overhead lights were low. The far wall was glass, and Colt saw that the building was a hollow square, several stories tall, with a center courtyard. He looked the guard in the eye and said, "We're tracking an arson suspect. He's been observed coming to this building during the evening."

"You are—?"

"Los Angeles County Fire arson investigator."

"We have people in and out 24/7."

"The suspect's distinctive. He's an albino. Wears black clothing. All buttoned up."

"Oh yeah," the guard said. "That sounds like Darkman. C'mon." He pulled out a ring of a dozen keys and used one to unlock the door to the security office. He held it open for Colt.

Colt entered a well-equipped room. Electronic monitoring screens covered two walls. He saw camera views of hallways, elevators, stairwells and the front entrance of the Nano Center. A second guard ate a sandwich and a bag of corn chips at a desk in front of the security monitors. The room smelled like tuna fish.

"This guy's an arson investigator," the little mustache said. "He wants to know about Darkman."

The second guard stood up. "I'm Ricky," he said. He pointed to the mustache. "And that's Bobby," He wiped his hand on his pants and extended it.

Colt shook his hand without giving his name and nodded to Bobby.

"Darkman's involved in arson?" Ricky said. "I always thought there was something weird about him. Just look at the way he dresses."

Colt could smell the tuna on Ricky's breath. At least he looked more like a real security guard than his partner. He was almost Colt's height, over 6 feet, and appeared to be in decent shape.

"What do you need?" Bobby asked.

"The investigation is still preliminary, but I want the name and address of ... uh ... Darkman."

"We just have names and university ID numbers," Bobby said. He pulled up a list on his computer screen.

"Whatever you have."

"Hell, Ricky," Bobby said, "what's his real name?"

"I dunno," Ricky said. "His first name starts with an M. Mike something."

"No, that's not right," Bobby said. He scrolled through the list to the M's. "I think it's Mark. Yeah, here it is. His first name is Mark. Last name Draper. Mark Draper." Bobby beamed.

"Thanks," Colt said.

"You want his ID number?" Ricky asked.

"No, I don't need that."

"He walks to work," Bobby said, "so he must live in the neighborhood."

"And he works in this building?"

"Lower level two. That's as far down as you can get." Bobby played with his keyboard and brought up a schematic map of lower level two, he pointed to an office. "That's it—LL2/3."

Colt studied the map. "What's this at the bottom of the fire stairs?"

"Entrance to the underground tunnel," Bobby said. "It connects parts of the campus. Students and faculty use it … on snow days." Bobby chuckled.

"What's this about?" Ricky asked.

"Is he starting fires?" Bobby asked. "Is he doing bad shit?"

"Sorry, it's confidential," Colt said. "I can't talk about an ongoing investigation, so please don't discuss my visit with anyone. If you see him, don't say anything."

"Oh we won't," Ricky said. He sat down to finish his sandwich.

"Do you know what this Mark guy does here?" Colt asked.

"I think he works part time, at night," Bobby said. "He's not one of the big-shot scientists."

"What do they do?"

"They're inventing little tiny things that go in your body." Bobby said.

"Yeah, they change your genetics," Ricky said.

"What does that mean?" Colt asked.

"They're doing stuff like this." Bobby picked up a Nano Research Center brochure and handed it to Colt.

Colt opened it and read aloud, "The Center is leading the research in di-polar molecular rotor crystals and nanocapsule vaults."

"Yeah," Bobby said. "That's what they do here."

"What I think," Ricky said, "is they're making better athletes. You know, faster runners, bigger muscles, stuff like that. They don't tell us, but that's what I think."

"OK, thanks guys," Colt said, concluding he wasn't going to get anything else from Dumb and Dumber. "The arson squad appreciates your help."

"No problem," Ricky said, stuffing his mouth full of chips. "I'll release the door for you."

When Colt walked outside, he realized he was damp with nervous sweat.

Impersonating a law enforcement officer wasn't easy, but he thought he had done a good job. He pulled out his cell phone and called 411. "In West Los Angeles, the number for Mark Draper."

The number cost 45 cents. The address, 410 Albion Street, cost an additional 45 cents. For less than a buck, Colt had the information he hoped would help locate Bibi's foot.

By the time he was halfway back to his truck, Colt's shirt was bone dry. He felt like he was walking into a blast furnace. The hot Santa Ana wind, a 50 mile-per-hour heat wave from the Nevada desert, had arrived in full force. He walked past the police and fire building adjacent to the hospital, stopped and turned around. Colt thought about the tunnel entrance to the Nano Center and wondered whether he could get to the albino's office on LL2/3 without going past the security guards. He decided to find out.

The campus police occupied most of the first floor. Colt had heard that the university had its own large police force but that their fire department wasn't much and relied on L.A. City Fire for protection. The campus fire department had an office at the end of the hall. When Colt entered, an older man, probably a retired firefighter from the city or county, looked at Colt's uniform and greeted him. "Hi brother, what can I do for you?"

"Evening," Colt said, letting his uniform speak for itself and not introducing himself. "I understand there's a tunnel system under the campus."

"That's right."

"Can I get a map?"

The man considered Colt for a moment. "We have an old one that shows where the tunnels are marked for above-ground standpipes and hydrants."

"That works."

"What's up?"

"My cousin's starting CU. I promised I'd get her a copy."

"Ours is about 80 percent accurate. She can get a better one in the bookstore. Tell her most of the students don't even use the tunnels. Hold on a minute." He went to a filing cabinet, searched one drawer, then another and withdrew a large Manila envelope. He pulled out a 12"x18" sheet and handed it to Colt. "Here you go."

Colt glanced at the map and saw how complex the passages were under such a large campus. "This'll do, thanks." He folded the map and tucked it into his pocket.

"Stay safe, brother."

Colt walked back to his pickup, looking at the map.

When Colt arrived home, it was just after four in the afternoon and Roy was already sitting on his cardboard mat under the stairs. "Hey buddy, what are you up to?" Colt said when he got out of his truck.

*"Munstaf binker tor,"* Roy answered.

As Colt approached the stairs, he saw that Roy held a wallet in his hand. "What's that Roy? Where did you get that?"

*"Binker tor,"* Roy repeated, and pointed to a pink backpack.

Colt snatched the wallet from Roy's grimy hand. He found a driver's license inside, and couldn't believe the picture he saw. A young woman with blue eyes stared back at him. Colt was certain he was looking at Bibi with long hair. He checked her name and address.

> *Darci Tierney*
> *895 Tobias Avenue*
> *Van Nuys, CA 91404*

"Roy, where did you find this?"

Roy stared at Colt.

"Where? Beach?" Colt bent down and walked his fingers on the ground. "At the beach?" He pointed north toward Malibu and looked at Roy.

Roy looked back at Colt.

Colt was certain Roy had found the backpack near the Surfrider Restaurant and he was certain Roy would never be able to tell him. Colt sat down on the stairs and searched through Darci's belongings. He pulled out a pair of jeans, tank tops, T-shirts, a sweatshirt, a pink brassiere, two pink thongs, a washcloth, a plastic bag with a toothbrush, toothpaste and sunscreen and two small books.

While Colt was busy with the backpack, Roy got up and headed for the beach underpass. *"Yinstoch wentel,"* was his final comment.

Colt opened one of the books. It had a pink and blue cover and the title was *Baby Names From Around The World*. In the girls' section, the "M" page was folded down and the names "Mai," "Maria," "Melissa" and "Micki" were underlined. In the boy's section, the underlined names were "Reilly," "Rod" and "Ryder." The second book was actually a small photo album. The plastic pages contained only two photos. The first showed a black and tan German shepherd, lying on a cement walk somewhere, looking up at the camera. The second picture was of Darci, with short blond hair, standing in front of an old Ford Mustang.

Colt again imagined the injured girl in the parking lot and heard her whisper "baby" in his ear. Her name was Darci, and she lived in Van Nuys, not Malibu. Colt marveled at the chain of events that led him to discover her identity, and began to wonder what kind of life Darci could have led in Van Nuys.

He took out his cell phone and searched his pockets for Nate Petruno's card.

# TWENTY-TWO

O N WEDNESDAY EVENING, before he left his apartment, Markus downed three more Vicodin. While it was in his bloodstream, it left him feeling light-headed, almost euphoric. When the drug wore off, the pain in his lower back and tailbone was acute.

He drove the short distance to Ocean Avenue, parked and walked under the neon sign down the ramp onto the thick rough wood planks of the Santa Monica Pier. A hot dry Santa Ana wind blew at his back, sucking the moisture out of the air. He was early for his meeting with Drakkar. The September days were getting shorter and at 7:20 p.m., the sun was setting into a pool of gold in the ocean. Seagulls circled the pier, crying out to one another. The warm weather had drawn a big weekday crowd to the shore and the last beach visitors stopped to wash sand off their feet before heading for the parking lot. Markus looked down and watched the breaking surf leave a sheet of white foam. It was high tide and the ocean rocked back and forth. Markus drifted along, moving with the water and the Vicodin toward the end of the pier.

The day people departed and the night crowd arrived. Salsa music blared out of RUSTY'S. Near the red plastic tables and umbrellas of the food court, the smell of the ocean mixed with the aroma of burgers, pizza and fried shrimp. When Markus walked beyond Rusty's, he smelled the odor of chemical toilets. Sounds of bells, whistles, electronic music and shouts and screams spilled from the Playland arcade. Gang-bangers with gold jewelry, wearing shorts that hung down to their ankles, stood around flirting with their girlfriends. Teenagers stood in groups, holding stuffed animal prizes and eating cotton candy. Tired, cranky children cried as their parents dragged them away from the games and the noise.

A Santa Monica police car rolled slowly through the throng and an officer in the passenger seat looked directly at Markus. A wave of panic washed through him and he thought of Audra. What if they arrested him for murder? Everything was going wrong. How had he gotten into this mess with Alexei? Was Grisha coming to hurt him? Would he be dismembered and sent to Africa in an ice chest? Would he ever get the China Doll's blood? Did he need surgery on his tailbone? For a moment, his life seemed out of control. His lower back throbbed. His head buzzed. His mind lurched from thought to thought. Markus wanted to curl up and let his mother hold and protect him.

In the fading sunlight, Markus looked down the pier. A figure dressed in black approached him. Was it Drakkar? He focused his weak eyes until he saw that it was someone in Darth Vader attire, carrying a helmet under his arm. The street performers in costumes, the artists, vendors and the musicians with guitars and metal drums were all finished for the day and heading home. Only the woman who advertised, "YOUR NAME ON A GRAIN OF RICE," remained at her stand.

Markus went in search of Drakkar. As he passed the small pier amusement park, the whole area erupted in illumination. Strobe lights everywhere began to flash. Neon beams—purple red pink white blue purple red pink white blue—pulsed along the spokes of the Ferris wheel. Bulbs sparked on and off on the rails of the small roller coaster. Two dolphin statues at the entrance to the fun house exploded with light. Blinded, Markus covered his eyes and moved as fast as he could manage toward the darkness at the end of the pier. He needed new sunglasses.

The farther he went, the quieter it became. Markus passed anglers carrying disassembled poles, tackle boxes and coolers. A few lovers sat on the benches kissing or leaning over the railing looking into the dark water below. At the terminus of the pier, the oversize windows of the Harbor Patrol station were black. A solitary red blinking light on a mast overhead shed a faint red hue. The sun disappeared on the horizon and a quarter moon began its journey across the sky. Markus listened to the waves crashing against the pilings below and waited for his friend. He had never been on the Santa Monica Pier, but this spot was so familiar. When he played *Vampire: The Masquerade* online, the game always ended in a confrontation at the end of the pier with Sebastain LaCroix, the leader of the Camarilla Clan in Los Angeles. Usually, Markus slashed LaCroix's throat and then waited for the Anarchs to arrive and then—

"Arrrrrgh!"

Someone screamed, lunged out of the shadows, grabbed Markus around the waist from behind and shoved him toward the rail.

GRISHA!

Grisha was about to throw Markus into the water. The Russian's tight grip caused a wave of pain to shoot up his back. Markus was too frightened to call for help. He could already feel the cold dark ocean swallowing him, dragging him under.

"Gotcha!"

Drakkar released Markus and laughed. "How you doing, white one?" He grabbed Markus in a bear hug.

"Oh shit, that's not funny. I thought I was going in the water." Markus waited for the pain in his back to ease and looked at his friend in the weak red light. Drakkar was tall and thin, almost skeletal. His face was drawn, cheeks hollow. Thick black hair hung down to his shoulders. "You losing weight?" Markus asked.

"I'm eating a lot and taking vitamins, but my chakras are out of balance. I need some new blood."

"I wish that were my only problem."

"What kind of trouble are you in?"

"I owe a fucking Russian some money."

"Not good. What for?"

"A hand."

"A hand? A hand? You've got to be kidding. You still messing around with body parts?"

Markus nodded. "Do you think it's possible to ship iced body parts from here to Tanzania?"

"How should I know? Are you starting a business?"

"I just wondered," Markus said.

"How's Audrey?"

"Audra? She took off." Markus wanted to tell Drakkar everything he had done. He wanted someone to share his burden, but he kept silent. "Listen, Drak, I have to come up with almost four thousand bucks as fast as possible, I need some help."

Drakkar walked over to the railing and looked into the darkness below. "Can you get the Bombay Blood?"

"Yes."

"How soon?"

"Right away, I think."

"Good. D'you know what I can do with it?" He turned to look at Markus and his gaunt face became animated. "I've got 30 nightwalkers in my blood family in San Diego alone who would kill to get an ounce of Bombay."

"That's great."

"Great? It's mystical. When you're feeling down, imagine what a spoonful could do for you. D'you know what I mean? It's life energy. A little sip once a week for extra strength, sexual stamina, spiritual nourishment, whatever. Every Goth girl in Southern California would kill to have a vial of Bombay Blood around her neck."

"Sounds good, but what I need to know is how much money I can get and I need it as soon as possible."

Drakkar nodded. "We'll go 50-50. I can probably get $100 an ounce. There's 16 ounces in a pint, right? So, I might be able to sell three or four pints. That would bring in about five or six thousand."

"So I would get three thousand? That's not enough. I'm still short. Is that all you can do?"

"On short notice? That's about it. Give me some time to get organized, and I can sell a lot more. Is this woman clean? She doesn't have anything, does she? I don't deal in blood that hasn't been tested."

"There's nothing in her medical records. She's from somewhere in China and she's working on her PhD. That's all I know. She's not a skank. All you have to do is look at her."

"Who knows what goes on in China? I can't just sell anything. I've got someone at a lab in San Diego who checks all my blood. "

"How long does that take?"

"A while. There's different tests."

"Drak, I can't wait a month for some retard in a lab to fiddle with a bunch of test tubes. I need the money by Monday."

"If you bring it down Friday, there's one test he can do right away. If it's clean, I'll take it to my feeding circle Saturday night. We're having a dusk-to-dawn event."

"It'll be there before lunch. I'll bring it down myself." Markus realized he couldn't wait to catch the China Doll in the tunnel next Monday. He would have to corner her tomorrow night in her lab.

"Have you thought about how you're gonna get three or four pints out of this woman?" Drakkar asked. "That's half her blood."

"I've got ether. I'll put her out."

"You'll kill her."

"Let me worry about that." Markus didn't care what happened to the China Doll. The important thing was to get her blood, and the money.

"You're right," Drakkar said, walking away from the railing, "I don't want to know any details. Leave me out of that part. Just deliver the blood."

"Don't worry, I will." Markus rubbed his tailbone with his hand and grimaced.

"What's the matter?"

"I hurt my back. Actually one of the Russians hurt my back."

"Man, what have you gotten yourself into?"

"Never mind. What're you doing here in LA?"

"I came up to see a guy who works at a blood bank, but now I think I'm gonna blow him off. If you can deliver the Bombay, I'm not really interested in donor blood. It's ordinary and it's expensive."

"I'll get the Bombay tomorrow night and leave you a message."

"OK. Good to see you." Drakkar gave Markus another hug.

"Careful," Markus said, and pulled away.

"Try to stay out of trouble." Drakkar started back along the pier.

"Too late," Markus muttered to himself. "Way too late."

Markus returned to an eerie apartment. When he entered, he thought he heard Audra moving around. He went to his desk, turned on the small lamp and eased himself into his chair. Out of the corner of his eye, he thought he saw her standing in the shadows. While Markus checked his e-mail, he heard a noise that sounded like Audra opening a drawer of the Victorian dresser. He struggled up from his desk chair and went into the bedroom. "Hello?" he said. He turned on the light on the night table and expected to see her sitting on the bed, pulling on her mesh stockings. The bed was empty. He thought he heard water running in the kitchen and went in to look.

A sense of dread settled over Markus as he stood by the sink. He was certain Audra's spirit had returned to punish him. Nothing in his knowledge of Goth lore told him how to combat a demon spirit from hell bent on revenge.

What was she planning?

A pillow over his face?

Rat poison in his yogurt?

A blow to the head?

No, Markus decided. Audra would sneak into the bedroom while he was asleep and sever his artery. She would stand over the bed while his blood drained out onto the sheet. She would awaken him when he was too weak to move. He would lie face up looking at her while his heart pumped the last drops from his body. Audra would laugh at him and say, "Fuck you." Darkness would rule.

Markus bent down to the kitchen sink and splashed cold water on his face. After a moment, he regained some clarity and realized he was hallucinating and decided he had to cut back on the meds. A moment later, a jab of pain in his lower back demanded more painkillers, not less.

Markus lurched through the shadowy apartment. He listened to Goth music, logged on to *Ghost in the Shell*, surfed Internet porn sites, and opened the freezer twice to admire the foot. Nothing worked. He became more stressed and anxious with each hour that passed. His nerves were as taut as piano wire. When he sat down, his lower back screamed in pain. When he stood up, his leg muscles began to twitch. Images of the China Doll, Audra, and Grisha shape-shifted through his mind.

Markus couldn't bear it any more and fled to the National Cemetery where he wandered aimlessly. Even his favorite gravestones and fantasies of Vlad the Impaler failed to soothe him. The air was hot and dry but sweat dripped from every pore on his body. He was drowning in his own perspiration. Markus tried to concentrate on how to harvest the China Doll's blood. He couldn't even consider the possibility he would be unable to find her. He would find her and drain her blood. He imagined her bent over a microscope in the lab, so absorbed in her work that she was unaware of him coming up behind her.

The hours of the night melted away while Markus wandered through the cemetery. It was early Thursday morning. Markus returned to his apartment as the sun came up in the east. The hot wind blew toward the ocean, bending eucalyptus branches and sending palm fronds sailing into the sky.

Markus unlocked his front door and listened for Audra. He went into the bedroom, pulled the heavy velvet curtains tight and stood motionless, wondering where she was lurking—perhaps under the bed or hiding in the bathtub. When he was confident he was alone, he swallowed the last three Vicodin without water and collapsed on the bed.

# TWENTY-THREE

Markus was still in a drug-induced sleep in his apartment when A Li awoke on Thursday morning. The unrelenting California sun was already shining into her small bedroom, the wind was still blowing and she heard the branches of a nearby tree brushing against the side of the house. Her sense of foreboding returned as she lay in bed. It was 8:15 a.m. and she realized she had overslept after studying late into the night.

Tired as she was, she forced herself out of bed, slipped on her robe and walked down the hall to the bathroom on the second floor of the home of her host, Professor Chen. She had 45 minutes to get to her CHESL class—Chinese English as a second language. Standing in front of the mirror, she touched her face and felt the tender, swollen spot where she had fallen to the floor of the lab Tuesday night. She unclipped her long black hair and gave it a few strokes with the brush. She had no time to braid it.

A Li hurried to the two-story building where her class met. She was 10 minutes late and wondered what would happen if she missed a session. In the United States, students were casual about going to class. In China, no one missed instruction; it was not an option. She hastened down the hall and silently opened the door to a narrow classroom with a blackboard in front and a mirror running along the back wall. Nine women and 14 men, all Chinese who spoke Mandarin, sat in a single row. The instructor, Miss Lloyd, stood in front of the class. She reminded A Li of a stork—she was thin and very tall, almost 6 feet, and towered over the shorter Chinese students. She had a pinched face and never smiled or seemed happy. She was, however, a good teacher. She grew up in Hong Kong, spoke fluent Mandarin and two other dialects and the students respected her language abilities.

When A Li slipped into the classroom, Miss Lloyd looked up, acknowledged A Li, glanced at her watch and looked at A Li again. A Li sat down and took out her workbook.

Miss Lloyd continued with the day's lesson. "Today, we're going to practice pronouncing words beginning and ending in R. That's RRRRR. Your inability to pronounce the American letter R will be the main cause of being misunderstood." She walked to the front of the room and wrote a 3-foot high R on the blackboard, pointed to it and turned to the class. "Pronouncing R at the end of a word, as in caRRR, is difficult. Pronouncing it at the beginning of a word, as in RRRat is extremely difficult. It's a skill you must master if you want people to listen to you and understand you."

The class paid close attention. The American R was very difficult and nothing like any of the four different R's in Mandarin.

"To make the R sound properly, your mouth must come forward and your lips must be tight. Look at my mouth," she commanded. "Watch me."

The students looked up and focused on her face.

"Now," she said, "practice saying OOOO. Turn around and look at your mouth and lips in the mirror. OOOO. OOOO. Now you try it."

A Li joined the other students. "OOOO. OOOO."

"Good," Miss Lloyd said. "Now say the word RAT. RRRat. Push out the R. Your tongue should not be right behind your front teeth."

The students struggled with RRRat.

"I can hear your tongues are not in the right place. Look at me." Miss Lloyd walked to the back of the room, stood by the mirror and turned sideways. "Bring your lips forward, like this, and stick your finger in your mouth. About 3 centimeters inside. It should touch your tongue. That's where your tongue should be. Push your tongue back." Miss Lloyd stuck her finger between her pursed lips. "Do it in front of the mirror."

The students watched themselves in the mirror, inserted their index fingers into their mouths and pushed their tongues back.

"Now, class. RRRat, RRRabbit. RRRock. Let me hear it."

As A Li gazed into the mirror with her finger in her mouth, the sound of her cell phone interrupted the exercise. Everyone stopped and looked at A Li.

Miss Lloyd exploded. "A Li, your cell phone must be turned off in class."

A Li reached inside her backpack for her phone. She was surprised, because no one ever called her. Could it be Tanay? She took the phone out, and, before she turned it off, saw a text message: A Li Jian. Please come immediately to the Office of the Dean of Graduate Students.

A Li felt a wave of panic as she hastened out of her class. Why was she summoned to the Dean's Office? Her sense of foreboding grew. Was there an emergency? Was something wrong at home, where it was 2:30 a.m.? She stopped and tried to call her parents but could not get through. She feared there had been an earthquake. A Li wondered if her recent apprehension foretold bad news from Zhongdian.

Oh sister, what has happened?

The campus, home to almost 25,000 students, stretched for more than a mile. Walking as fast as she could, it took 20 minutes to reach Dean's Hall. She didn't wait for the elevator and took the stairs two at a time to the second floor. Her hand trembled as she opened the door to the Dean's Office. She walked in and blurted out, "I got a message to—"

"Are you Miss Jian?"

"Yes."

"Come in." A secretary led A Li to the Foreign Graduate Students Assistance Office, knocked and opened it. "Miss Jian is here," she said.

An older woman, her gray hair pulled back in a tight bun, stood up from behind her desk and pointed to a chair. "Miss Jian, please."

A Li sat down. Her heart was pounding. "What's happened?" she asked.

"Ah, Miss Jian … I have bad news. We received a communication last night from your Provincial Government Office. Apparently there's some problem with the telephones and they forwarded a message from your mother." She picked up a sheet of paper from her desk and read from it. "Your father has had a heart attack and fell down a flight of stairs. His condition is critical. Your mother requests you come home as soon as possible."

A Li gasped.

Sister, is our dear honorable Pa Lags knocking on the door of death?

"The Yunnan Government has paid for an airline ticket." The woman came around her desk and put a hand on A Li's shoulder. "I'm very sorry. I know how hard this is, especially when everyone is so far away. There's a reservation for you on a flight to Beijing tomorrow afternoon at 4 and a connection on a flight to ..." She looked again at the paper. "... Zhongdian through Kunming." She handed A Li the information. "The ticket will be here late this afternoon; you can come by and pick it up."

"Thank you," A Li said, stunned.

"Do you want to call home?" the woman asked.

"I've tried." A Li's lips began to quiver as she tried to control her emotions.

The woman looked at A Li. "The side of your head is swollen. Did you have an accident?"

"I fell in the laboratory." A Li fingered her temple.

"Why don't I leave you alone for a few minutes?" The woman took A Li's hand and squeezed it, then left the office.

*Oh sister, our Pa Lags is dying. We must be with him.*

A Li sat alone in the Dean's office. She felt crushed by the weight of her problems: her loneliness and isolation in Los Angeles; her dissatisfaction with the way Dr. Murray treated her; her unrelenting study and work program; her second-rate status among the other Chinese students; her poor English skills; the money she owed her government. Now her beloved Pa Lags was ill and she was halfway around the world. She tried to keep control of herself, but it was too much. All of the insults, slights, and disappointments of her entire life filled her mind. Tears leaked from the corners of her eyes, then became a torrent. She gave in to her despondency and sat, with her head bowed, letting the tears fall.

*A Mei, give me strength.*

After several minutes, she stood up, took some tissues from a box on the dean's desk and wiped her eyes. She went to the window and tried to compose herself as she looked out at the mid-morning sunlight shining on the campus. Soon she would be back in the cool mountains, in the fields and pastures of her homeland and she felt comforted by the thought.

A Li walked out of the office and down the hall. She had so much to do in the next 24 hours before her flight to Beijing. Pa Lags' illness meant an approaching tsunami of medical bills. She thought about the gold rush going on in China. The economy was booming and people were getting rich in so many different ways. Everyone in her generation was becoming a capitalist. She knew the value of the stem cell research data in Dr. Murray's laboratory. She could return home with it and use it to become wealthy and important. She could use it to help her family. The Communist Party might even welcome her as a member. Her friends would call her Big Bucks Jian. She could solve so many of her problems by taking the stem cell information home to China.

She thought of Tanay and felt regret. She would have to tell him she was not staying in the United States.

# TWENTY-FOUR

*YUSUMBICH MYSPOR TAKFF! CHEMEE TAKFF!* When Colt woke up early Thursday morning, he heard Roy down on the street shouting. Another voice screamed back. Roy was having one of his arguments with Max, the bearded beggar who often stood on the far side of Chautauqua and panhandled for small change when drivers stopped at the light. They had their own language and Colt couldn't understand a single word they were bellowing. The argument went on for another 10 minutes before both vagrants ran out of steam and fell silent. Colt cursed them for starting up so early, rolled over, pulled his pillow over his head and tried to go back to sleep. It was too late, he was wide-awake.

Three hours later, Colt drove south on the 405 Freeway, going to his performance review at PTI—the Paramedic Training Institute of Southern California. He turned off the freeway and drove through Carson, a low-income community with gang problems and a sky-high homicide rate.

Southern California Hospital had closed two years before Colt began his paramedic training, leaving the area without a major health-care facility. He passed the deserted hospital and turned down a narrow driveway that led to the paramedic training center, a one-story building that once housed the human resources department. Colt looked at his watch and realized he was early—something of a miracle in a city where the average speed on the freeways was less than 20 miles per hour. He parked among the motorcycles, cars and pickup trucks with firefighter license plates and red and yellow stickers from the California State Firefighters' Association. The lot was almost full. Classes met four days a week. On the other days, they studied and practiced skills and techniques. Colt thought the nine-month course was the hardest thing he had ever done and wondered how the men with wives and children found time for their families.

Colt had 15 minutes to kill. He walked across the parking lot and slipped between a gap in the temporary fence that ran around the hospital. The deserted facility was depressing. The buildings, none more than four stories high, were spread over two city blocks. Once colored pink and rust, neglect and oxidation had changed the outside walls to shades of dirty brown. Colt wandered around the perimeter, looking in at the deserted rooms, treatment centers and hallways. He saw bulletin boards still covered with outdated announcements posted on colored sheets of paper, but there was no sign of life. The hospital was empty, stripped of equipment, furniture and anything else that could be salvaged. In a few places, a lonely chair or a stray box of files remained unclaimed. Colt found it unnerving to look through the windows of the buildings and see the street on the far side. The grass was faded to the color of straw and the shrubbery had withered. Only the largest trees were green, somehow surviving in the dry Southern California climate. Even in the bright, hot sunshine of mid morning, Colt thought the facility screamed decay and death.

He turned and walked back through the breach in the fence to the training center. Outside the entrance to the school Colt saw the familiar blue cases containing the life-sized upper body dummies used for airway management training. Although they were identical, each dummy had a crazy name written across its forehead. Every class changed the names, creating a little humor and diversion to relieve the stress of the hours spent learning endotracheal intubation—insertion of a breathing tube into a patient's windpipe. It was a difficult and critical procedure and Colt had wondered at the time if he would ever be able to do it when someone's life hung in the balance. The instructors assured everyone that paramedics intubate hundreds of patients during their careers and that it would become second nature.

After hours of training on the dummies, Colt's class had gone to San Diego to practice on a real cadaver before a group of medical students dissected it. When the paramedics entered the OR, they saw a body on the table covered from the waist down. From across the room Colt recognized the round yellow disk secured to the corpse's right ear. He moved closer and confirmed that it was the same identification tag used on cattle. It carried a serial number and as Colt knew from experience, it was almost impossible to remove without tearing off the ear.

Under the bright lights, the man's skin had a gray-brown pallor. His chest looked emaciated. The shoulders and arms were skeletal, the underside of his body a dark red-purple color where the blood had pooled. His head was bald, his eyelids closed. The mouth, with withered, cracked lips, was slightly open, revealing the tip of the tongue. It was clearly an older person and the body appeared diminutive—Colt guessed it was no taller than 5 feet 1. He wondered about the high points of this man's life. Had he loved someone? Did he have a family? Was he a war hero, a great scientist, a famous criminal? What were his last thoughts?

Someone in yellow scrubs joined them in the OR. "Let's get started," he said. "I'm Dr. Davis and I teach gross anatomy to first-year medical students. This is called the 'Gross Lab.'" He paused to see if anyone appreciated the joke. He got no reaction and proceeded to hand out a black and white diagram of a cross section of a throat. "Study this. By the time your training is over, you'll need to know the terms for the anatomy of the larynx."

"Where did the body come from?" one of Colt's classmates asked.

"That's always the first question," Dr. Davis said. "We never know anything about the cadaver except that before death it was donated to medical research."

"So the person knows what's gonna happen?" another paramedic asked.

The doctor nodded. "Full disclosure and a half-dozen legal forms." He bent down, touched a button and the operating table rose. "Step closer please."

They edged nearer to the body.

"To provide a realistic dissection," the doctor said, "the body remains in its natural state. It's been refrigerated, but not embalmed. When you finish your intubation practice, my first year medical students will cut out each organ and study it. When that's over, the body and all its parts will be cremated and given a respectful burial." He paused for a moment and put his hand on the forehead of the corpse. "First-year med students sometimes get spooked about lingering spirits and souls from their cadavers. The funeral gives them closure too." He looked at the paramedics standing around him. "Don't you guys get any crazy ideas." He looked at Colt.

Doctor Davis slipped his hand under the head of the cadaver. Long past rigor mortis, the body was limp. He lifted the head and rested it on a Styrofoam support. "For a successful intubation, the head should be in what we call the 'sniff position,' tilted back with the chin up." He looked around. "Who's first?"

He held up a handful of plastic breathing tubes in front of the assembled group. "Help yourselves."

Each paramedic had a few minutes, assisted by a partner, to use the laryngoscope—a flat blade with a tiny light at the tip—to push the tongue aside, open the larynx and vocal cords and insert the flexible breathing tube into the windpipe. Even after all the practice on the dummies, the first effort on a real body, even a dead one, was difficult.

Doctor Davis hovered nearby, looking over their shoulders and giving instructions. "Take your time," he said, "and learn to do it right. Just don't let your patient run out of oxygen."

When Colt stepped forward and bent over the head, he smelled a faint unpleasant odor through his mask. When he opened the mouth, he saw that most of the teeth were missing. On the first try, Colt couldn't get the tube into the windpipe. It kept sliding sideways and getting caught in the folds of the vocal chords. Finally, he withdrew it, smeared it with more Vaseline and tilted the head farther back to get a better look into the throat. On the second attempt, the tube slid into the trachea without a problem.

Afterward, as they prepared to leave and the medical students arrived for the dissection, Dr. Davis pulled aside the sheet covering the lower half of the cadaver. Colt was surprised to see it was a woman. Her toenails were ragged and untrimmed, but still showed traces of gold polish.

Colt lingered for a few minutes to watch the beginning of the dissection. The medical students stood in a tight group around the operating table and watched Dr. Davis run a small saw around the skull, remove the top half and take out the brain. Next, he cut away the ribcage with a tool that looked like a big garden clipper. Colt watched as her heart was removed, dissected and passed around for examination.

Colt departed, imagining the end of the session when all the woman's organs, sliced and diced, were piled on a table, leaving her body a hollow shell of bone and skin. He wondered why anyone would donate their body to be cut up and passed around, piece by piece, by a group of medical students. When Colt applied for his California driver's license, the DMV asked whether he wanted to sign up to be an organ donor. The thought had troubled him at the time. His own death was somewhere far into the future and he wasn't ready to think about his organs being "harvested." He couldn't imagine his heart pumping someone else's blood. He told the clerk he might consider it some other time. Colt had no immediate plans to die.

While he stood by the entrance to the paramedic training center, still day-dreaming about the cadaver dissection in San Diego, the door swung open and someone Colt's age, wearing a suit, white shirt and dark tie, nodded and headed to the parking lot. As he walked past, Colt saw the standard-issue firefighter boots and knew the man had just finished an admissions interview. Colt walked into the reception area and the first person he saw was Nick, the receptionist.

"Hey, Colt," Nick said. "Welcome back. How's it going?"

"Can't complain," Colt said. He had only been gone a few weeks, but felt strange coming back. It already seemed like another lifetime.

Nick checked his computer screen. "You're here to see Sandy?" He glanced at the closed door with the SANDY HAYES nameplate. "Take a seat. You're early and she's running late."

"Thanks," Colt said. The reception area was furnished with ergonomic stenographers' chairs commandeered from the hospital after it closed. They were uncomfortable and he knew from experience that the back supports were loose. He sat down gingerly and leaned forward. Colt gazed at the pictures of graduating classes hanging on the walls. Three classes a year passed through the paramedic school. Colt graduated in Class 25 and saw himself in the class picture hanging at the end of the hall.

Sandy's voice boomed out from behind her closed office door. "So when you're called to a convalescent home, Earl, what do you find?"

Colt heard a low, indistinguishable answer. He looked away from the door. Sandy sounded angry and he didn't want to listen while she slammed a fellow paramedic intern.

"What you're gonna find is some poor patient who's 85 or 90, has six things wrong and is taking two dozen different meds. The medical history file could be an inch thick and your patient could have dementia, or may just be confused. Okay? You can't just take the vitals and start a treatment. What look like terrible vital signs may be normal for someone in a convalescent home. So what do you do, Earl?"

In spite of himself, Colt strained to hear a response. Nick glanced at Colt and gave a tiny nod of his head, acknowledging that he too was listening and commiserating with the guy inside. Colt realized that Nick had probably been sitting at his desk listening to these closed-door conversations for years.

"You get one of the nurses, Earl. The first thing you do is you get one of the nurses and you ask her why you were called. Understand? The nurses in those homes will disappear the minute the paramedics arrive. You have to round them up and ask questions. Got it? You don't have time to read through a big file."

Colt shifted around on the stenographer's chair. Earl, whoever he was, was catching hell.

Sandy went on. "If the patient's failing, Earl, what do you do next? What you do is, you ask them if there's a DNR. If the patient is about to take his last breath and he's left a DNR, it means you don't try to do anything heroic. You don't just jump in and start a full workup until you find out."

Down the hall, Colt heard other voices. It was the mid-morning break and the interns were coming out of the classrooms and practice areas for a breather. They congregated in the hall and dining area or stepped outside for a smoke. A ping-pong game began immediately—the quickest way to relieve the stress. Above the commotion in the hall, Colt still heard Sandy.

"Your preceptor says you know your stuff, Earl, and I agree." Sandy's voice grew calmer. "I'm gonna add eight more shifts to your internship. Next time, I want a good report. Okay? You just have to pay attention to the details and be more assertive out in the field. Got it?"

There was silence for a few seconds and the door to Sandy's office opened. A red-faced paramedic, wearing a patch from the Vernon Fire Department, walked past Colt, head down, not making eye contact.

Sandy stood up behind her desk. "You're next Colt," she said and waved him in. "How are ya?" She greeted him with a strong, firm handshake.

Colt sat down and felt the body heat left on the seat.

"Gimme a minute," Sandy said, and glanced through the pages of Colt's file.

Colt watched her face, looking for some indication of her response to Brian's report. She gave nothing away until she finished. Finally, she closed the file, dropped it on her desk and smiled at Colt. "Sounds like you and Brian are doing well together."

"Brian's a good guy," Colt said, relaxing. "I'm learning a lot from him."

"He's one of the best preceptors we have." Sandy leaned forward and put her hands on her desk. "You know the biggest problem I have with new paramedics?"

"No, but you're about to tell me, right?"

"Right." She smiled again. "I spend most of my time telling gruff firefighters and military men with combat experience to be gentle and show compassion to their patients. I keep saying, 'Your patient doesn't care how much you know, but wants to know how much you care.' It's a struggle to get the new guys to slow down and make personal contact with the patient. I have to tell them a dozen times to treat each one like a family member until they hand them off to someone else."

"Brian said that's my problem?"

"No, just the opposite. Brian's concerned you're getting emotionally involved."

"You're telling everyone else to show more compassion, and you're telling me to be indifferent?"

"Not indifferent," Sandy said. "But you're already way up on the sensitivity scale. In your case, you have to learn to keep some emotional distance. It's just a matter of time. You'll learn not to let things get to you."

"I hope so."

"Learn or burn. I say you'll learn."

"Thanks for the vote of confidence. I'm looking forward to becoming a regular hardass."

"So you had an incident last week and a girl's foot was severed and she bled out?"

"Sunday. Someone walked off with the foot."

"Brian says you're looking for it?"

Colt looked at Sandy but said nothing.

"Colt," she said, looking him straight in the eye.

"Some moron hit a light pole. It came down and took off her foot. There's a dozen sheriff's deputies, a dozen firefighters and medics and somehow somebody steals her foot. She was all alone and we were responsible for her. It's not right. It's just not right." Colt paused. Sandy was still looking at him. He realized Nick was probably listening to every word he said.

"Look Colt, stuff like this will eat you up if you let it. You don't really want to get involved in other people's lives. That's what families are for, and you're not family."

"She was all alone. You know, my mother ..."

"Your mother what?"

Colt sat back in his chair. "Never mind."

Sandy shifted around in her chair. "OK, enough of that. Another thing you have to learn, along with everyone else, is to manage the stress. The tones go off 10 times a day, five times a night and each time you get an adrenaline dump. You have to stay fit, exercise and relax on your days off. Try to keep things in balance. Have some fun. Are you doing that? Have you got a girlfriend?"

"Just broke up."

"Well, a girlfriend helps smooth out the highs and lows. I'm sure you won't be alone for long." Sandy stood up "You're doing fine, but you're such a serious guy. Loosen up a little." She gave Colt another strong handshake. "I'll see you once more next month, and that should be it. Stay safe and think about what I just told you."

When he walked out of Sandy's office, Nick gave him the thumb's up sign. He had heard every word.

# TWENTY-FIVE

Aᴛᴇʀ ʟᴇᴀᴠɪɴɢ Dᴇᴀɴ'ꜱ Hᴀʟʟ, A Li walked back across the campus to face the ogre. She had been in Dr. Murray's office in the Molecular Sciences building a few times and had dreaded each visit. His workplace was small but imposing. Reprints of articles he had authored in scientific journals filled an entire wall of shelves. Diplomas, honorary awards and pictures of the great doctor with important politicians and scientists covered the space behind his desk. Mementoes of his travels around the world rested on his desk. Plastic knick-knacks from pharmaceutical companies filled a small table. A Li always struggled to find her voice in these surroundings. She knocked and opened his door wide enough to stick her head inside.

"A Li, good morning." Dr. Murray was working on his laptop. "What can I do for you?"

She expected him to ask why she wasn't at work in the lab. "Good morning, Dr. Murray. I am here to tell you … I must return to … to China tomorrow afternoon. My father is … sick … he has … a heart attack. I must go home. I am sorry, my work … will … uh …" Her English was failing her. Every word seemed wrong. Could he even understand what she was trying to tell him?

He stopped his work, was silent for a moment, looked up at her and said, "Your father is ill? Then you should be with him. Family comes first, research comes second."

He spoke in an even pitch. In Chinese, tone and emphasis told everything. A Li couldn't determine whether he was sympathetic, disappointed or angry.

He glanced at the calendar on his desk. "Today is Wednesday, the 16th. If you are gone more than a week, we will …"

The old man was estimating how her absence would affect the timelines of the other research projects. A week was no time at all. Pa Lags might need her for a longer time. She might have to comfort him in his last days. It could be a month, it could be longer.

He pushed his glasses to the top of his head. "I know you must think I'm very harsh, but I do value what you are doing. I understand that your father needs you now, but just remember that I need you here in the laboratory as well. Your work is important. We're doing critical research and it's behind schedule. Everyone's input counts."

A Li waited for him to say something more, perhaps express a wish for Pa Lag's recovery.

"Send me a message as soon as you can and let me know when you're coming back." He held her gaze for a moment, then turned back to his laptop. "Have a safe trip."

A Li backed out of the office. That was it? That was all he had to say? Did he ever do anything but think about his precious research? She wished Dr. Murray a short reincarnation as an insect struggling in the beak of a hungry bird.

Outside the Molecular Sciences building, A Li tried again to call A Ma. Her hand trembled and her fingers tripped over the buttons on her cell phone. On the fourth try, she managed to punch in the correct string of numbers and after a few seconds of silence, her mother answered.

At home, it was almost 5 a.m. Friday. A Li listened to her mother's tiny, sad voice, so far away on the high plateau in Zhongdian. A Ma had been awake all night, worrying about Pa Lags and waiting for the hospital to open so she could go to his side.

"The news is not good," A Ma said. "Pa Lags suffered a massive heart attack at home. He fell down the stairs from the second floor."

A Ma was crying and A Li strained to hear what she was saying.

"His hip is shattered. They fear he has a serious concussion as well. He is semiconscious and they say he is in critical condition."

"Where is he?" A Li asked.

"He is here in Zhongdian. There is no intensive care unit, but the doctors want to stabilize him before they risk moving him to Lijiang. I don't trust them—they know nothing and they are stupid. I don't know what to do. I am so worried. A Li, please come home immediately. Pa Lags needs you. I need you. Who knows how long he will live?"

"I will be there soon. I am flying to Beijing tomorrow and I will be home the following day. I will pray for Pa Lags. A Mei will pray for him also." A Li began to cry. "A Ma, do you have money? A Ma ..." A Li heard the long-distance silence. "A Ma?" She tried to call again but was unsuccessful. She prayed she could reach Pa Lags' side before it was too late.

Honorable Pa Lags—I am coming. A Mei and A Li will soon be with you. Please wait for us. We love you.


A Li stood in the middle of the campus, trying to decide her priorities. She had 24 hours before her departure, and so much to do. It would take hours to organize her research data and prepare a detailed outline of the status of her work for the lab manager. She had to pack her belongings and talk to her host, Professor Chen. She also needed to leave messages for her other professors and her few friends.

Her thoughts returned to Tanay. Could she leave without seeing him again? There were things she had wanted to say to him, but now it no longer mattered. She decided it would be best if she simply left him a message of goodbye.

A Li sat down on a bench under a jacaranda tree. She felt powerless to help her father and her anger and frustration began to rise. Her status as a minority from the TAR was the cause of most of what was wrong in her life. She could not join the Communist Party and it loomed in front of her like a wall she could not surmount, blocking her path and making her life more difficult. She was jealous that she could not enjoy the status and economic benefits of a Party member. She was angry because her family had no money and knew none of the influence peddlers or power brokers who could help Pa Lags obtain the healthcare he deserved. There were places in China where Pa Lags would be comfortable and have a chance to survive, but everything in China was now a matter of money and connections. Some Chinese were beginning to enjoy the kind of privileges and well-being that Americans had enjoyed for years. There were modern hospitals in cities like Guangzhou and Beijing where the rich and well-connected received the best of care, but Pa Lags was relegated to the decrepit health facility in Zhongdian.

It was not right. It was not fair. Now aged 67, Pa Lags had suffered a hard life, living through the birth of modern China. He was 7 years old in 1950, when the People's Liberation Army launched the "peaceful liberation" of Tibet and established what became the Tibetan Autonomous Region of China. He endured the havoc of the Great Leap Forward in 1958. In 1966, Pa Lags' life was turned upside down again when the Cultural Revolution brought violence, investigations, denouncements and the creation of re-education camps where millions lost their lives. Tibetan monasteries were ransacked, universities were closed, intellectuals were sent to do manual labor, propaganda replaced learning and the chairman's favorite phrase was, "The more knowledge a person has, the more likely he is a counter revolutionary."

Pa Lags' name as a child was Bright Sun, because he loved learning. In 1967, after he had struggled to become a science teacher, the Red Guards dragged him from his classroom and beat him. They sent him away from his new wife to a remote farm where he spent the next six years studying Chairman Mao's books, reading his letters of self-criticism to the other workers, listening to military music and affirming his faith in communism and his love of the motherland. In addition to undergoing a political re-education, he suffered physically, spending hours each day planting rice in ankle-deep water. While he was away, his wife nearly starved to death and sold their few possessions to survive.

When Pa Lags returned home in 1973 at the age of 30, everyone said he looked 20 years older. His health was ruined and his body was frail. His hair was starting to thin and turn gray and he had deep lines in his face. Pa Lags and A Ma were impoverished and struggled to rebuild their lives. They tried to have a child for years and then gave up all hope. It seemed like a miracle in 1982 when A Ma discovered she was pregnant and that they would have a family after all.

After the birth, Pa Lags, once again a teacher, struggled to take care of his baby daughter A Li, and build a secure life for her. Above all, her parents wanted their beloved child to be happy and to grow up without the anxiety and tumult that had plagued their own lives. They pushed her to become a top student— a good education was the greatest gift they could provide for her. A Li tried to meet her parent's expectations, but life in China was hard for everyone and sometimes it was difficult to be optimistic. The pressures from her academic efforts added to the stress. She often retreated into a fantasy world where her imaginary sister was a great comfort.

Now, near the end of his sad and difficult life, Pa Lags lay in critical condition in a rural hospital with only basic medical care to sustain him. The family's health insurance would barely cover the cost of his heart attack. If he survived, the cost of surgery, medication and care for his other injuries would consume what little money they had managed to save. If he died, or was unable to continue his work as a teacher, they would be penniless. The only good news was that they had deposited a quantity of their rare Bombay Blood for just such an occasion.

Pa Lags had done everything he could to help A Li with her education. It was her duty to repay him by becoming a great success. Lately, she had begun to feel like a failure and wondered if she was on the right course. All she had accomplished so far was to burden her parents with the debt to the government for her college and graduate education. A Li made an important decision. In 24 hours, she would be on her way to Beijing. First, she had to spend a few extra hours in Dr. Murray's lab.

# TWENTY-SIX

THE LAWS OF PHYSICS had been repealed. Markus floated in space, looking up at angry red clouds above him. Sheets of bloody rain soaked him. He couldn't close his mouth. He choked, drowning in blood. He knew he was dreaming and kept trying to wake up, but could not. His terror exceeded the bounds of the dream.

It was 4:00 p.m. The Thursday afternoon sunlight crept in around the edges of the thick bedroom curtains. As soon as Markus moved, his back hurt. He felt dizzy when he stood up and staggered into the bathroom. His head spun. His mind was a windmill. His thoughts were a jigsaw puzzle. Markus had no idea how many painkillers he had taken in the last two days. He opened his medicine chest and discovered he had used all the Vicodin. He searched through the cabinet until he found a bottle of Percocet. The prescription had expired years ago, but he emptied three of the blue pills into his palm, tossed them into his mouth and washed them down with tap water. The water had a metallic taste he had never noticed. He looked at himself in the mirror. The haggard face looking back belonged to an old man. His red eyes were sunken deep into his skull. His face looked terrible—it was puffy and lined and his pure white skin had red blotches. His white hair lay limp and damp on his head.

Markus returned to the bedroom and opened the closet. He dressed and slipped on running shoes without socks. When he pulled out his duffel bag, a pair of Audra's jeans, torn at the knees, came with it. Markus thought of her beautiful long legs for a moment and tossed the denims aside. Looking through the bag, he checked the bottle of ether, the washcloth and the sterile syringes with needles capped in blue plastic. In the back of the closet, he kept a box of four dozen blood collection tubes. He wrapped his favorite Alien Sex

Fiend sweatshirt around the box to protect the glass inside and placed it in his duffel.

Markus' mind drifted. He stood staring into the closet when he heard a knock on the front door. His body began to shake. No one ever knocked on his door.

GRISHA!

This time it had to be Grisha. Markus imagined Grisha swinging a machete, cutting off his arms while he was still alive, and then pulling out a pocketknife to cut off his most important parts. Before he could move, Markus heard another knock, more insistent this time, followed by pounding on the thin wood door. Markus saw parts of his body, locked in an ice chest in the back of a truck, headed for the LAX cargo terminal. On his hands and knees, he crept into the living room, edged up to a window and pulled the curtain aside just far enough to see who was on the porch. He was shocked to see Jack Wyatt, the manager of the Alley Kat.

Markus opened the front door partway. The late afternoon sun shined directly into his eyes. "Hey Jack. What're you doing here?"

"Dude, I haven't seen you at the club for quite a while."

"I've been busy at night. I work at CU."

"CU? You're the man."

"What's up?"

"I'm looking for Audra."

"Audra?"

"Audra."

"Haven't seen her in weeks."

"I thought she lived here with you."

"Nope. She moved out a couple weeks after we got together. She missing?"

"We haven't seen her at the club for two nights. A lot of customers are asking about her."

I'll bet they are, Markus thought. "Sorry, I can't help you. Haven't seen her."

"You're sure she's not here?"

"I said no."

"Can I come in?"

"Look Jack, I'm in the middle of something. Tell Audra I said hello. I'll come by the club sometime." Markus tried to close the door.

Jack put his shoe on the threshold, blocking the door. "I don't believe you, douche bag. Where's Audra? She said she was living here."

"I don't know." Markus leaned against the door and managed to push Jack's shoe back. As he did, he saw a pickup truck parked on the street. From the second floor, with his weak eyes and the glare from the afternoon sun, it was hard to see clearly, but it looked like there were two men inside. Markus closed the door and waited for Jack Wyatt to knock again.

After a moment of silence, he peeked out the window. Jack was gone, but the truck remained. Someone opened the passenger side and got out. The guy was huge, bigger than Grisha. He looked like King Kong. He bent to speak to the driver through the side window of the pickup and then looked up toward Markus' apartment. Markus couldn't see who was inside the truck, but it had to be Grisha. Two of the biggest Russians on the face of the earth were outside waiting to cut him up.

Markus went into the bedroom and sat down on the bed. He winced at the pain in his back. He wanted to curl up in the dark under the bed. He wanted to put his head in his mother's lap and let her protect him. He wanted a lightning bolt to strike the pickup, fry the Russians, and send them to a dirt nap. He tried to concentrate and think clearly through the effects of the Percocet. Vicodin created a buzz. Percocet created a haze. Why were the fucking Russians outside now? Today was Thursday, the day he planned to collect the China Doll's blood. Or was it?

Markus held his head in his hands. He had to bail, somehow ditch the Russians and hang out at the Nano Research Center until he could find the China Doll. Once he had her precious liquid, all of it, every drop, he could head directly to San Diego. He would get $4,000 from Drakkar—even if it was more than his share. They were bound by ancient blood ties and his friend would give it to him. Once Markus had the money, no one could hurt him. Grisha wouldn't touch him. Markus would hold up the cash like a silver cross in front of a vampire.

It seemed like a plan.

Markus opened his closet. The least he could do was leave a surprise for the Russians. He didn't like guns—the idea of a shotgun booby trap in his closet had always seemed too dangerous. A true Goth might have rigged a swinging halberd, a large ax-like blade that could take off an intruder's head, but there was no room in the shallow space for anything like that. Markus had devised his own protective device. He reached into the closet, armed it and carefully closed the door.

Markus dragged his duffel from the bedroom into the bathroom and opened the medicine chest. He swallowed two more Percocet and placed the remainder, along with aspirin, drops for his eyes and sunscreen in the pack. He went into the kitchen, stuffed his car keys and cell phone into his pocket and put on his hat and extra pair of dark glasses.

He opened the freezer, took the foot out and looked at it for a moment. There was no way, no possible way, that he would leave it behind. He used three additional plastic bags, one inside another, to create layers of insulated air space. He then filled a larger plastic bag with packages of frozen peas and what little ice he had and placed the foot, in its multiple containers, inside. He shoved the entire package down to one end of his duffel.

He went back to the front door and cracked it open. King Kong was back in the pickup talking to the driver. Time to go!

Markus shut down his computer and went into the bedroom. He pulled aside the heavy curtains and noticed a spider web with several dead flies in a fold. Daylight streamed into the room for the first time in months. Markus clenched his teeth against the pain in his lower back as he struggled to lift the window. Wood scraped against wood as he worked it up partway, wide enough to escape. Marcus dropped his pack out onto the roof of the carport and squeezed through. At the edge of the carport roof, he looked down at the alley. It was a 10- or 12-foot drop to the cement and he knew what it would do to him. He lay down on the roof, dangled the duffel over the side and let it fall, praying the glass tubes wouldn't shatter. Markus slid over the edge, feet first, and did his best to hang on and lower himself as far as possible before letting go.

Although he had expected the surge of pain when he hit the ground, it was so excruciating that he lay gasping, unable to move. It was the fear of King Kong coming around the corner that finally caused him to stand up and drag himself and the bag to his car. When he lifted his arm to the door handle, a jolt of pain shot from his back up to his shoulder and down through his leg. Markus shoved the duffel onto the passenger seat and crawled behind the wheel.

The ache in his lower back was a white light before his eyes. He clenched the steering wheel, backed out into the alley, turned right on Albion and accelerated away from the two Russians parked in the pickup in front of his apartment.

# TWENTY-SEVEN

"So how was the meeting with Sandy this morning?" Moose asked while they sat in Colt's pickup in front of Markus' apartment on Albion.

"No problems with my skills," Colt said. "Brian gave me a good report, but he said I'm too sensitive."

"What does that mean?"

"I'm supposed to stay detached from the people I rescue."

"That's it?"

"If I don't fuck up, five more shifts and my internship's over."

"Attaboy." Moose reached over to grind his knuckles against the side of Colt's head.

Colt pushed his hand away. "Hey, there goes the albino. That's him in the PT Cruiser." He pointed toward the alley.

"Great."

"I'm going in."

"Going in? I thought this was a surveillance mission. That doesn't include breaking and entering."

"I'm going in to get the foot. Her parents are gonna claim her body pretty quick. I want to get the foot to the Coroner before that happens."

"No way." Moose reached across and shook him. "Earth to Colt."

"What?"

"Brother, have you lost your mind? What're you thinking?"

"I'm getting the foot back."

"How do you know this guy even has the foot? I think you're imagining this."

"I'm not imagining anything. He has it."

"You're risking your career. Do you understand that? Half the firefighters in the country would kill to work for L.A. County Fire Department. Not only that, but you're a paramedic. I could never get through that program. The best I could do is three years in the Marines. You've got it made and now you're breaking into someone's apartment? That's a crime. If you get caught, you're shit out of luck and you lose everything. For what?"

Colt sat quiet for a moment, looking straight out the windshield. "He was there with her. After the accident he deserted her and took her foot."

"Where are you getting all this crap?"

"Believe me, I know. He's the kind of scumbag who would do something like that."

"Colt, she's a cadaver now. You did your best and she didn't make it and that's all there is to it. Over and out."

"The girl was abandoned. She was all alone. No one was with her. I showed up and held her hand, and then I let her down."

"Stop. This is such bullshit. Forget about whatever her name is. Get a new girlfriend and get laid. Don't risk everything you've got for someone you don't even know." Moose leaned over, turned the key in the ignition and started the engine. "C'mon, let's go."

"What if I just go in and make sure he has it? If he does, I can tell the Sheriff's Department. They can retrieve it."

"What're you going to tell them? You broke into someone's house?"

"Someone has to do something." Colt turned off the pickup's engine

Moose exploded. "Let her parents find the damned foot. It's their daughter. Look, man, I'm not getting involved in this. I have a fiancé and I'm not gonna screw up my life for this. You know I've got your back in any emergency. If you were in any kind of trouble, I would risk my life to save you." He opened his door. "But you're on your own on this one."

"She had a name, Moose. It's Darci. She's a person, a real person and she should be buried with her foot."

"She *was* a person."

"This is no big deal, Moose. The albino's not home. All I have to do is go in and find it. It has to be in his freezer. After that, I'm done."

"Whatever," Moose said, "but I'm out of here."

"Hang on for a minute. You're a Marine, you can handle this. Just wait in the truck. If he comes back, honk the horn. You won't be involved."

Moose got out of the pickup and leaned in the window. "See you later, bro. I'll just walk back to your place to get my car."

Colt exhaled. "Catch up with you later."

Moose started to walk away, turned and came back to the truck. "You're still coming for Thanksgiving, right?"

"Right."

"No date?"

"Not unless lightning strikes in the next two weeks."

"Don't do anything stupid, Stupid." Moose walked off down the middle of the street.

As soon as Moose disappeared, Colt got out of his truck and stood on the sidewalk. The neighborhood was quiet; there was no traffic and no one outside walking around. He climbed the front stairs to Unit 2, knocked on the door and waited. He knocked again and still there was no response. He tried the door handle, but it was locked. He hit the door with his shoulder and it popped open. So much for breaking and entering.

"Hello?" Colt called. "Hello?" He entered a dark cave decorated with black lace and red candles. Thick curtains covered the windows in a small living-dining room. Wrought iron porch chairs circled a table covered with computer equipment. Colt had never seen so much electronic gear—and the tangle of wires, cables, plugs, surge protectors, and power outlets violated every known fire code. He understood the darkness—Mark Draper was an albino—but the place was eerie.

Colt went into the kitchen, turned on a light and stood in front of the refrigerator, thinking of Darci Tierney. He opened the door to the freezer and saw several packages of frozen peas but no foot. He pushed them aside and found two plastic bags, which he pulled out and laid on the counter. The first bag contained what looked like the head of a brown squirrel, teeth bared, eye sockets empty, the fur around the neck frozen and stiff like small quills on a porcupine. Colt picked up the second bag, expecting to see the foot. Instead, he found a left hand, fingers bent, frozen in the shape of a claw. Colt dropped it on the counter and stepped back, trying to make sense of what he saw before him. What kind of lunatic was the albino? Colt had seen heads of trophy animals shot in Wyoming and some people carried a jackrabbit's foot on a key ring, but this was sick. In front of him was proof certain that the albino was some kind of body-parts freak, just the kind of person who would pick up Darci's foot. The problem was, the foot wasn't in the freezer. Colt looked again. Aside from the frozen peas, all he found was a package of turkey burgers, crusted inside with ice. He put everything back, checked the refrigerator and saw nothing but a dozen containers of yogurt. He leaned against the kitchen counter, trying to decide what to do next. Plan B was to go to the albino's office in the Nano Research Center.

Colt wandered into the bedroom. It was another weird room with a few pieces of heavy wood furniture. A box of Real Feel colored condoms had been dumped out on the floor. The dresser drawers were open and a girl's clothes were lying on the floor. The black drapes were pulled aside, admitting a shaft of late afternoon light and exposing a partially opened window that led onto the top of the carport in the alley. A sheet pulled from the bed lay crumpled on the floor. Colt nudged it with his foot and saw stains on one corner. He bent down to look more closely. The dark brown spots looked like dried blood.

Colt started out of the bedroom, stopped, went back and opened the closet door.

AAAARRRRRRRRRRRRRRRRRRRRRRRRRR.

The siren mounted on the inside door jamb erupted into a wail. Although Colt had learned to distinguish the sirens of various emergency vehicles, this blast of sound, inches from his ear, was like nothing he had ever heard. He slammed the closet door and staggered back, hands over his ears. The siren stopped, but the noise was replaced by a roar that continued into the center of his brain. Colt closed his eyes and tried to blot out the pain in his head. "Fuck," he shouted, kicked at the bloody sheet on his way out of the bedroom and went for the front door.

Colt sat in his pickup for half an hour. The roaring sound began to subside, but was replaced by a high-pitched ringing-buzzing sound that was just as bad. He wondered if his eardrums had been broken.

Driving home, Colt didn't see Moose anywhere on the street. When he reached Chautauqua, Moose's car was gone and Colt felt relieved. He had a terrible headache, could barely hear and was in no mood for a discussion about breaking and entering or about the severed foot he didn't find in the albino's apartment. The little bastard albino must have taken it with him when he ran off.

# TWENTY-EIGHT

WHILE COLT DROVE HOME with his ears ringing, Markus entered one of the university parking structures in his PT Cruiser. It was early evening and the structure was half-empty. He parked head-in against a cement wall, on the lowest level.

The pain in his tailbone was unrelenting. He looked through the windshield at the gray wall moving before his eyes. He tried to focus his eyes and align his thumb with a large crack in the concrete. His thumb shook and the crack moved without moving. Markus felt dizzy. He was nauseated and thought he might throw up. He leaned forward and rested his head against the steering wheel to take the pressure off his spine.

The cement wall disappeared.

For two hours, the hard plastic rim of the steering wheel pressed against Markus' forehead while he slept. When he opened his eyes, he saw the winged Chrysler logo in the center of his steering wheel. He sat up, rolled down his window and inhaled the stale garage air. He rubbed his forehead and felt the impression from the steering wheel.

Too much Percocet!

Markus didn't know how much was too much, but it didn't matter. He needed something to get him through the evening. He took two more blue tablets from his shirt pocket, collected his saliva on his tongue and swallowed them. Once he paid off Alexei, there would be plenty of time to see a doctor to find out what was wrong with his back, stop the meds and get a life overhaul. First, he had some important business in a third-floor laboratory.

Markus rolled up his window and got out of his car. He took the duffel from the rear seat. As he wobbled over to the parking structure elevator, he regretted the extra weight of the foot, the bags of frozen peas and the ice.

Markus exited the parking structure at ground level and slowly made his way to the Nano Center where he sat down on a bench near the entrance. He tried to concentrate on the evening's mission. He opened his bag and checked everything. The blood collection tubes and the bottle of ether were intact; nothing had broken when he dropped the pack into the alley. Syringes, tubing, washcloth—everything he needed was there.

A tall man wearing a white lab jacket approached the entrance to the building and Markus recognized him as one of the nano scientists. Markus grabbed his duffel and followed the man inside without registering his presence with his own ID. Once in the lobby, he ignored the security guard office and concentrated on walking a slow, straight line to the elevator. He didn't stop to look at the brass plaque with the quote from Francis Crick.

On LL2, the silent elevator doors opened and Markus walked, sliding one hand along the wall to steady himself. Once inside his office, he slumped down at the desk nearest to the door.

# TWENTY-NINE

WHILE MARKUS DOZED in his office, Colt woke up in his apartment. The first thing he heard was the ringing in his ears. The next thing he heard was more ringing in his ears. He rolled out of bed and went into his bathroom. He turned on the cold spigot, splashed water on his face and watched the whirlpool of water as it ran off into the drain. Fully awake, he dried off and ran his hands through his hair. The high-pitched sound was worse in his right ear, but it seemed slightly softer than it had been when he fell asleep.

Colt sat down on his bed and considered what to do next. His father's favorite phrase, "In for a dime, in for a dollar," summed it up. Confronting the albino at the Nano Research Center wasn't any worse than breaking into his apartment. Colt still had to retrieve the foot and deliver it to the coroner in time to be buried or cremated with Darci's body. After the siren blast, the little prick albino also deserved a punch in the head—let him listen to his own ears ring for a while.

Colt unfolded the 12" x 18" map of the CU tunnel complex and studied the layout. He located the underground entrance to the Nano Research Center and found the nearest street-level access to the tunnels, next to the Student Housing Administration building on University Drive. He drew a line along his underground route with a bright yellow marking pen. At the first tunnel intersection after student housing, a left turn would take him under the Birney Computing Center. He would then continue straight until he came to a second intersection under Structural Engineering Sciences. At that point, he would make a right and follow the passageway under Earth and Space Sciences, directly to the sub basement entrance to the Nano Research Center.

There was no scale of distance on the map, but it didn't seem like a difficult trip—just the first left and the second right. It appeared to be no more than a 15-minute walk, a piece of cake. Even if the structures weren't marked in the tunnel, the numbers of the above-ground standpipes and hydrants were indicated. Colt circled the numbers nearest the buildings along his route in case he became lost. He was confident he could navigate the maze. He had an excellent sense of direction above ground. Colt had never been lost on the Indian reservations or on the vast energy fields in northern Wyoming and as a child, he could find his way home alone on horseback from distant places in the Powder River Basin, navigating in dust storms or snow, in daylight or moonlight.

Colt dressed. Tonight he wanted to look like a student, not a firefighter. He put on jeans and a University of Wyoming sweatshirt. He decided to wear his cowboy boots and his father's rodeo belt. When he wiped away the dust with a dirty T-shirt, the boots gleamed with a deep brown gloss from years of polish and wear. In Wyoming, he had lived in these boots, but when he pulled them on, they were stiff and pinched his feet, as though he had never worn them.


On his way to the CU campus, Colt thought about how surprised the albino would be. He was determined not to take any lip from the freak. It would be a quick discussion, like an in-and-out with plenty of air left in his SCBA. All Colt wanted to do was get the foot and look directly into the albino's eyes while he explained why he abandoned Darci at the Surfrider. Colt decided not to hurt him unless he asked for it.

When he arrived on campus, the map of the tunnels didn't help Colt find the Student Housing Administration building. Once again, the size of the university overwhelmed him. He was nowhere near the hospital or anything else that looked familiar and the darkness didn't help. He discovered that University Drive was a main street, which circled around half the campus. It took 30 minutes driving back and forth before Colt arrived at his destination.

He parked on the street, left his paramedic card on the dashboard and crossed to the cement blockhouse that housed the access door to the stairs. Colt held the map in one hand and shined his halogen flashlight on it. He turned the paper 90 degrees, lined it up with the street and got his bearings.

The blockhouse door was unlocked and well oiled. Colt entered and descended two flights of metal stairs, his boots pinching his toes at every step. At the bottom of the stairwell, a sign indicated STUDENT HOUSING ADMINISTRATION. So far, so good. He knew exactly where he was and it appeared that each building would be marked on the tunnel wall. He looked up to confirm that the stairs had taken him in a half circle. He turned his map again and aligned it with the turn of the stairs. Colt looked into the tunnel, an 8-foot-wide half circle lined with cement. He expected fluorescent lights, but saw only bare overhead bulbs encased in metal cages secured to the ceiling. They were spaced far apart and the light was dim. The air was cool, damp and stale. Colt set off toward his first landmark, standpipe 460, which was half the distance to the left turn under the Computing Center. In the silence, the ringing in his ears seemed much louder.

Walking through the tunnel, Colt thought of a tragic search and rescue incident years ago in Sheridan. Two teenagers, boys he knew at school, decided to explore one of the abandoned gold mines in the hills outside of town. The old mines were extremely dangerous—the ceilings and walls were weak and the passages contained toxic gas and snakes. When the boys failed to return later in the day, near hysteria ensued in Sheridan. Fire and Rescue was dispatched with a full complement of equipment—breathing apparatus, protective gear, special lights, ropes and radios. They spent 24 hours searching, but were unable to find the teenagers. A special team flew in from Denver and the following day they recovered one boy's body at the bottom of a shaft. The second body was never found. For weeks, people in the area talked about how stupid it was to enter the old tunnels. After that tragedy, the entrances were sealed. Colt had never forgotten the incident.

Walking underground without reference points, Colt found it hard to judge how far he had gone, but he thought he had covered quite a distance. The semicircular shape of the passage had become a rectangle. The smooth cement walls abruptly ceased, replaced by large stones held in place with mortar. Moisture seeped through the walls in places, running down over the rough rock and collecting in small puddles. Colt continued. It seemed that the tunnel was on a slight incline. He passed a point where a passageway connected from the right. Colt stopped to refer to the map. He hadn't yet made the left-hand turn under the Birney Computing Center and the map showed no intersecting passage before that point on his route. In this underground world of half light, time as well as distance seemed to melt away. Colt checked his watch. Could he have been underground for half an hour? He walked farther and approached a set of stairs and a sign for PARKING-WEST.

PARKING-WEST? Colt studied the map. Where was he? Did he pass the Computing Center? Where was the spot where he was supposed to make a right turn under Earth and Space Sciences? He looked for PARKING-WEST on the map but couldn't find it. There were several rectangles and squares marked PARKING, but without further identification. He started up the first set of stairs and saw a fire-hose connection labeled Standpipe 472. He studied the map again and swore. He was on the wrong side of Student Housing. Colt Lewis, excellent navigator of the high plains of North Central Wyoming, had somehow managed to set off through the tunnel in the wrong direction.

# THIRTY

MARKUS AWOKE. This time he had slept in his office with his head resting on a computer keyboard. He looked at his watch. It was almost midnight and time to get moving. He stood up, grabbed the duffel bag and hurried out of the office. As he staggered down the hall, he felt terrible. On the first landing of the fire stairs, he put his duffel down and waited until the dizziness subsided. He pulled out the plastic bag with the foot and removed the sacks of frozen peas and ice cubes. The extra weight was killing his back; he could stop on the way to San Diego and buy ice later. He dropped the pea packages and cubes down the center of the stairwell and heard them strike the cement at the bottom.

Markus took several deep breaths, pulled the brim of his hat farther down to eliminate the reflected light overhead and started up another flight. When he finished the five-flight climb, every part of his lower body hurt, his back muscles were locked in spasms and his head was in a fog. He lay down on his stomach, reached up and pushed open the third-floor fire door. He wiggled through the doorway, pulling his duffel along behind him. Markus knew the angles of the security cameras were off. The retard guards were probably asleep, but even if they were watching, the video screen would only show the top half of the door.

He inched his way into the hall and the fire door swung shut behind him without a sound. Markus lay in the hallway and listened. In a building designed for silence, he could hear his labored breathing and pounding heart. He felt drowsy and wanted to go to sleep right there on the floor, but the thought of Alexei and Grisha kept him going. He stood up and dragged his duffel bag through the hall until he stood outside the door marked:

### 301
### PETER T. MURRAY, MD PhD
### LABORATORY

He removed the bottle of ether and the dark green washcloth. The last face it touched was Audra's—the next face would be that of the China Doll. Markus took a deep breath. He pulled out his master key, unlocked the door and crept inside the laboratory.

Only the lights on the far side were on. He saw the China Doll, just as he had imagined, with her back to him, bent over a laptop. No one else was in the lab and the setup was perfect. In a few seconds, she would be lying unconscious on the floor. He would insert the IV, drain her blood and it would be over. It was a piece of cake, a done deal. Alexei and Grisha would be off his back. At last, things were going his way. He could soon resume a normal life.

He opened the small bottle and emptied the remaining ether onto the cloth. In a haze, he inched his way along a row of workbenches and approached the China Doll from behind. His running shoes made no sound, but he never considered that the smell of the ether would precede him. He was still 10 feet behind her when she sat up, raised her head slightly and sniffed the air like a wolf sensing the scent of blood.

A Li had just finished downloading as much information as she could get from Dr. Murray's research database. It was 12:30 p.m. and she was anxious to finish and get out of the lab. She had copied into her laptop most of the data on successful reprogramming of stem cells into blood cells by the insertion of new DNA; she wasn't interested in the experiments that had failed. She now possessed the information from dozens of successful mouse and human cell reprogramming efforts, the genetic instructions and molecular models, as well as the details on the particular viruses used to introduce the new DNA into the stem cells. What remained was to copy the summary of recent work on the errant cells that caused cancer in mice, which Hisao described in the last lab meeting. The information was still locked in his laptop. She sat with it in front of her on his workbench. Her attempt to access his files was taking too long.

While A Li tried to circumvent the security codes on Hisao's computer, a strange smell wafted through the lab.

Sister? A Mei?

Markus watched her as she turned, saw him, stood up and screamed. He couldn't understand what she shouted, but he saw the fear in her eyes. He tried to spring forward, but his head was spinning and his body moved in slow motion. The China Doll backed away from him, bumping into what looked like a gray Humpty Dumpty squatting on the floor. He reached out toward her and tried to press the ether-soaked cloth against her face.

What creature from hell was this with red eyes? What infernal smell came with it? Every evil spirit from her childhood rose up in A Li's memory.

Sister, are you doing this?

By the time her scream bounced off the insulated walls of the laboratory, she came to her senses and realized it was the strange man dressed in black. She had never been close enough to see his red eyes. He was a *Bai Hua Bing*, an albino, and he was coming after her with a cloth saturated with ether.

A Li backed away. While her mind tried to make sense of what he was doing, her instincts called for defensive action. The first thing she thought of was the metal thermos bottles containing liquid nitrogen, kept on the counter next to the tank. She grasped one by the handle and swung it at the albino's head. He was too far away to strike, but the top of the container flew off, releasing the contents in a spray of vapor and sub-zero liquid. A small amount of the N2 touched her lower leg and she felt a sting on her flesh.

She swung one of the thermos jugs. Markus saw a cloud of white mist and liquid coming at him. Was he hallucinating, or was it boiling water? When it hit his right ankle, ran through the mesh on his running shoe and touched his bare foot, he knew it was something else. Markus looked down and it was only nanoseconds before a liter of liquid nitrogen, at a temperature of -270 degrees Celsius, boiled on contact with his skin.

The pain receptors in his body reordered their priorities. The lower back pain signals were old news. The first-order neurons in Markus' skin sent out a new alarm to his central nervous system. The signal reported tissue trauma from a heat burn. By the time the second-order neurons sent additional acute pain information up through his spine, the signal had changed to one of extreme cold—his skin was freezing. The impulses reported that a cryogenic burn had occurred. Once his brain became conscious of the injury, it shifted into damage control. A message went back down his spinal cord to increase respiration and to block the pain sensation with the release of endorphins. Markus' heart rate and blood pressure, depressed from the painkillers, shot through the roof.

The pain suppression lasted 10 seconds.

Markus screamed as he had never done before. The goddamn Chinese bitch had burned him! He wanted to choke her. He wanted to kill the she-devil slut and drain every drop of her blood. He reached out for her neck, but managed only to lurch sideways and crash into a workbench. The impact knocked down a shelf of glass chemistry utensils. Beakers, flasks, jars, burettes, test tubes and dishes rained down on him, smashed on the floor and sent a shower of glass fragments everywhere. He stood amid the sea of broken glass, looked at her and screamed, "You bitch. I'll bleed you dry!"

The Bai Hua Bing screamed when the liquid nitrogen touched his skin. He staggered toward her, his red eyes full of fire, calling her a bitch. A Li backed away toward her workbench. She looked for another weapon and saw a pipette syringe on the ledge above Tetsu's bench. She reached up, grabbed it in her fist and in the process, tipped the entire shelf. Another shower of glass crashed onto the floor. With her thumb resting on the plunger, she stepped toward the albino and swung her arm in a horizontal arc that ended at the base of his throat. She jammed the business end of the syringe into his *Yan Hou*, the soft indentation at the base of his throat. On impact, her thumb came down on the plunger.

When the pipette needle penetrated his skin, Markus felt a stinging sensation in his throat and began to cough. By the time he pulled the syringe away, the sodium azide, $NaN_3$, a poisonous substance with acute toxicity, was already in his bloodstream. Markus tried to hold on to the top of the bench, but he fell to the floor, gasping for breath. While the $NaN_3$ combined with his hemoglobin, blocking oxygen transport in his blood, Markus' lungs worked furiously to provide his body with air. He groaned. He heaved. He sucked air and it rattled through his throat. He felt steel bands around his chest, drawing tighter and tighter. The pain was excruciating. His lungs burned. Bubbles of saliva formed on his lips. He wheezed, gasped and clawed at the steel leg of the lab bench while a few drops of blood oozed from the puncture wound in his throat. He looked up at the China Doll—not even her rare blood could have saved him at that moment. When his own blood, devoid of oxygen, failed him, Markus suffocated on the floor of the lab, lying on a carpet of glass fragments.

A Li stood frozen in the aisle of the lab. The Bai Hua Bing lay motionless—she was certain he was dead. The empty pipette syringe lay on the floor, inches from his body. A dark green washcloth was also on the floor, covered with shards of broken glass. Most of the ether had evaporated, but she could still smell traces of its distinctive odor in the air. After the chaos, the screaming, the shattering glass and the sound of the albino gasping for air, only the hum of the refrigerators remained.

A Li steadied herself against a bench and tried to comprehend what had just happened. Whenever there was an emergency, the Americans yelled, "Call 911." A Li thought about it. She could not call 911. The police would come, there would be an investigation and she would be detained.

She heard someone open the door to the lab. A chill came over her.

A Mei?

# THIRTY-ONE

COLT DESCENDED the PARKING – WEST stairs into the tunnel and started to retrace his path. He had now wasted 45 minutes and began to walk faster. His boots pinched at every step and he wondered how he had ever worn them. As he proceeded, the tunnel still seemed to slope upward. Shouldn't it be going downhill if he were going back in the opposite direction? He thought the incline might be an illusion; it was hard to maintain a sense of up and down walking through the long tunnel. The rough-hewn stone on the walls was familiar, but after a few minutes, Colt noticed water pipes and conduit running along the ceiling. He was certain he had not seen that before. He passed an unmarked Y-shaped intersection. He looked both ways. Fluorescent light illuminated the passage to the left. The other passage was dark. Had he passed this way before? Ahead, the tunnel once again had a smooth cement lining, but a large metal air duct emerged at ground level and ran along the ceiling. Nothing looked familiar. He looked at his watch—now it was close to midnight. He had somehow spent another 30 minutes underground. Colt realized he was losing track of time as well as distance.

He walked for a few minutes and began to feel claustrophobic. The tunnel now sloped downward and the farther he went, the steeper the descent. He stopped, looked behind him, looked ahead and knew he was lost. The walls around him were marked with drawings and words. Colt saw a crucifix, coffins, daggers, and wolves and humans with bared teeth. Next to the images were words written in red: *BLOOD, BLUT, KREW, LE SANG, KHUNA, DUGO, LA SANGRE* and *KROVI.* Beneath the drawings and words, on the cement floor of the tunnel, he saw a large red stain. It could have been red paint, but Colt thought it looked like dried blood. He bent down and placed his flashlight on the ground, the beam shining on the discoloration. He looked at the spot more closely and scraped at it with his fingernail, bringing up bits of red flakes. He was certain it was blood.

While he rubbed the substance between his fingertips, a sound of voices broke the silence. He listened, straining to hear above the ringing in his ears. He thought he heard the screams of a woman and then a man. The sound bounced off the walls and reverberated through the tunnel. Colt had no idea from which direction it came and saw no one. While he listened, a blinding burst of light came from the sloping passage ahead of him. The bulb in the ceiling shattered. For several seconds, white spheres drifted across his eyeballs. When the spheres disappeared, Colt was in total darkness. He had encountered the pitch black of the flash chamber after the doors were closed for fire training, but this was thicker and deeper than anything he had ever experienced.

His flashlight was gone. He knelt down again and patted the floor, trying to find it in the darkness. He wished for his fire helmet with the high-power headlamp. Colt crawled around. He was having difficulty breathing. He was smothering, running out of oxygen. He couldn't see the walls of the tunnel, but felt they were closing in on him and would soon squeeze the air from his body. He was caught in an underground maze and would never see daylight again. He would turn to dust and not even the men at 88s would ever find him.

Firefighter paramedic Colt Lewis felt nauseated; his heart was pounding and a cold sweat washed over his body. He had survived many dangerous situations, but now he was having a panic attack, knew it, and could do nothing to prevent it. He slumped to the floor of the tunnel and tried to take deep breaths. He remembered a moment from his childhood when he had accidentally locked himself in a closet at the ranch. After a few minutes, he was screaming and pounding on the door. He couldn't have been more than 4 or 5, and his mother hadn't left him yet. She rescued him from the terror of the crushing darkness. In the dark tunnel under the CU campus, he knew there was no one to rescue him.

As his respiration slowed, he began to recover and saw his flashlight, just inches away. Had it been on all this time? He took hold of it, stood up and watched the beam flutter in his shaking hand as he stumbled to a juncture in the tunnel where the overhead light glowed. The passageway was level.

The walls were free of graffiti and the only image was an arrow that pointed down a passage marked STADIUM. He followed it to the exit, climbed three flights of stairs, pushed open a metal door and emerged into the dry California night.

# THIRTY-TWO

"A Li? Hello?"

She heard his voice.

Tanay came past the row of refrigerators and dropped an olive-colored duffel bag on the floor. He looked at the body lying amid the fragments of glass. "What happened? Who is this?"

A Li's mouth hung open. She was trembling and hyperventilating, unable to say anything.

"A Li?" Tanay shook her gently. "A Li!"

"He attacked me." She began to cry. "He wanted my blood. I ... I think I have killed him." Her voice was almost a whisper.

Tanay pulled her to his chest. A Li felt his strong arms around her. He held her until she calmed down and her breathing slowed.

"Did he hurt you?" he asked, releasing her.

She shook her head.

Tanay looked at the man with the white hair and pale skin lying on the floor. "An albino? I've never seen one." He pushed some glass away with his shoe, bent down, looked at the body and checked for a pulse. "He is dead." Tanay stood up. "What happened?" he asked again.

"He came into the lab with ether. He wanted to drug me." A Li picked up the green washcloth. She shook off the splinters of glass and held it to her nose. "Yes, ether." She held it out to Tanay. "He was shouting about taking my blood. There was something wrong. He came after me, but he could barely walk. I stabbed him in the throat with a pipette syringe."

"A pipette syringe?"

She nodded. "From Tetsu's bench. Filled with sodium azide."

"Someone attacked you and you were able to do this? Tanay looked into her eyes for a moment and she met his gaze.

A Mei, do not be angry ... A Mei, stop it!

Tanay pointed to the duffel. "This was outside in the hall." He unzipped it and dumped the contents onto the floor. A few articles of clothing, a white Nano Center ID card and a plastic bag containing a gray object fell from the duffel. A glass bottle containing a small amount of ether and several blood collection tubes tumbled out and shattered, adding to the pile of broken glass. The smell of the anesthetic drifted through the lab.

"I have killed him." A Li began to hyperventilate once more. "I will be arrested. *Rogs pa byed, rogs pa byed, sdug cag las. skur srung ba 'phebs—*"

"Stop." Tanay dropped the duffel, put his hands on her shoulders and shook her, harder this time. "Speak English! What are you saying? Do you know him?" Tanay bent down and picked up the ID card that had fallen from the duffel bag. "Mark Draper. He works here in the building, on LL2." He picked up the object encased in several plastic bags. A layer of moisture had collected between each layer of plastic, making it hard to identify. "It looks like a—"

"Help me Tanay. If the police ..." A Li gulped air and struggled to gain control of herself. She touched his arm.

"Have you called 911?"

"No. We can't."

Tanay placed the ID card and the object in the plastic bags on Tetsu's bench and turned to A Li. "We've got to call security," he said. "And the police. You can tell them what happened. He attacked you. You defended yourself."

"No! I have to go home to my father tomorrow. If the police come, they will arrest me and keep me here." A Li was terrified of the police. In China an investigation could drag on for months, possibly even years, and the police could be brutal. At home, she would be imprisoned and rot in a cell for months or years before she was even charged with an offense. It might be the same in the United States and she would never see her father alive. "I must go to my father. He needs me. He may die. We can't call the police."

Tanay stared again at the albino on the floor. "His skin is so white, almost transparent. I've never seen such skin."

"I have seen the Bai Hua Bing in the Center." She looked again at the syringes and broken tubes on the floor. "Somehow, he must have found out about my blood." A Li turned to Tanay. "Why are you here?" she asked.

"I got your message. I wanted to see you again before you left. I wanted to ..." He looked past her to Hisao's workbench. The LOG IN page was displayed on the screen of Hisao's laptop. Next to it, A Li's laptop screen showed DNA data. "What are you doing?"

She stared at him.

"Are you taking research data?"

She gave a tiny nod.

"A Li, you can't do this. It's wrong. If you take this information, you can't ever come back." He went to Hisao's laptop, turned it off and closed it. "Are you coming back?"

A Li still didn't speak.

Tanay continued, "You have to return. You have to finish your research; you're part of the team. I want you to come back. Please. I want you to come back."

A Li was overwhelmed. Everything was happening at once. Her entire life was in chaos and conflicting emotions swept through her. She was overcome with fear and anxiety—she had just killed someone and the police might arrest her. She was worried about her Pa Lags, who might be at death's door. She had just copied into her laptop some of California University's most valuable stem cell data, which she planned to take back to China. Now, to complicate everything, Tanay had just told her he wanted her to come back.

Tanay held her for a moment. "A Li," he whispered, "I'll help you." He released her and smoothed her hair with his hand. "Did you come in the front entrance? Did the guards see you?"

"Yes."

"I came through the tunnel." He sat down on the stool at A Li's bench. "Let me think."

She touched him on the shoulder. "I don't know what to do. I have to go home. I must leave tomorrow."

Tanay exhaled. "In India, people are killed and their bodies just disappear. There are over a billion people. Life counts for nothing. No one cares. There are no records and no one tells the police anything." Tanay looked around the lab.

"It is the same in some parts of China," A Li said, "but this is the United

States. When people disappear here, the police investigate."

Tanay wasn't listening. "Old. Young. Bodies rot on the streets. Bodies are cremated. Ashes are thrown in the Ganges River. What is one life out of billions? Especially a bad life? Who cares?"

"Cre-may-ted?" A Li said. "Cre-may-shun?" Her English was improving. She knew what the words meant. She pulled her wallet out of her backpack and found the card the big man in the blue suit had given her at the Flower Mart. "Gates of Heaven Mortuary," she read aloud. "We specialize in memorial services and cre-may-shuns." She handed it to Tanay.

Tanay took the card and looked at the address. "Burbank?" He paced up and down the aisle of the lab, pulverizing the glass on the floor with his large shoes. "OK, I have an idea, I can take care of this. You'll see your father. Start cleaning up." He went to the far end of the lab and entered a storage room.

A moment later, A Li heard a rumble and Tanay returned, rolling one of the square green metal disposal containers. Each side was marked with a black skull and crossbones in a red circle. BIOHAZARD, TOXIC WASTE, DISPOSE PROPERLY appeared in large white letters. Tanay opened the cover, lifted the limp body off the floor and dropped it into the empty bin. It made a soft thud. Tanay looked at it for a moment and then closed the lid.

"Don't forget the duffel bag," A Li said. She stuffed the clothing, the tubing and the needles back inside the bag, lifted the lid and dropped it in on top of the body.

Tanay started to push the bin down the aisle of the lab. He stopped, came back to A Li, pulled her close and kissed her lightly on the lips. It was tentative, but it was a kiss. He looked at her. "Please, come back."

Without thinking, A Li pulled Tanay's face to hers, kissed him again and pressed against his body. With a single kiss, he had breached the wall within her that held back a lifetime of secret longing and desires.

A Mei, please, do not be angry.

Tanay held her tight for a moment, sighed, turned away and began to roll the container down the aisle again. He paused, took one of the long white lab jackets off a hook on the wall, and put it on. "What time is your flight?" he asked.

"Three-thirty in the afternoon."

"I'll call you. Clean up and go home. Get some sleep. Don't worry about this. It didn't happen." Tanay pushed the biohazard container toward the door.

"Thank you for helping me, Tanay." With all that was going on, with all that was at stake, A Li still felt the touch of his lips and the feeling of Tanay's body against hers.

He turned back again to look at her. "Please don't take that data."

A Li didn't respond. She just stood and watched him push the biohazard container out through the front door of the lab. She glanced at the debris on the floor, then went to the janitor's closet and took a broom, a bucket and a dustpan back to her bench. When she began to sweep up the glass, she noticed the ID card and the plastic bag that Tanay had forgotten on Tetsu's bench. A Li looked more closely at the object encased in plastic bags. Could it be what she thought it was?

She opened the bags, one after the other. The first three contained moisture. When she opened the fourth bag and looked inside, she saw a frozen human foot. She shuddered. Where had it come from? Why would the Bai Hua Bing be carrying a foot around in a plastic bag? Had he stolen it from one of the anatomy labs? She looked at it more closely. It belonged to a female. Above the ankle, the bones of the leg were exposed and broken; the foot had been cut off, but not by a surgeon. It was starting to defrost.

She sealed the foot back inside the plastic bags, wrapped it in paper towels and deposited it in the container marked BIOHAZARD – GENETICALLY ALTERED MATERIAL. A Li then carefully swept the broken glass from the floor and dumped it in the trash. The Bai Hua Bing's ID card was still on Tetsu's desk. She slipped it into her pocket.

It was close to midnight. A Li was emotionally and physically exhausted. So much had happened in the last 24 hours. She wanted to go home and sleep. She picked up her backpack, turned off the lights and left the lab.

Be quiet A Mei.

As she walked down the quiet hall to the elevator, she didn't want to think about her sister—she wanted to concentrate on Tanay.

# THIRTY-THREE

"**S**CREW IT," Colt muttered. In a rage, he balled up the map and threw it into a 6-foot high stand of oleander bushes by the tunnel exit. He sat down on a low stone wall that ran along the sidewalk. His heart was still pounding. He couldn't believe it. After all the frightening and demanding things he had done as a firefighter, how could he have a panic attack walking through a goddamned tunnel? Colt rubbed his eyes. His ears were ringing, he had a headache and it was time to go home.

A low rumbling sound broke the late night silence on the campus. Colt heard it above the other noise in his ears. As it seemed to come closer, he looked around and wondered if he was hallucinating, or whether his hearing had just taken a turn for the worse. Colt turned on his flashlight. A man wearing a white lab coat pushing a rectangular trash container emerged from the darkness. Colt shined his halogen beam at him and the man held out his hand to shield his eyes from the light. He had dark hair, dark eyes, and a dark, golden-brown skin. Colt dropped the beam to the trash bin. It was a green container marked with a black skull and crossbones in a red circle. The words BIOHAZARD, TOXIC WASTE, DISPOSE PROPERLY appeared in large white letters.

"Hey," Colt said, and turned off his flashlight.

"Good evening, sir."

Colt wanted to ask why he was pushing a toxic waste container across the campus at midnight. He settled for, "Warm night, isn't it?"

"Yes sir." The man stopped and the deep-pitched rumble of the bin's wheels on the rough cement ceased.

"What's in the container? Radioactive waste?"

"No sir."

"Dead body?"

"Dead body, sir?"

Colt laughed. Just kidding. "Are you a doctor?"

"A lab technician, sir. Yes, a lab technician ..." He looked up at the dark sky. "... I work for Stericycle. We collect medical waste."

"At midnight?"

"At midnight, sir. When everything is closed down. We bring the containers out to the trucks."

"What do you do with all that stuff?"

"Incinerate it, sir."

Colt wondered where the burning was done and what kind of crap was escaping into the air, but it was really none of his business. "Where you from?" he asked.

"India, sir."

"India? I know some Indians, but they're Cheyenne."

"I'm not an American Indian." He leaned against the container and began again to push it down the street. "Good night, sir."

"Don't spill anything," Colt said and watched this member of the United Nations of California University push the green waste bin down the street. "Hey!" Colt shouted.

The lab technician stopped and turned. "Sir?"

"Where's the Nano Center?"

"The Nano Research Center?"

"Yeah, the Research Center."

The technician walked back toward Colt. "Why do you ask?"

"Just tell me where it is."

The technician pointed in the direction from which he had just come. "It's that way. See that?" He pointed.

Colt looked and saw a dark multistory building with a few lights glowing inside.

"It's right behind that building," the technician said.

"Great, thanks. And if I want to go via the tunnel, how would I do that?"

The lab technician came even closer to Colt and regarded him again. "It's quite simple. You enter here." He pointed at the spot where Colt had emerged moments before. "You walk about 25 meters. It's the only direction you can go.

When you come to an intersection in the tunnel, you turn right. You can't miss it. The entrance to the Center is marked with a sign. Why don't you just walk down the street?"

"I like the tunnels," Colt replied. "Thanks for the directions." Colt turned back toward the tunnel entrance.

# THIRTY-FOUR

INSIDE THE ELEVATOR, A Li realized her mistake and put out her hand in front of the electronic eye to stop the doors from closing. When they reopened, she ran back down the hall to Dr. Murray's laboratory. Still fearful of a police investigation, she wondered what would happen if someone found the foot in the disposal container. She couldn't take the chance. They would know which lab it came from and it might lead to her involvement. The foot had to be retrieved and left where it belonged—in the Bai Hua Bing's office on the lower level. Let the police find it there. It was his problem.

Back in the lab, she went to the biohazard bin and opened the lid. The foot, encased in its plastic bags, lay on top of a mound of dissected mice and white paper towels covered with spots of blood. A Li fished the foot out, stopped at a sink, sprayed the plastic with disinfectant and washed her hands. When she returned to the elevator, she punched the button for LL2.

In the basement, when the doors opened again and she walked down the silent hall to office number 3, she realized she had gone past it every Monday night for weeks on her way from the lab to the tunnel. A Li swiped the albino's white ID card and opened the door. The small windowless office was dark, illuminated only by the glow of several computer screens. The space felt claustrophobic and she wondered how anyone could work in such a confined space.

A Li placed the foot on the first desk, took a tissue from her backpack and rubbed the plastic bag. She had seen one of the crime investigation programs on American television where a criminal wiped his fingerprints off a doorknob with a handkerchief. Through the plastic, the foot felt like it was beginning to defrost.

She slumped down on the desk chair. A Li was exhausted, more tired than she had ever been in her entire life and wondered if she even had the strength to get home.

What is it, sister? I don't want to talk to you right now.

A Li willed herself to stand up.

Are you jealous because Tanay has chosen me instead of you?

She picked up her backpack and walked out into the hall. She wiped the handle and walked to the elevator without closing the door.

I can get through this without you. STOP IT!

She hoped she would never see the office on LL2/3 again.

I can grow beyond you, sister. I can become strong myself.

# THIRTY-FIVE

COLT MADE THE UNDERGROUND TRIP from the stadium to the Nano Research Center in three minutes. As he walked through the tunnel, he wondered whether the albino would be locked inside his office and how he would get him to open the door. He couldn't just shove the door and break the lock, like he had done at the apartment.

He opened the steel fire door and entered the lower level hallway of the Center. It didn't take long to find office LL2/3—the door was wide open. Colt stuck his head inside the dark space and called out, "Hello?" There was no answer. He listened carefully, heard nothing and turned on the lights. It was hard to imagine anyone working in the tiny, confined, windowless spot. The office contained a half-dozen desks with computer equipment, a chair and a wastebasket for each.

On the top of the first desk, Colt saw a plastic bag and knew immediately what was inside. He opened four bags, one inside another, and the last one contained Darci Tierney's right foot. Colt felt a moment of sadness when he looked at it. Once again, he remembered the image of her lying on the blacktop, bleeding out. It was Thursday night, only five days had passed, yet Colt felt like he had been searching for her foot for weeks. He touched it with his finger. It was still hard and cold, but it was beginning to defrost. He had to get it into a freezer or under an ice pack immediately.

Colt looked around again and wondered if the albino had gone out to pee. He went down to the far end of the hall to check the men's room. When he opened the door, the automatic lights went on. It appeared deserted. Colt got down on his hands and knees and looked under the stalls, just to make sure the albino wasn't playing games. He checked the ladies' room as well, and walked back to the empty office. The albino could be anywhere in the building and Colt wasn't about to search for him. He had what he came for—the foot. He felt vindicated. The weird little creep had picked it up at the Surfrider. Colt was certain he would have a chance to confront the albino again, some other time; it didn't have to be tonight. He could always visit him, now that he knew where he lived. Right now, the most important thing to do was get out of the building and put some ice over Darci's foot.

When Colt again emerged from the tunnel at the STADIUM exit, he realized he should have also asked the Indian for directions back to the Student Housing building. He had no idea how to get to his truck and figured it was probably on the other side of the campus, half a mile away.

He shined his light on the thicket of oleander where he had thrown the crumpled map. After several minutes, he saw where it had caught near the top of some branches. He waded into the thicket, began shaking the bush and finally dislodged it. When he smoothed out the map and located the stadium, he saw that Student Housing was a few streets away, no more than a 10-minute walk.

On Santa Monica Boulevard, he stopped at a convenience store, purchased an insulated Igloo container and filled it with a sack of ice. Back in his truck, Colt placed the Igloo on his passenger seat and shoved the bag containing Darci's foot down into the ice. Colt felt a small sense of fulfillment. During a single week, he had lost two patients, but at least he had rescued a foot. His mission, his crusade, was just about over. In the morning, he could stop by to pay his respects to Darci's parents and then drop the foot off with Nate Petruno. Colt decided if Darci's parents said anything about the missing foot, he would be vague about where it was found.

Colt was certain he would have a good night's sleep with no nightmares, if only the ringing in his ears would stop.

# THIRTY-SIX

"*Shto?*" Alexei asked, watching Grisha come up the wooden steps of the porch after opening the heavy iron gates at the front of the mortuary. Alexei repeated, "What?"

It had been a very tough night. Alexei had spent several hours in the basement dismembering a woman's body and packing the parts in two large ice chests. He thought he should have used more ice, but he had none left and the van was waiting. Too tired to clean up afterward, he left a small pile of leftovers—skin, hair, and bones—lying on the white tile floor.

Upstairs, he stood in the shower and welcomed the hot, almost scalding, cascade of water running over his body. He saw the accusing eyes of the dead woman looking up at him from the embalming table. He felt bits of her flesh, thrown off the teeth of the small chainsaw, clinging to his skin. He thought droplets of her blood had seeped through his pores, finding their way into his own bloodstream. Alexei had scrubbed his body until it was raw. When he emerged from the shower, he still felt dirty. In his bedroom, Alexei couldn't go to sleep. He poured a glass of vodka, then another and another. Soon he was looking at the bottom of the bottle.

This morning, Alexei's eyes were bloodshot, his head was pounding and his tongue felt like it was covered with the hair of a Russian mink.

"What?" Alexei asked Grisha for the third time.

"The albino."

"What about?"

"He won't be paying us."

"Then you go for visit and mayhem."

"No," Grisha said, "It's not necessary. His body was outside by the front gate."

# THIRTY-SEVEN

AFTER RETURNING FROM THE LAB, A Li lay on her bed propped against the headboard, watching the blue digital numbers on her clock mark the progression of time. Her body cried out for sleep, but her brain would not allow it—too much had happened.

The events in the lab played in her mind like a movie. The attack by the Bai Hua Bing ran in slow motion. She watched in exquisite detail and relived her panic. As he came at her, she swung the thermos and then stabbed him. He collapsed on the floor of the lab, red foam on his lips, and died at her feet. The slow-motion terror dissolved and a love scene played through a soft-focus lens as Tanay entered the lab. In the darkness of her bedroom, A Li again felt his first gentle kiss on her lips and their second, more exciting kiss. Soon, her sister joined in, expressing her anger. A Li wanted to stop the movie, savor Tanay's kisses and skip everything else, but it was a loop and the images started over again with the Bai Hua Bing coming after her.

A Li reached for her laptop on the nightstand. She switched it on and the glow of the screen cast a small circle of silver light around her. She looked at the titles of the dozens of scientific files she had copied and thought about what this information would be worth in China.

You can't do this. It's wrong, and you can't come back if you do.

She turned off the computer and returned it to her nightstand.

The first hint of light appeared in her window at 5:45 a.m., three hours after she crawled into bed. Before she finally dozed off, she thought about Pa Lags and A Ma, and how lonely she had always been as a child. A Li wondered how her life might have been different if she had a real sister.

It was only 11:00 a.m. A Li's flight to Beijing didn't depart for another four and a half hours, but Professor Chen wanted to take her to the airport early. A Li felt like she had sand in her eyes. She struggled to stay awake in the car while the professor conducted a one-sided conversation. Usually a man of few words, her host had a special message for her before her departure. Driving down the freeway to LAX, he spoke with enthusiasm about China and America, about how both countries were great, expressing his pride as a Chinese living in America. A full professor in the Chemical Engineering Department, he told A Li she should be proud to be attending CU, a center of research and learning with a worldwide reputation. He told her she should be especially grateful to be working with Dr. Murray, the famous genetic researcher.

Just as she was about to doze off, Professor Chen asked, "When do you expect to return?"

A Li yawned. "It depends on Pa Lags' health."

"I'm sure Dr. Murray wants you back as soon as possible."

"Yes, I'm sure."

A call on Professor Chen's cell phone interrupted the conversation. He listened for a moment, and then said, "I'll tell her." He put his phone in his shirt pocket, slowed the car and moved into the right-hand exit lane. "That was my wife. You've forgotten your laptop, it's in still in your bedroom." He looked at his watch. "We have time to go back."

"No, it's OK. I don't need it," A Li said. "I can do without it until I return."

Professor Chen moved into the left lane and sped up.

When they stopped at the International Departures terminal, Professor Chen took A Li's small suitcase out of the trunk and helped her shoulder her backpack. "I hope for the best for your father," he said and clasped her hand. "Let me know when you are returning. I will try to pick you up."

"Thank you," A Li said. "You and your wife have been very kind. I'll be back as soon as I can. I have so much to do."

She didn't watch Professor Chen drive away. She was anxious to check in and call Tanay.

Sister, I have found someone. Do not be angry. We will share him.

# THIRTY-EIGHT

O̶N FRIDAY MORNING, Colt drove across Victory Boulevard in Van Nuys and turned onto Tobias, a small street in a poor neighborhood. The Igloo container with Darci's foot and a fresh sack of ice rested on his passenger seat. Colt planned to drop it off at the coroner's office after his visit with her parents. He parked across the street from number 895 and looked at the Tierney home. It was not what he had imagined. It was the furthest thing from a serene glass-walled house overlooking the Pacific Ocean from the bluffs of Malibu. The small windows were covered by wrought iron grills to keep out intruders. Except for a blue tarp covering a corner of the roof, the house was indistinguishable from all the other dilapidated little dwellings on the block, every one of which needed paint. Several auto body parts—bumpers, side panels, hoods, doors, and an assortment of hubcaps—lay in a jumble near the driveway of 895 Tobias Street.

Colt reviewed what he wanted to say to the Tierney family. At the end of paramedic school, Sandy had spoken to the class about compassion and sensitivity in dealing with bereaved families and friends. First, she had emphasized, do not get involved with an accident victim or friends and family. Then she went on to say that if it was unavoidable, be a good listener and just express sympathy and support. Phrases such as "I understand," and "I know," were to be avoided because at the time of loss, the bereaved don't believe that anyone can comprehend their grief. That, Sandy emphasized, should be the absolute limit of a paramedic's personal involvement in any rescue incident.

Colt thought Darci's mother and father would be grateful to know that someone was with their daughter and had tried to help her. That would certainly comfort them. If they asked, he would lie and tell them she felt no pain at the end of her life. He would also play dumb about the fact that she was pregnant. He was certain Darci's parents would want to see her body whole before they buried or cremated her; it would help with their sense of closure. Closure was a term Colt had never heard of until he attended paramedic school.

While he sat in his pickup, an unshaven man came out of the house wearing grease stained pants and a Jake's Towing Service T-shirt that barely covered a beer belly. When he bent down to pick up the morning newspaper, he glanced at Colt's truck. Could this be Darci's father? Colt watched him turn and walk back into the house.

When the front door closed, Colt jumped out of his pickup and headed up the walk.

The doorbell didn't work. Colt pressed hard with his finger, but the button was stuck. He opened a screen door with the mesh torn away from the frame at the bottom and knocked on the unpainted wood. He tried to look through the small glass window, but it was covered with a film of dirt. Colt waited a moment and knocked again. His knuckles were about to hit the door a third time when the man wearing the Jake's T-shirt opened it.

"Mr. Tierney?"

"Yeah?" The man stared at him with clouded brown eyes.

Colt had the brief thought that Darci's ocean blue eyes must have come from her mother. "Uh, my name is Colt Lewis. I'm a paramedic with the L.A. County Fire Department."

The man said nothing. He continued to stare and opened his mouth slightly. Colt saw teeth that matched the color of his eyes. Ranch hands in Wyoming had teeth that color, stained from a lifetime of chewing tobacco tucked into their cheeks.

"I responded to … your daughter … uh … the accident … she had in Malibu. Can I come in?"

The man stepped aside. "Sure, but I gotta go to work in a few minutes."

Colt walked directly into a small, messy living room, which connected to a kitchen and dining area. Newspapers were strewn on the floor around a battered brown couch. Two unmatched chairs faced the sofa. In between, a coffee table was covered with half-full ashtrays, empty beer cans, coffee cups and a plate of unfinished food. A dark green rug looked as though it had never been vacuumed. An ancient black and white television set, the sound on mute, showed a local news broadcast. The house smelled of cigarette smoke and other stale odors that Colt couldn't identify.

"Who's at the door?" A beefy woman with pasty skin came into the room, leaving a bedroom door open behind her.

Colt saw rumpled sheets and a blanket lying on the floor. The woman wore a robe over a yellowed nightgown. Several ugly blue varicose veins protruded from her legs. Her ankles were thick and puffy. Colt immediately thought edema.

"Who're you?" she asked. She held a cigarette and exhaled a cloud of smoke.

"He's from the fire department. Went to Darci's accident," the man said.

"Oh?" She walked over to the couch, put her cigarette in an ashtray and sat down.

Colt watched her push aside some dishes with a bare foot and rest both legs on the table. Her robe and nightgown hiked up and he got a view of two fat inner thighs he didn't care to see. He dropped his eyes. "I just wanted to tell you that we did everything we could to save your daughter." Colt was dumfounded. He refused to believe this was Darci's home. Could these people be Darci's biological parents? They were pigs. Maybe she wasn't as pretty as he remembered. Didn't she have blond hair? The mother had 3-inch gray roots in hair dyed several shades of blond and her eyes were a washed out, dirty gray color. Colt remembered Darci's vivid blue eyes, the color of the T-shirt. Could they have really been the same polluted color as her mother's eyes? Was his memory so unreliable? He turned and searched for a photo. All he saw on the living room walls were cheap pictures of cats and children with black eyes, painted on purple velvet.

"Do you know God?" the man asked Colt.

"God? Uh ... I guess so," Colt replied.

"Darci didn't know God. We took her to church for years, but she wouldn't pray. She was Satan's child." The man folded his hands across his stomach as though he were rejecting the memory of his daughter. He looked at his wife and showed his brown teeth again.

"We ain't seen her in almost two years," the woman said.

"The girl was evil. Even God couldn't save her," the man said.

"Sir, I—"

"She took off to work in a restaurant," the woman said, taking her legs off the table and sitting forward on the couch. "That's the last we ever heard from her. Sometimes she thought people was after her."

"Well, her friends wasn't after her," the man interjected. "Because she didn't have none. Pissed 'em all off. And the fuckin' doctors—"

"Our daughter was sick," the woman said. She looked at her husband and then at Colt. "No one could help her. They said she was bipolar and they gave her all kinds of pills. It cost us a fortune, but nothing worked for long." She paused to take a deep drag on her cigarette, blowing the smoke out in a cloud from her nose and mouth.

Everything Colt had planned to say disappeared from his mind. Were they talking about the same girl he tried to save at the Surfrider?

"She was probably hooking," the man said. "She was too lazy for work, but she had enough energy to run around day and night." He scratched his neck. "She was Satan's child," he repeated.

This wasn't the existence Colt had imagined for Darci. He didn't want to hear any more about it. If this were her reality, he preferred to remember her life the way he had invented it.

"What exactly do you want, Mr. … uh?"

"Lewis." Colt thought for a moment. "Well, I just wanted to tell you how sorry I am, how sorry the whole department is, about what happened to your … uh … Darci." He stopped and waited for an expression of grief or sorrow. They had only learned of her death yesterday from the Coroner. Were they in denial? The mother put her head down and rubbed her eyes. Colt thought she might be about to cry.

"Yeah, thanks," the man said. "We didn't want to see her again, did we Dora?" He looked to the woman for agreement, but she looked away. "It wouldn't fix nothing," he continued. "Just bring back a lifetime of bad memories and all the screamin' and fightin'. There wasn't anything good to remember. We told the coroner to cremate her and he's gone and done it. Saved us the expense. There wouldn't be anyone to say prayers or come to a funeral anyway. Just us, and we already prayed all we could." He disappeared into the kitchen.

There was a silence while the woman smoked and looked at Colt. Her eyes were damp. She said, "I just wish—"

The man returned from the kitchen with a cup of coffee and said, "Dora, when you gonna get the dishwasher fixed?

"I said I would, didn't I?"

"What's wrong with today?"

The woman didn't answer, but gave Colt a sad look. She stood up, went to the television set and turned on the volume. News of a shooting in South Central Los Angeles boomed through the living room.

"Anything else?" the man asked Colt.

Colt shook his head. "That's it, I guess."

"I always liked firemen," the man said, and stuck out his hand. "Good people. I've towed cars from lots of accidents and made money doing it. Real good people."

Colt shook hands with the man and went to the door. He turned to say goodbye to the woman, but she had already disappeared, leaving a cloud of cigarette smoke hanging in the living room.

Colt closed the front door and walked out to his truck. When he looked at his watch, it was 8:30 a.m. He had been in the Tierney house for less than fifteen minutes. So much for the life of the girl who lived in the glass-walled house on the bluffs of Malibu. Colt tried to visualize her growing up on Tobias Street in Van Nuys with a pile of used auto parts at the end of her driveway. He tried to visualize her friends. He tried to see her with the German shepherd in the picture. Colt drew a complete blank. He couldn't imagine a single thing about Darci's real life except her unhappiness. His dream of the girl with the ocean blue eyes had been blown away by the Santa Ana winds.

Colt sat in his pickup and listened to the ringing in his ears. The rest of Darci's body was already reduced to ashes—her parents and the coroner didn't waste any time—but her foot was still in the Igloo container on his passenger seat. What was he supposed to do with it now? Colt pulled out his cell phone, turned up the volume so he could hear over the ringing in his ears and called Nate Petruno. Petruno didn't answer and Colt left a voicemail message: "Nate, it's Colt Lewis. Darci's father told me she's already been cremated. What happened to the blue T-shirt? If you still have it, hold on to it. I'm on my way to your office to pick it up. Please call me as soon as you get this message. Thanks."

# THIRTY-NINE

IT WAS SUNDAY MORNING, September 19, a week since the 88s responded to the accident at the Surfrider. The hot dry Santa Ana winds continued to blow in from the desert and Southern California baked in triple digit temperatures. Colt's one-day shift was due to end at 8:00 a.m., but the tones dropped an hour earlier for a call about a rattlesnake in a backyard. The engine and squad responded.

Moose was the first off the engine and ran into the yard with a fire ax. Moments later, when Colt arrived in the squad, Moose was about to cut off the snake's head.

Colt looked at the snake and shouted, "No, leave it. It's a king snake, they eat rattlers."

Moose paused.

The homeowner was hysterical. "I don't care what it is, get rid of it," she screamed. "Get it out of my yard."

Colt pushed in front of Moose. "Yes ma'am, we'll take care of it," he said, bending down to pick up the snake. It twisted around in his hands as he carried it out of the yard and across the street to a vacant lot. He walked a few feet into the weeds and dropped it.

When the crew returned to the station, the men from C Shift were eating breakfast in the kitchen, waiting to go on duty. Captain Ames briefed them on the calls and problems of the last 24 hours. Moose and Brian joined them for coffee before heading home. Colt left the station immediately.

At his apartment, Colt took off his uniform and put on his jeans, a T-shirt and his father's rodeo belt. He left his cowboy boots in the corner and wore his fire boots. He picked up the Igloo and Darci's blue T-shirt and went out to his truck.

On his way to the freeway, he stopped at a convenience store and bought a large bag of ice, which he dumped into the cooler. As Colt drove east, the air conditioner in his old truck struggled. In Sheridan, the "warm spot" of Wyoming, it would be around 55 degrees and the beginning of the winter snow would be only weeks away. Traveling across the floor of the San Gabriel Valley, Colt watched the gauge indicating the outside temperature rise from a relatively cool 89 degrees at the coast to 103 degrees. By the time he exited the 210 Freeway and wound his way along Foothill Road through the communities clustered at the base of the San Gabriel Mountains, the temperature stood at 106 and waves of heat shimmered on the soft blacktop. Colt thought a cold beer would taste incredible, even at this hour of the morning, but kept driving. He checked the Igloo to make sure the ice wasn't melting.

In La Canada/Flintridge he turned up the steep Angeles Crest Highway, a 40-mile road running through canyons and along mountain ridges in the Angeles National Forest. A year earlier an arson fire started near the ranger station became an angry 165,000-acre blaze feeding on the thick brush and trees. Colt missed all the action in what became the largest fire in Los Angeles County's history. While he was in the middle of paramedic training, 3,000 firefighters spent seven weeks fighting what became known as the Station Fire. Two firefighters trying to escape the flames died when their truck plunged off a cliff. A thick cloud of smoke visible on weather satellite images from space, billowed four miles into the sky. Ash and soot rained down on the city of Los Angeles. After containment, mop-up went on for several weeks, with helicopter crews using thermal imaging to find smoldering spots deep in ravines and canyons while inmate fire crews worked to clear the burnt debris from wilderness fire roads, trails and campgrounds. Caltrans closed the entire Angeles Crest for months while it replaced guardrails and parts of the road destroyed by the fire. Soon after the road reopened, the winter rains came and tons of mud and debris flowed down the bare mountainsides, eroding the slopes and destroying more of the highway. A year later, reconstruction was still underway.

A mile up the Angeles Crest, Colt came to a line of white and orange barricades and a large sign that said:

## FIRE DAMAGED AREA
## PUBLIC ACCESS PROHIBITED

A lone Highway Patrol cruiser was parked on the shoulder, partially sheltered by the shade of a tree. When Colt stopped and got out of his truck, the heat pressed down upon him. He had never thought of temperature in terms of weight. The freezing cold in Wyoming weighed nothing, but this unbearable heat in California had a heaviness he had never felt before. He walked over to the cruiser. The engine was running and when the officer lowered his window a couple of inches, Colt felt a tiny blast of cold air.

"Afternoon," Colt said, and held up his fire department badge.

"A scorcher, isn't it?" the officer said. "Where you headed?"

"Red Box."

"Be careful up there, there's a lot of construction equipment parked on the side of the highway."

"Thanks."

The officer raised his window.

The view on the ascent was bleak. What was once a spectacular panorama of the rugged San Gabriel Mountains was now a moonscape. As Colt climbed the steep, two-lane road, he looked out at a black carpet where skeletons of pine and conifer, oak, birch and cottonwood covered the hillsides. Colt tracked the direction of the fire where it had raced uphill in different places. Many trees, charred on the side where the fire approached, still had a few brown, dried clusters of pine needles or leaves on the sheltered side. Scorched pinecones hung from the high branches of the tallest trees. The massive blowtorch had seared away the manzanita, chapparal and sagebrush from the ground, leaving stumps, scorched earth and blackened rock. As he climbed higher, Colt saw a few patches of green where the wall of fire jumped over patches of trees and brush tucked into deep folds in the landscape.

Colt continued up to Red Box, a 5,000-foot high junction of three highways named after the large wood container where firefighting tools were stored at the turn of the 20th century. Just after he moved to Los Angeles, Colt had visited Red Box and remembered the place clearly. The San Gabriel Mountains weren't as rugged as the Rockies or the Tetons, but he thought the spot was beautiful. It was the perfect place for a burial.

He parked in the deserted turnout near a line of picnic tables and got out of his truck. The early afternoon temperature had dropped from triple digits at the base of the highway to 88 degrees. Colt walked across the road, listened to the crunch of the gravel under his fire boots and looked down into the canyon at the drainage of the San Gabriel River. The winter rains had caused rock and mudslides to cascade hundreds of feet down the hillsides, ripping out what vegetation was left and scouring the earth. Above, the sky was pale blue, fading into a white mist at the horizon. Several jet contrails crisscrossed and two hawks made lazy circles in the canyon, riding the air currents, barely moving their wings. The wind made the only sound. For a moment, Colt was a child again, sitting on his horse Flash, looking up at a cloudless sky above the mountains in the Powder River Basin.

The California heat and low humidity was insidious. Colt walked back to his truck and drank a bottle of water. He took the Igloo container and the blue T-shirt, went around to the bed of his truck and grabbed a Pulaski—the half ax, half hoe that wildland firefighters use. He started up the steep hillside beyond the picnic tables, using the Pulaski for balance. As he climbed, he saw how the earth had begun to repair the damage from the fire and prepare for a cycle of regeneration. The sunlight, once filtered out by heavy brush, overhanging branches and an accumulation of leaves, now touched the ground and nurtured new growth. Pine cones, awaiting a fire, had burst open and spread their seeds. Green shoots of plants and bushes were already pushing up through the burnt ground. In five years, a lush carpet of green would cover the mountainside again. In 10 years, there would be no trace of the Station Fire. In 25 years, the mountainside would be overgrown once again and it would be time for another big fire.

Colt climbed until he came to a small level spot on the side of the mountain. A 3-inch conifer sapling grew off to one side. With a few swings of the Pulaski, he dug out a hole deep and wide enough to contain a girl's foot and a blue T-shirt. He opened the ice chest, took out the plastic bag and emptied the half-melted slush on the ground. Colt unzipped the bag and looked inside at the still frozen foot with the painted red nails for the last time. He placed the open bag in the hole. On top of the bag, he placed the neatly folded blue T-shirt.

"Rest in peace, Ma. Rest in peace, Darci." Colt was certain they both would have liked this spot. "Wherever you are now, I hope you're happy and at peace."

He looked out at the hazy horizon and listened to the silence in the mountains. Everyone had a different explanation for what happened at death. If nothing else, when the bones of her foot turned to dust, Darci would become part of the earth. Some part of her would reside under the spot where the 3-inch conifer would grow into a majestic tree. Somewhere, some trace of his mother resided in the earth as well. He would choose to believe that it was in this place.

He pushed dirt into the hole with the Pulaski. After he filled it, Colt picked up pieces of shale and pressed them into the spot with the heel of his boot. He piled more dirt on top of the shale and rolled a large rock in place on top of everything. He looked around once more, then picked up his Pulaski and the Igloo and descended to his truck. In the turnout, he tossed the cooler into a trash barrel. When the head of the Pulaski hit the bed of his truck, the impact of metal on metal broke the silence. Colt got behind the wheel and rolled up the window. He felt a weak gust of cool air from his air conditioner when he started the engine.

Driving back across the San Gabriel Valley, Colt pulled to the side of the road and got out of his truck. Using Moose's military binoculars, he focused on the Angeles Crest. He wasn't certain, but he thought he could see Red Box, the place where he'd just buried Darci and said goodbye to his mother.

Colt got back in his truck and headed home. He needed a new love interest; he also needed a new pickup truck. One would be easier to acquire than the other. He tallied his paramedic scorecard. So far, he was 0 for 2. After losing Darci and Tyler, it was time to even the score. He had to rescue someone. He had to resuscitate someone on the verge of death. He was a trained fire paramedic. It was his job to save people, not lose them. He knew there would be days when he would see victims in great pain and near death. Some would die before his eyes despite his efforts, but he had a long career ahead of him and he knew he would save people. Maybe once in his life he would even do something miraculous.

# EPILOGUE

*LOS ANGELES TIMES*
*October 14, 2010*

"Cadaver Ring Arrested"

*BURBANK, Calif.:* Law enforcement officials in California announced the arrest of several Russian immigrants in connection with a nationwide funeral home network that secretly dismembered more than 700 cadavers destined for cremation. The group sold organs, corneas, arteries, bones, and even skin to surgeons, medical laboratories and research labs. Funeral directors received up to $50,000 for the parts of a body, depending on their condition and use. The leader of the ring, Aleksei Korsakov, is still being sought.

The Los Angeles County Sheriff's Department reported that the investigation had been ongoing for almost two years with the help of the FBI. The first break in the case came from a hospital identification tag on an arm found in a medical laboratory, allowing authorities to identify an individual whose death certificate certified that the person was cremated.

\*\*\*

"Paramedic Saves Child"

*MALIBU, Calif.:* A Los Angeles County Fire paramedic was credited with saving the life of a child found at the bottom of a swimming pool in Malibu.

Six-year-old Sabrina Sanger was unresponsive when her father pulled her from the shallow end of the family pool. He didn't know how long she had been in the water.

Paramedics arrived and began CPR, but after several minutes, they failed to revive her. "We were hysterical," Sabrina's mother said. "We were certain we had lost her." Colt Lewis, a newly trained paramedic with the County Fire Department, refused to give up. He continued to administer CPR to Sabrina long after the maximum time to revitalize a drowning victim. Lewis was eventually able to revive the child and she began to breathe unassisted. Sabrina was transported by helicopter to the California University Hospital where she was reported to be in satisfactory condition.

Paramedic Lewis said he is thankful whenever he has the opportunity to save someone's life. "It's a great feeling," he added.

# ACKNOWLEDGMENTS

My sincere thanks to so many people who helped me write this book.

To the C Shift at Los Angeles County Fire Station 88 in Malibu—Captain Lenny, Gene, Fletcher, Tim and Phil—thank you for the time each of you spent telling me stories, instructing me on paramedic procedures and welcoming me for morning coffee. Stay safe, brothers! Also thank you to Captain Brian Savage and his men at Culver City Station 1.

To the Los Angeles County Coroner's Office, for the visit to the basement.

To Kefu Fu and his wife Weiji Huang, who helped me understand what it is like to grow up in China and aspire to world-class post-doctorate scientific research.

To my editor, Denise Middlebrooks, who did an incredible job.
To Captain Tony Duran at the Los Angeles County Fire Department for technical editing.
To my wife, Connie, a former script supervisor, who doesn't miss a thing.
To all those who read and suffered through the different drafts of the manuscript.
To my many friends at that great university in Westwood, CA.

# ABOUT THE AUTHOR

Malibu, California resident Kurt Kamm has written a series of firefighter mystery novels that have won several literary awards. His newest novel, *The Lizard's Tale*, provides a unique look inside the activities of the Mexican drug cartels and the men dedicated to stopping them. Kurt has used his contact with CalFire, Los Angeles County and Ventura County Fire Departments, as well as the ATF and DEA to write fact-based ("faction") novels. He has attended classes at El Camino Fire Academy and trained in wildland firefighting, arson investigation and hazardous materials response. He has also attended the ATF and DEA Citizen's Academies. After graduating from the DEA Citizen's Academy in 2014, he began work on *The Lizard's Tale*.

Kurt has built an avid fan base among first responders and other readers. A graduate of Brown University and Columbia Law School, Kurt was previously a financial executive and semi-professional bicycle racer. He was also Chairman of the UCLA/Jonsson Comprehensive Cancer Center Foundation for several years.

Visit Kurt Kamm's website at **KurtKamm.com**

# ALSO BY KURT KAMM

## ONE FOOT IN THE BLACK – A Wildland Firefighter's Story

"Kurt Kamm has been there with the firefighters, step by step,
and you will feel in the pages of this book that you are right there
in the middle of a firestorm as well."

—DENNIS SMITH, author of *Report From Engine Co. 82* and *A Decade of Hope*

"With **One Foot in the Black**, Kurt Kamm has used the tools of popular
fiction to shine a light on the inner workings of the wildland fire service.
The tortured main character, who tries to pull a brutalized life together
by joining Cal Fire, the Golden State's fire protection agency, takes us
on a journey from training ground to fire ground that vividly captures
the sense of family, of pulling together, of physical challenge and
mortal danger that go with this increasingly vital occupation."

—JOHN N. MACLEAN, author of *Fire on the Mountain* and other fire books.

## RED FLAG WARNING – A Serial Arson Mystery

A serial arsonist tries to burn down Malibu.
Can the Arson Squad stop the fires?

"NiteHeat is memorable—another lunatic out setting fires."
—MIKE COLE, CalFire Battalion Chief, Law Enforcement

*Red Flag Warning* won two FIRST PLACE
national mystery competitions:
The Written Art Awards – Mystery/Thriller 2010
Royal Dragonfly – Mystery Category 2011

### *HAZARDOUS MATERIAL*

A firefighter battles painkiller addiction and
the Vagos outlaw motorcycle gang.

*Hazardous Material* won several literary awards:
Best Novel 2013 – Public Safety Writers Association
2012 Hackney Literary Award for best novel of the year
Reader's Favorite 2013 – Finalist – Urban Fiction

### TUNNEL VISIONS

As California faces its driest year in history, terrorists threaten
the Los Angeles water supply.

"A chilling read about a fascinating subject.
I thoroughly enjoyed this book."
—CHRISTOPHER REICH, *New York Times* bestselling author.

*Tunnel Visions* was a finalist in the 2014 USA Best Book Awards.

### THE LIZARD'S TALE

Author Kurt Kamm has done it again with his most exciting crime novel to date. From the jungles of Guatemala to the Coast of Southern California, *The Lizard's Tale* follows a cast of characters more colorful than a box of crayons. Drugs, lust and high-stakes wit will leave you wishing for more!

"An exciting trip through the violent world of the drug cartels. Realistic enough to be true"
—MIKE BANSMER, DEA Special Agent, ret.